Dreams of the Red Phoenix

UNBRIDLED BOOKS

Dreams of the Red Phoenix

VIRGINIA PYE

This is a work of fiction. The names, characters, places and incidents are either the
product of the author's imagination or are used fictitiously, and any resemblance
to actual persons living or dead, business establishments, events,
or locales is entirely coincidental.

Unbridled Books

Library of Congress Cataloging-in-Publication Data

Pye, Virginia.
Dreams of the Red Phoenix : a novel by / Virginia Pye.
pages ; cm
ISBN 978-1-60953-123-2
I. Title.

PS3616.Y44D74 2015
813'.6--dc23

2015011742

1 3 5 7 9 10 8 6 4 2

Book Design by SH ● CV

First Printing

For John,
after all and before much more

"But whether true or false, my opinion is that in the world of knowledge the idea of good appears last of all."

PLATO

"If I knew for certain that a man was coming to my house with the conscious desire of doing me good, I should run for my life."

H. D. THOREAU

"If you want to know the taste of a pear, you must change the pear by eating it yourself. If you want to know the theory and methods of revolution, you must take part in revolution. All genuine knowledge originates in direct experience."

CHAIRMAN MAO

NORTH CHINA

SUMMER

1937

Part One

One

At dusk, the pigeons came home to roost in a flurry of white wings and damp air. The rains had finally stopped, and Charles and Han waited on top of the wall to reward them with seeds from their palms. After the birds landed and strutted about, the boys gripped their trembling bodies and stuffed them into the coop.

"You were right," Charles said. "They came back."

Out beyond the upturned tile roofs of the town stretched fields of millet and hemp that had never produced a bountiful harvest. The pear and apricot orchards begrudgingly offered up shriveled fruit each summer, and further in all directions stretched rocky ground that to the west ended in forbidding mountains. In winter, wind swept across the plains, carrying dust from the Gobi Desert. The ground stayed hard and crusted with snow for months, cracking into fissures that healed only with the spring rains.

But on this day, the arid earth glowed as new leaves softened the landscape. This brief, bright, promising moment in June wouldn't last long. Soon the sun would beat down and turn the fields brown, the trees limp. Rain might return in autumn, although the farmers knew not to count on it. This part of North China remained dry and desolate for much of the year, nothing like the lush visions Charles carried in his mind of America, where he had seen fields of tasseled corn so green it hurt his eyes.

As he gazed out at the countryside now, he felt more convinced than ever that he belonged in that other, distant place he still called home. The harsh landscape before him had caused the Carson family nothing but heartache. Six weeks before, Charles's father had died on the trail in the mountains west of town, his body not yet recovered. Reports pointed to a deadly fall in a mudslide, the cruel earth swallowing the Reverend Caleb Carson and offering little in return.

At his funeral, his fellow ministers had reminded the congregation that he was in a better place now: heaven, they said, not the hard ground, held the Reverend in its embrace. Charles had been raised to believe that, but it seemed just as likely to him that his father hovered somewhere over the plains like the terrifying characters in his amah Lian's bedtime stories. Those frightening spirits swooped down and skimmed the earth, flying senselessly from place to place, impossible to catch and impossible to contain. Charles feared that his father's spirit would be forever trapped in this restless purgatory known as North China.

"Where the devil is our last bird?" he asked his friend now.

"You have to be prepared to lose one or two on the first run," Han said. "They fly off into the wilds, or someone from the market snatches them and claims them as his own. It is to be expected."

"But not our Little Fat One. He's too clever to be caught."

"No, not Hsiao P'angtze. He will return."

"I would never let anyone steal my birds." Charles crossed his arms over his narrow chest. "You can't let people walk all over you, Han. You need backbone."

"So you have said, Charles."

"It's high time you people got rid of these bastards. It's been more than five years since the Japanese occupied the North, and no one's doing anything about it. This would never happen in

America. Every farmer in Ohio would tote out his rifle and shoot the Japs right off his land."

Han let out a little puff of air and turned again to the countryside, his eyes scanning the horizon. Charles knew his friend saw things out there that he never could. The Chinese were uncanny like that, which was why the situation seemed so galling.

"You think maybe the Reds will finally get rid of them?" Charles asked. "Guerrilla tactics seem the way to go."

The corners of Han's mouth rose, and he let out a slight laugh. "What do you know about the Communists, Charles?"

"Not much." He shrugged. "Father said they're hiding up in the hills to the west."

"You should believe what Father says. Reverend Carson was a very wise man."

"But I want to know what *you* think, Han. There's something you're not telling me. Like what are all these Reds doing in our town all of a sudden?"

"Putting on plays."

Now it was Charles's turn to laugh. "Those are the strangest performances I've ever seen. Imagine thinking that people would want to watch a play about land reform? Back home in America, they'd be hooted off the stage, but here, everyone loves it."

"That show was not so good. The one about the death of the landlord was much better."

"The Reds must be doing more than just putting on plays. I bet they're itching for a fight."

"And on what basis do you make this deduction?" Han asked.

Charles threw up his hands and said, "I don't know. Maybe I'm itching for one. I wish something would happen around here." Then, to show Han he meant what he said, Charles stepped forward, tossed back his head, and spat over the wall.

Han grabbed his sleeve and yanked him away from the edge. "What are you doing?" he shouted.

"They'll never know who did it. They're too dumb."

"American fool," Han said, his black bangs shaking from side to side. "You'll get us in trouble. You're too impulsive. You never think things through."

"And you sound like a crotchety old maid. Are you Lian? Is that who you are?"

Charles spun away from Han and spat again, this time with a full mouth. The outraged cry of a Japanese soldier rose from the street below, and Charles said, "Direct hit. Damn, I'm good." He could curse only with Han, and it always felt excellent.

"Damn *you*," Han hissed as he crouched low. "You'll get us killed!"

A shout came up to them. "Who for stands on our wall?"

"Not your wall," Charles shouted back as he ducked down beside his friend. "This wall is as American as I am. Belongs to the Congregational board, headquartered at number 14 Beacon Street, Boston, Massachusetts. You can write them a letter of complaint if you want."

"Go home, America!" the Japanese soldier shouted. "Get off our wall."

Charles popped up again and leaned over the side. He tipped his golfing cap and said, "Hey, mister, can you spare a dime?"

The soldier shook his rifle in the air. "American missionary boy very bad. Come down from our wall."

"Told you, not your wall," Charles said again. "It's one hundred percent American property."

6

"We come up and arrest American boy and teach him whosoever owns wall."

"'Whosoever'?" Charles repeated. "Big word, soldier. But in this instance, that whosoever is me."

The Japanese soldier gave up on his sorry English and resorted to ranting in his native tongue. Charles smiled down at Han, who still huddled on the brick walkway at the top of the wall. Beads of sweat had appeared on Han's forehead, and he rapped his knuckles against his knee. Charles switched to the local Chinese dialect to set his friend at ease. "Don't worry, they can't bother me. I'm not the enemy. And besides, I'm going home soon. You knew that, didn't you? Mother and I can't very well stay in China with Father gone."

"You are lucky to leave, Charles, and even luckier that no one ever attacks your country," Han said. "But you shouldn't be so cocky."

"Of course no one attacks America. They wouldn't dare," Charles said and began to whistle.

Down below, the voices of the Japanese soldiers blended with the rattling of wooden carts over the rutted road, the calls of peddlers heading to market, and the braying of mules in a field nearby. The day carried on, uninterrupted. The Chinese went about their difficult business, trade as paltry as ever. The Imperial Army had paved the road leading in and out of town, so now more travelers stopped, though, finding little there, they quickly moved on.

Still, even the lowliest of merchants felt he had gained from the occupation. Opium dens, prostitutes, and bars selling rotgut and sorghum wine did their best to unburden the Japanese soldiers of their meager salaries. The Mandarins tried to play their cards right, secretly pledging their allegiance to the invaders, whom they declared their liberators, even as they were appointed to be officers in the Chinese Nationalist Army. When Chiang Kai-Shek placed the nephew of ancient Tupan Feng in charge of his forces in the region, everyone knew that the warlord system of bribes and levies would continue, only now with the constant threat of conscription as well. As farmers and coolies shuffled past the American mission compound on their way into town, they kept their heads down to escape the interest of their own army more than that of the Japanese.

"So where the devil is our Little Fat One?" Charles asked.

Han stood again. "Patience, Charles. He is coming."

"How can you be so sure?"

Han might have offered any number of answers, for he had learned a great deal about pigeons. His father, the Carson family cook, had taught him before he'd headed out on the trail with Reverend Carson. New pigeons must be treated with care. For days before their release, the trainer should place cloths over their heads so that the birds remained blind, their initial flight as fraught as a baby's first steps. When they returned, they must be rewarded amply, especially if the trainer intended to use them again, and for a greater purpose.

The finest of the flock finally swooped down, and Han reached into his pocket for seeds. Hsiao P'angtze glided over the wall and landed. The pigeon's cooing grew louder as it paced and then preened, cautious and yet eager—ready for whatever was needed of it next. Han felt the same way. He fed the bird from his open hand and prepared for what came next.

Two

A final chord hung in the air as Shirley closed the lid on the piano keys. The other ladies gathered up their things and thanked her, then slipped across the front hall and out the screen door. During practice, they had spoken in hushed tones and hadn't even raised their voices on the stirring chorus. Shirley appreciated their delicacy but realized that if the choir were to regain its singing vigor, she would need to convince them that she was all right now—or at least all right enough to endure a full-throated rendition of a song. She doubted she'd ever be fully all right again.

Mrs. Carr stacked the hymnals, and Mrs. Reed set the floral Chinese teapot and cups on the lacquered tray for Lian to clear. The missionary ladies knew a hundred ways to be of help, Shirley thought, and yet none of their efforts over the past weeks had eased her pain. After word had come of her husband's death out on the trail, the ladies had taken turns in shifts outside her bedroom door. But, receiving little encouragement from her, they soon drifted off and sent their servants instead with suppers in straw baskets and stacks of devotional readings—dog-eared passages from the Gospel and scraps of sentimental poetry torn from Christian ladies' magazines. None of it had suited Shirley, not here in China nor back in the States, not while married nor now as a widow.

Her friend Kathryn appeared at her elbow and patted her sleeve. "Good to have you back, my dear. But next time, the choir should meet in the chapel. You don't need us traipsing through your home."

"I must grow used to it again."

"They say it's good to have people around after a certain amount of time," Kathryn offered.

"But what amount of time, they never say."

Kathryn brushed a stray curl from Shirley's forehead. "You look better. Your eyes are less puffy."

Shirley doubted it but thanked her as they made their way to the front door, opened the screen, and stepped out onto the wide verandah. She noticed for the first time that full summer was well upon them, the night air thick and close with no breeze from across the plains. Crickets already sawed madly in their fever, and in the lantern light that shone from the Reeds' front porch, silhouettes of a few spindly stalks of corn and sturdy sunflowers rose above the communal vegetable garden: proof that time and the world had carried on without Shirley, without Caleb. Lost in mourning, she had somehow missed the month of June altogether.

Her husband had always been the first with a hoe and rake, but Shirley could see now that this year someone else had stepped in to take over the task. Shirley wished it had been she. Instead, she had passed the spring and early summer beneath her bed's silk canopy, tangled in embroidered sheets and tossed about on a sea of tears, sleep, and morphine-induced oblivion. If concern for her teenaged son had not periodically bobbed to the surface of her mind, she might still be lost to the shore.

"You haven't seen Charles, have you?" she asked.

"Not to worry, we've all got our eyes out for him." Kathryn tucked an arm into hers. "He and your cook's son have been hanging about up on the wall."

"I hope they aren't getting into trouble."

"I can't imagine a flock of pigeons causing trouble. Just be thankful he's not like us at his age. He could be lolling about in opium dens or gambling with the White Russians in town."

"We were never as bad as that. A cigarette behind the bleachers hardly compares."

"Or a flask in hand," Kathryn said as she squeezed Shirley to her side. "But he's a young man now, and you should be aware of the proliferation of prostitutes since the Japanese influx. There's one on every corner, and that's during the day. I can only imagine what goes on at night. Russian, Japanese, Chinese, you name it, there's a girl of every nationality. A young fellow like Charles can get the clap just by stepping outside."

"Please, Kathryn." Shirley let out a soft moan and pressed her cheek against her friend's bony shoulder. "I just thank heaven he's still a boy. By the time he reaches that age, we'll be long gone."

Kathryn offered a discordant grunt. Although two years younger and almost a full foot shorter, with straight raven hair instead of Shirley's light-brown curls, Kathryn had always been Shirley's match in intellect, if not in appearance or opinion. The two often locked horns but only became closer for it, their devotion to one another deepened by their differences.

"The Lawtons offered to take him out to the countryside with their brood, but he refuses to go."

"He doesn't want to leave you. He's worried about you. We all are."

"But I'm worthless to him. I'm worthless to everyone so long as I'm here."

"It'll be different back home. We just need to get you there."

"God help me if Cleveland has become my salvation." Shirley shifted away and went to the porch railing. "Have a cigarette handy?" she asked.

Kathryn laughed a little. "Lighting up in plain sight now? Mourning has changed you. I think Caleb would be proud of your independent thinking."

"Oh, please," Shirley said. "He had far more important concerns." She looked out at the empty courtyard. "Besides, no one seems to be around at this hour, and even if they were, they'd leave me alone. When you're in mourning, you can get away with practically anything. I could have stayed anesthetized in bed for another half a year, and no one would have bothered me."

"Not true. Charles and I were already conspiring to drag you out of there."

"You were, with Charles?"

"I did my duty as a loving auntie while you were laid up," Kathryn said as she rummaged in her Chinese silk purse. "I came around quite often to make sure the boy wasn't going hungry. I even told him he needed to start shaving. I think he was mortified, but someone had to point it out."

She placed a monogrammed flask on the porch railing, pulled out the matching monogrammed cigarette case, then dropped the flask back into her purse and yanked shut the silk tassels. Shirley smiled at the familiar sight of the tarnished silver. Before China had ever entered Kathryn's plans, she had cavalierly broken off an engagement to a lackluster college boyfriend and accidentally driven her coupe into a ditch after too many old-fashioneds at the country club. As her father prepared to roundly discipline her, Kathryn concocted a punishment far greater than any he could have mustered: she announced her intention to take up the Christian cause with, in Cal James's words, a group of uptight, sanctimonious teetotalers halfway around the world. Before she left America, he gave her the monogrammed silver set and a bottle of fine Kentucky bourbon. Shirley would have liked to reassure him now that Kathryn had come to care deeply for the Chinese children she had gone all that way to teach.

Kathryn handed Shirley a cigarette, took one for herself, and shimmied up onto the porch railing, her pencil skirt straining as she crossed her long legs. She really was a fine-looking gal, Shirley thought, deserving of far more attention than she received here in this hinterland. It was all for the best they were heading home before Kathryn's window of opportunity began to close. Shirley would set her mind to finding Kathryn a good catch once they got stateside. Wasn't that the sort of thing that a widow did with her time? They thought of others instead of themselves.

She inhaled slowly, her head bent and spirit worn. "Caleb was always so generous and so full of life and vitality. Far more than I am."

"Oh, now, that's not true," Kathryn said.

"I've always been too—" Shirley looked at her friend, whose cheeks in that moment appeared especially rosy, her blue eyes sparkling. Really, she thought, not for the first time, Kathryn and Caleb would have been better suited to one another. They were easygoing and warm, nothing like Shirley in temperament. "I've been stingy with my heart," she announced. "I'm sure Caleb stayed out on the trail because of it. I didn't show my love for him nearly enough. And this is my punishment. I will never love again."

"Oh, for goodness' sake, " Kathryn said, "don't talk nonsense. You're my oldest friend, and you know perfectly well how to be loyal and dear. Your husband has died recently, so of course you're miserable. But you must eventually face the fact that your own life is not over."

"It might as well be."

"That decides it." Kathryn hopped down from her perch on the railing. "Tomorrow morning, I'll impress upon Reverend Wells the need to hurry our papers along. We can't wait another month. He has to find us passage sooner. And it's time for you to focus on something else. How about your son for starters?"

Shirley let out a sigh. "Don't remind me what a negligent mother I've been. But do tell Reverend Wells I'm concerned for Charles. This is no place for a teenaged boy without a father."

"According to my father," Kathryn said, "this is no place for anyone. Another telegram came from him begging me to return home. Apparently everyone but us knows that we're living in a danger zone."

Shirley turned and studied the still courtyard. It seemed remarkably peaceful. The tan brick pathways divided the yellow soil where ginkgo and cherry trees had been planted thirty years before. A calm and idyllic setting, she thought, just the way the early missionaries had envisioned it: the Congregational mission resembled a quintessential small college campus, dotted with fanciful Chinese elements to gently remind the visitor of what existed outside the high brick walls.

The Chinese Boys' School loomed at one end of the quad and the Girls' School at the other. Just across the way, in the center of the mission, the chapel resembled a pagoda with an eccentric, Chinese-inspired steeple. The roofs of the buildings flipped upward at the corners, and ornate lead decorations climbed each ridge with colorful sculpted dragons at the peaks. On each wall, moon windows intersected by Chinese wave patterns balanced nicely with standard Western-style rectangular frames. And at the entrance to the wraparound porch of each mission home stood a moon gate, etched with Chinese characters that offered words of welcome and promises of good fortune to all who entered.

Shirley shut her eyes and pictured Caleb dashing through their moon gate, bounding up the steps to kiss her on the lips. When she opened her eyes, her lashes were moist again, and a frightening stillness surrounded her. No one stood gazing up at the evening stars or strolling on this summer's eve. Earlier, Shirley had assumed that the choir ladies had slipped out quickly after practice to be sensitive to her, but now she wondered if they had hurried home for another reason.

"Are we under a curfew?" she asked.

Kathryn took her hand. "Oh, my dear, you really haven't been paying attention, have you? Of course we are. I've spared you the news, but things don't look good for our Chinese friends."

As Kathryn began to explain the situation, Shirley intended to listen but quickly became distracted by the sight of the chips of glossy paint littered across the porch floorboards. She loved the red-coffered ceiling and the intricately painted timbers of her home and the gaudy gold details around the heavily carved front door. But apparently in her weeks of mourning, her house had started to crumble around her. The heavy spring rains could do that—peel the paint right off the walls.

Caleb had always seen to upkeep. It didn't matter to Shirley anymore how the place looked except that its demise served as a reminder that he was truly gone. She let out a final stream of smoke and flicked her cigarette over the railing and onto the courtyard ground. In the past, she would have hidden her extinguished butts under the porch, but now, she didn't care who knew about her unladylike habits. So little mattered anymore except that Caleb was gone, and she would be leaving soon, too.

"Even though they're supposed to be united, they hardly trust one another," Kathryn was saying, and Shirley realized she had missed her friend's subject altogether.

"Sorry, who is united?"

"The Nationalists and the Communists, dear. At least that's their intention, but out here in no-man's-land, it's all up for grabs."

"And people think it's good that they're united?"

"A desperate move." Kathryn stubbed out her cigarette on the porch railing and flicked it under the porch. "But necessary."

"All right, then, a united front it is," Shirley said and tried to rally some enthusiasm. "They'll sweep the Japanese out in no time."

"Not likely. The Japanese are pouring in from the north."

"From the north? You mean, near here?"

They both turned to gaze again at the courtyard.

"The young warlord, your Tupan Feng's nephew, has appointed his usual cronies. They love to strut about, but rumor has it they're as ineffectual and greedy as ever."

Shirley gave a weak smile. "Old Tupan Feng finally has a reason to wear his dress uniform."

"Skirmishes are taking place out there somewhere. Japanese

supply lines and railroads and such are being attacked by the Nationalist forces. Or perhaps the Communist ones. Honestly, it's all a muddle to me." Kathryn straightened Shirley's collar and smoothed her flyaway hair. Their hands found one another again and swung ever so slightly, as if they were the schoolgirls they had once been together. "Some people say the Chinese don't care who rules their country," Kathryn continued. "I can't imagine that's true at heart. They're just highly pragmatic. And the poor peasants are worked to the bone and haven't time to look up from their plows. I think they assume they'll remain miserable under any government. While meanwhile, the higher-ups take Japanese bribes until a better option comes along. They're cagey, always hedging their bets, but who can blame them, with so many factions in our sorry little province?"

"I wonder what the Japanese are offering?"

"To let them live, I suppose," Kathryn said with an arched eyebrow. "The alternative, I gather, is not so good."

"But the Japanese seem decent enough," Shirley said. "One of the young soldiers started sweeping our back steps after Cook disappeared. I didn't see any harm in him doing it."

"But have you asked yourself *why* Cook disappeared?"

Shirley didn't know what to say. She should have wondered. Of course she should have. "Is it possible that he joined the Nationalist Army? He was always patriotic and absolutely hates the Japanese."

"True, but if he's like everyone else, he hated his own government almost as much. And besides, if Cook had joined, they would have sent him off with whatever feast they could manage. Candles would be lit for him, and we'd probably know his whereabouts."

"Then perhaps he joined the Reds? I remember Caleb saying they weren't far from here, up in the hills to the west, I think."

"The Red Army has been around these parts for months, recovering from their escapades across the country. It's possible that Cook may have joined them and not the Whites. Did you know that they call them the White Army?"

"Who?"

"The Nationalists. The ones who aren't Red. Although now that they've supposedly combined forces, I assume they'll start calling them the Pink Army! Oh, it's all so ridiculous. I can hardly believe we're stuck in the midst of it. Remember when our greatest concern was which chapeaux to wear to Sunday service?"

Both women shook their heads.

"The point is," Kathryn continued, "while we are still here, we must do our best to help hold off the Japanese. Most likely, my dear, *they* are the ones responsible for your cook's disappearance."

Kathryn let go of Shirley's hand and patted her charming cloche into place. She opened her purse and pulled out her lace gloves in the same forest green as her hat. Shirley marveled at her friend's style, even here in this distant outpost and with the other American women so little inclined to care about such things. Shirley felt certain she was the only one who saw Kathryn for who she really was: a smart, snappy future career girl who had made a wrong turn and wound up in China for her own stubborn reasons. Once she got back to America, she'd find a job and a husband. The rest of the mission might be deluded into thinking that Kathryn cared about China's endless troubles, but Shirley knew better, because now that Caleb was gone, she felt similarly worn out with the whole mess.

"I'm so sorry to have abandoned you these past weeks, my

love," Shirley said as she bent to kiss her friend on both cheeks. "Let's make a pact. We'll take tea with one another every afternoon until it's time for us to depart. We can start tomorrow. We'll review the latest news and make our plans. There's much to be discussed. As our professors used to say at Vassar when the bell rang, 'Ever more learning tomorrow, fine ladies!'"

"Yes, ever more learning. I remember it well. Now, get some rest. Your eyes do look awfully puffy."

As at so many partings since girlhood, the friends let go with outstretched fingers. But at just that moment, from around the corner came two young Japanese soldiers with an officer marching a few paces behind. The men halted before the moon gate in front of the Carson home. The two younger men looked identical, their khaki uniforms the same and their blank expressions in the shadowed light unchanging, until Shirley realized that the one on the right was the young fellow who had swept her back steps. She offered a nod, but his expression remained unchanged. The officer stepped forward through the gate, snapped his heels together, and bowed quickly.

"Good evening, American madams," he began in stilted English. "I am Major Hattori, Fifth Division, Japanese Imperial Army. Does American mother know whereabouts of boy with red hair?"

Kathryn retreated up the steps and stood next to Shirley.

"Is everything all right?" Shirley asked. "He isn't hurt, is he? I assume he's somewhere around the compound, but honestly, I'm not sure where exactly."

"American mother does not know whereabouts of son. Very bad. I have reports American boy is rude and should be punished."

"Oh, thank goodness," Shirley said. "I thought he might be injured."

"From high on wall, American boy spits on Japanese soldier."

"Good Lord," Kathryn said under her breath.

Shirley raised her chin. "Why, that's terrible, Major. I'm awfully sorry. I will speak with him. But you must realize that boys will be boys."

Kathryn squeezed her hand.

"American boy learn bad manners at home. But bad boy not reason for visit. I come to confiscate your two-way radio."

"My what?" Shirley asked.

Kathryn whispered something she didn't catch.

"We believe radio in house used by Red Army. We intercept signal. American missionary woman is spy!" He raised both his voice and his eyebrows with his pronouncement.

Shirley burst out laughing. She pulled her hand free and ignored Kathryn's worried expression. Her friend quickly regained her arm, but Shirley straightened her spine and thrust out her chin. At five feet eleven inches, she would have been noticeably taller than Major Hattori had they stood nose to nose. Looking down at him from the porch she felt had an even better effect.

"Everyone knows that radios get terrible reception here," she said. "No signals can make it over the surrounding hills. My husband tried to find my beloved opera on the dial but gave up years ago. And perhaps you did not know this, Major, but he is no longer with us. Our house is in mourning, so I will ask you to respect our peace."

Shirley's mind drifted for a brief moment into the chasm left by Caleb's death. A familiar wafting loneliness sucked her downward. It swirled and engulfed her in its chilly calm. Her arms went limp at her sides, and she had to work to keep her knees from buckling. But instead of leaving her completely floored, as it usually did, she could feel the sorrow somehow bolstering her courage and helping her to rise back up again. It was as if the undertow was buoying her, the way a candle sucks down heat before flaring upward into light.

"I'm quite certain that my husband gave that old thing away years ago," she continued, her voice growing stronger. "Or if I do still have it, I have no idea where it is."

"Don't be foolish, my dear," Kathryn whispered, her pretty cheeks flushed. "Give the man what he wants. These people don't mess around."

The officer marched up the steps and placed himself before them. "Madam," he said to Shirley, "bring radio to me."

She had spotted his saber in its hilt at his side, his revolver tucked into the leather case on his belt, and knew she was supposed to be impressed by them and by his crisp uniform and shiny boots, but the fact that she literally towered over the man seemed to contradict all that. She turned and strode into her house, calling back over her shoulder, "I shall return in a moment."

Kathryn clasped her hands together and looked off at the courtyard and then up at the black and starless sky, anywhere but into the stony faces of the officer and his two soldiers, who remained like sentries blocking the bottom step. "Reverend Carson died quite recently, you see. Mrs. Carson really isn't herself."

The major did not respond or acknowledge Kathryn's words, and she wondered if perhaps his English was rudimentary. She was about to try the local Chinese dialect when the screen door flung open again and Shirley reappeared in a flurry, her black satin mourning skirt swishing and her arms upraised. She had a broom in one hand. With a dramatic gesture, she placed it on the floorboards and began sweeping. As she did, she sang an off-key, airy tune: "Don't sit under the apple tree with anyone else but me. Anyone else but me. Anyone else but me."

As Shirley continued to sweep and sing, Kathryn's jaw slackened. The broom whisked right up to the edge of the major's polished boots and kept going, as if they were merely annoying debris that had fallen onto the otherwise tidy porch.

Major Hattori shuffled back. "American woman most impertinent. She and son must be punished!"

Kathryn reached for the broom and tried to pull it away, but Shirley held on and surprised them both with her strength. She thought she must have been storing it up all those pointless, painful weeks since Caleb's death, when she had repeatedly come to the conclusion that there was no reason to go on living. For, as she yanked the broom back from Kathryn, she remembered her husband's words: *Face the foe*, he had said. A silly phrase he had heard from British military passing through. He had meant it tongue-in-cheek, spoken in a teasing and irreverent manner, but Shirley had known that at heart, he had meant it. Caleb had wanted her to be brave.

She planted the broom and announced, "You may go now, Major Hattori. Good evening."

Kathryn rocked back on her heels, and the major let out a growl.

"I will return," he said and hurried down the steps. His soldiers followed closely at his heels as he strode across the courtyard and was gone.

Shirley let the broom fall from her hand, and Kathryn caught it. Shirley's arms trembled, and she felt perspiration snake down her sides. She leaned against the carved post and gripped the railing.

"Good heavens, who ever knew I had that in me?"

Kathryn offered no congratulations and no reassurances. She simply stared at Shirley with a concerned expression. Shirley didn't expect her friend to understand. Kathryn had not endured the hollow sensation that coursed through Shirley's veins all the time now, its meaning only beginning to come clear to her.

Three

The screen door wheezed shut, and Shirley paused in the front hall, her pulse still thrumming in her ears and her thoughts addled. One of the thick muslin curtains in the dining room wafted, though there was no breeze. She let out a gasp, but it was only Charles. He slipped out from his favorite childhood hiding place and scurried after her as she moved unsteadily into the parlor.

"Bravo!" he whispered. "You were wonderful, Mother. But is it true? You aren't really a spy, are you?"

"Please, darling, I need a moment to collect myself. How long were you there at the window? You really shouldn't eavesdrop like that. I've told you before."

Her hands were shaking as she gave her maid, Lian, the broom. The older, dignified woman offered to bring tea, and Shirley thanked her, then tossed herself down onto the wicker sofa. It creaked and complained as she settled into the silk pillows.

"Mother must rest now," Lian said. "Ladies' Choir very big effort. Leave her be, Charles-Boy."

For the first time in many weeks, Shirley said, "It's all right, Lian; he isn't bothering me."

Charles ignored his amah, anyway, and knelt down before the sofa. Shirley tousled his thick red hair, so like his father's, she thought with a sigh. Then she leaned back again and shut her eyes.

"Brilliant tactic, sweeping that old goat off the porch. I almost let out a cheer when he left."

"That wasn't a tactic, son. That was complete idiocy on my part. I'm far too impulsive, and you are, too. You get it from me. Tell me you didn't actually spit on a Japanese soldier."

Charles sat higher on his haunches. "In one of his sermons, Reverend Wells said we should do all that we can. So I did."

Shirley swung her legs around, placed her oxfords on the carpet, and patted the spot beside her. Charles hopped up to join her. His long legs stretched out past hers, reaching the coral-colored cherry blossoms in a sea of blue on the Chinese rug. She noticed for the first time that not only his socks showed above his too-short trouser legs but his bare and surprisingly hairy calves as well. She turned to get a better look at him. What used to be pale peach fuzz above his upper lip had sprouted into actual coarse dark-red hairs. They had appeared below his bottom lip as well. Her son seemed to be growing a rudimentary goatee. His bony wrists protruded from his rumpled linen jacket, and his shirttails were out. Shirley thought that the young man seated beside her wasn't unattractive. He just appeared un-cared-for, like someone who had no parents and must survive by his wits alone.

"This is serious, my boy. You could have been arrested. Or worse, gotten Han arrested."

He patted her knee. "I know, Mother, but I think Father would have been proud of us."

Shirley slumped back against the pillows.

"Father was no coward," Charles continued. "Remember how he used to put on that fake British accent and say, 'Don't fire till you see the whites of their eyes'? He was kidding, of course, but he wanted me to be brave and stand up for what I believed in.

It's a manly thing, but you did swell just now, too."

"Charles, you're as wrong-headed as you could possibly be. Your father did not believe in fighting. He wanted everyone to cooperate and trust one another and work as one. And he absolutely understood that women can be as brave as men and, in fact, must be. Such foolishness, my darling."

Shirley smoothed his wild hair again and realized that with his irrepressible grin, her son was trying to buck her up, not the other way around. Charles had always had a buoyant personality. A chuckling baby, a toddler who raced forward on stocky legs, then an angular little boy covered in freckles and grins from ear to ear. But a sensitive soul, too, whose sunny disposition could quickly cloud over when criticized or corrected. So she simply hadn't. It was too painful to see him crumple into self-doubt. He had run wild and carefree throughout the compound, without oversight or direction. All had been grand for him for so long. He must have been completely floored when word had come of his father's accident, Shirley thought. Nothing remotely like it had ever happened to him before.

"How are you, Charles?" she asked. "Without Father, I mean."

The smile on his face evaporated, and he appeared baffled by the question.

"I'm so sorry that I've neglected you," she said softly.

Her son's large, angular Adam's apple rose and fell. She sensed he had no idea how to respond.

"I suppose, though," she said, attempting a smile, "it's good that you're feeling strong enough to take on the Japanese Imperial Army." Then she added more firmly, "But I believe you need to be put to some purpose this summer instead of strutting about like a useless rooster. We'll begin a new regimen tomorrow morning."

Charles's shoulders sagged, but Shirley thought she had finally hit the right note: he needed rules to butt up against in order to regain his fiery gumption.

"I intend to keep a closer watch over you. There will be duties for you to perform around the house."

"Chores, Mother? When the country is practically at war, you want me to clean my room?"

"Discipline begins at home," she said and couldn't help remembering the Japanese officer's words.

Charles scrambled to his feet and stood far above her. When had he gotten so tall? she wondered.

"Han lives on his own now," he said. "No one tells him what to do anymore."

"That's not something to envy. Your friend's father has gone missing. I'm sure his uncle and grandmother and other relatives are keeping a close eye on him. Chinese families are terribly close-knit."

"I know, but it's pretty keen that he gets to come and go as he pleases."

"That's enough, now. Get ready for bed."

Charles bent low and kissed the air near her cheek. It wasn't until he had turned and walked from the room that she realized she had meant to offer him a good-night hug. His footfalls struck firmly on the stairs, and Shirley realized that the moment for comforting her boy had passed. He was practically a young man now.

Lian appeared at the door to the parlor with the black lacquered tray, bamboo-handled teapot, and lidded cup. As Caleb had instructed their maid, she did not bow but nonetheless entered quietly. That seemed to be how all the Chinese women walked in their thin slippers, although Shirley's husband had enjoined Lian to speak up and rattle the dishes however she liked. He was forever encouraging the Chinese to be themselves in his presence, though Shirley had often wondered how a foreigner would know the difference.

Lian set the tray on the teak side table, poured tea, and, after allowing it to steep, handed a cup to Shirley. Although Lian was a bulky woman, she settled delicately into the wicker rocking chair opposite the sofa and tucked her long tunic under her. Out of respect for the formality of the setting, she had removed her apron before entering. It wasn't customary for servants to sit with their masters in the living quarters, and Shirley knew it made Lian uncomfortable, but Caleb had insisted on it. *We are all congregants,* he had said, *each the same in God's eyes.*

Since her husband's passing, Shirley had been grateful for his eccentric demands on their servants—essentially, that they all behave as equals under this roof. Lian and even the young and silent girl, Dao-Ming, had offered Shirley kindness and comfort. Lian had become a true friend, Shirley thought, or as true a friend as their dissimilar circumstances would allow.

"Does my son seem all right to you, Lian?" she asked now. "You have brothers. Were they this difficult when they were his age?"

"He is American boy, nothing like Chinese. Our boys behave, or else."

"Or else what?"

"My father beat them every week whether they deserve it or not."

28

"That's terrible."

They are responsible men now."

"And you would do the same if you had a son?"

"I have no son."

Lian touched a finger to the simple cross she wore around her neck. Shirley couldn't envision her maid raising a belt to a child, but Lian had no children of her own, so it was a moot point—or, more accurately, a sore point. A barren woman here seemed to be of a lower status, marking a stain upon her for her loss. Shirley undid the laces of her oxfords and slipped them off. Lian pulled her seat closer, lifted one of Shirley's feet into her lap, and began to rub.

"As young man, Charles needs father more than ever," Lian said, "but now he has none!" She let out a forceful laugh.

Shirley tried not to be affronted. Her maid meant well. She was blunt, that was all, not unlike Shirley's mother, another older woman with a decidedly ungracious manner. Though in Shirley's mother's case, the sourness went all the way through. As Lian continued to rub, Shirley recalled how her mother was accustomed to being waited on hand and foot. The irony that she thought of this while her maid was waiting on her was not lost on Shirley, and yet she felt certain that she and her mother were utterly unalike. Her mother complained about her servants constantly. Shirley was uneasy with her servants at best and had accompanied her husband to China in part to help ensure that she didn't inherit her mother's selfishness. Performing good works, as Caleb called the efforts here, was the best antidote to such upper-class self-preoccupation and snobbery.

"You must find new uncle here in mission," Lian suggested. "Other ministers do good job with boy."

Shirley leaned forward and whispered, "Not a single one of the other reverends is half the man Caleb was. They're fine people, but they lack character. Charles would hoodwink them. They'd wind up doing his bidding. My son is a thoroughbred—good-natured, high in spirits, perhaps too cocky, but with awfully thin skin."

Lian looked up from her rubbing. "What is trouble with boy's skin?"

"An expression. He bruises easily."

"Ah, yes, Charles-Boy is baby! I know this. You should consider the belt."

Shirley put down her cup. "Can you imagine? A boy who's never heard a raised voice in his life. He'd be shocked out of his wits." She placed her stocking feet on the carpet. "Honestly, going forward, I mean to do better by him."

A phlegmy cough sounded from the hallway, followed by the tap of a cane. Old Tupan Feng stood teetering in the doorway, waiting to be announced.

Lian rolled her eyes and said in a teasing tone, "Ancient Warlord Feng enters!"

He cleared his throat again and spoke in fine, British-accented English. "No need to bow," he said as he hobbled in. "In the modern fashion, I no longer require that of my subjects."

Lian stood, slapped her skirt, and began to clear the tea set. Back when Tupan Feng had been an active warlord, he had punished any servants who weren't silent at their tasks, so Lian made as much racket as possible now. She stood before him, and he blinked at the tray in her hands.

"Is it tea time already?" he asked.

"We finish now."

"I'm sure Lian would be happy to make you tea, Tupan Feng," Shirley offered.

He turned his head slowly, as if only now recalling her. He often seemed to forget that this was the Carsons' home and not his own. "Very kind of you, Mrs. Carson, but I could not possibly. It is bad for the humors to drink at this hour."

"And what hour is that, Old Feng?" Lian asked, her nose practically touching his.

He waved a hand to shoo her away and relied on the cane. "In my day, I instituted the regulation of the hours. All subjects rose at 6 a.m. My Early Rising Society saw to it! Excellent for productivity."

"Perhaps it is morning then, hmmm? Do you hear birds outside? Time to rise?" Lian pressed.

"That's enough, Lian," Shirley said.

Tupan Feng paused as if considering the time of day but then determining the topic beneath him. He set off again in mincing steps toward the rocking chair that Lian had just vacated. Shirley hopped to her feet to catch him before he sat; otherwise she'd be forced to stay up with him until he dozed off again. The old *tupan*, or warlord, slept at all hours of both day and night, roaming the house when the spirit struck him. In her own nocturnal ramblings since Caleb's death, Shirley had slipped into darkened rooms to discover his spindly frame curled on chairs or atop makeshift beds, even stretched out beside the cold hearth. He seemed as partial to the sunny window seats in the dining room as were the cats. As she studied his tiny frame now, Shirley tried to recall if she'd ever seen him eating and wondered if he wasn't perhaps starving.

But, to his credit, old Tupan Feng never complained. He

was stoical and upright, though half bent now. Over his years as warlord of this province, he had professed an amalgam of philosophies—most committedly to Confucianism because of its effectiveness at inculcating respect for authority. He also adhered to Buddhist sensibilities on occasion, and even some Taoist beliefs to appease the old spirits. But because he had ambled into church somewhat regularly, and during his reign had proclaimed his province a welcome bastion for Christians, Reverend Carson had offered him a small room at the back of the house in his less-substantial older age. Being a man of curiosity about the broader world, and also temporarily homeless, Feng had taken the Reverend up on the offer. He wished to observe the American Christians firsthand. He had come to suspect that the self-sacrificing aspects of their religion explained the physical and moral strength of Westerners overall, something he had wished to propagate in his own people.

Shirley took his arm, and he froze in midstep and swayed, his ceremonial sword in its black sheath grazing her long skirt. His uniform was badly stained, many of the brass buttons missing and the collar frayed. But the braid on the epaulettes somehow miraculously had remained in place, giving his shoulders a perversely broad appearance. He was so profoundly hunched that the top of his balding head didn't quite reach Shirley's chest.

"Off to bed we go," she said. "And wouldn't you like to take off your jacket when you recline? It could use some freshening up. I'm sure Lian would be willing to launder it, wouldn't you, Lian?"

Lian let out a chuckle. "Good luck peeling it off him. He will be buried in that ratty thing."

"Must keep it on," Tupan Feng said. "You never know when the moment will arise."

"And what moment is that, Old Feng?" Lian asked with a slight smile.

He turned to look at her, and his face went blank. A long moment later, a bolt of light came back into his eyes, and he licked his lips. "Battle!" was all he said.

Lian hooked his arm into hers. "Come now, Old Tupan, I walk you back to your room."

"Kind of you, Lian," Shirley said.

"Very bad nephew of Old Tupan should buy him new coat, not to mention his own house, after all the *taxes* his family took from the people."

Hearing that word, the old man summoned a surprisingly stentorian voice. "It is necessary and prudent, though not pleasurable, to impose levies on all transactions."

"Enough!" Lian said, and he went quiet again. When they reached the door, she turned back and asked, "Mrs. Carson, did you see flag raised high today?"

"Flag? What flag?"

"American flag at entrance to compound above gatehouse."

Shirley shook her head.

"The servants think it means something, but no one knows what. We hear Reds infiltrate Japanese Imperial Army supply lines. We worry they will retaliate here."

"The Japanese Imperial Army will squash all enemies!" Tupan Feng perked up. "They have very fine leaders. Excellently trained at top-notch military academies."

Lian pulled him tighter to her side to keep him from listing. "We know all about you and the Japanese."

"I am Number One Student from Tokyo Military Academy. Prize ceremonial sword proves it!" His palsied hand flailed around to find the sheath on his hip.

Lian ignored him and explained, "Many relatives from countryside come to town with everything they own."

"But I thought people were moving south, escaping in that direction. Why would they arrive here when the Japanese occupy our town?" Shirley asked. "Wouldn't they rather go where there aren't any Japanese?"

"Yes, where to go is big question!" Lian exclaimed. "They come to American mission. It is safe haven, remember?" she asked and added the exasperated tsking sound that Shirley had dreaded ever since she and her family had first arrived. She must have missed something painfully obvious. "We think," Lian continued, "American flag flies higher today to make Imperial Army remember America is neutral. Also, Japanese not attack same town where they live. No, it is safer here than countryside." She shook her head. "Out there very, very bad. Missus understand now?"

Lian stared at Shirley and seemed to be waiting for her to say something. The tray in the solid woman's hand wobbled.

"Yes," Shirley said, "I see," when really she didn't see, hardly at all. "Is there something else you'd like from me tonight, Lian?"

Her maid let out a long stream of air and finally said, "No, I leave now. Good night."

Lian turned and shuffled out of the room, dragging the old man along beside her, his saber clinking at his side and her long, narrow dress rustling as she went. Just to fluster Shirley even more, Lian's little helper, Dao-Ming, suddenly ducked her head out from behind one of the muslin curtains and dashed after Lian across the hallway on her thick, ungraceful legs. Apparently, the girl had been spying again.

The little scamp, Shirley thought. The young girl was forever popping up and surprising Shirley. It couldn't be helped because she was Lian's charge and a pathetic young thing: a true Mongoloid with the enlarged head, deeply recessed eyes, and rotund body. Back home, she'd have been put in an institution, but they didn't have such options here. She could no doubt in the end be shuffled off to the poorhouse, but Lian, out of the goodness of her Christian heart, had taken the orphan in. Caleb, whose heart had also been warm and malleable, had agreed to permit Dao-Ming to hang about. The sight of her never bothered him, and, to the girl's credit, she rarely made a peep, but those spooky hooded eyes, overly pink cheeks, and odd little grin all gave Shirley a chill.

She took a final sip of tea and tried to understand what had just transpired with Lian. Communication between foreigners and Chinese was always fraught, Shirley thought: sometimes barbed, other times overly serene, as if nothing had transpired at all, when clearly it had. Tomorrow she would try to make sense of it all. She might even venture out and see what was going on outside the mission, returning in time for her reward of tea with Kathryn. They would discuss every maddening incident and together parse the unintelligible. But for now, Shirley's head spun. She needed rest.

She started toward the stairs, but her fingers instinctively reached to graze the chipped keys of her beloved upright piano that stood in the front hall. She wished she could play the rousing chords of a choir hymn, but such noise at this hour would alarm her already concerned neighbors. On the entrance table, she pulled the brass chain on the cloisonné lamp, and the hallway went dark. The timbers of her home settled and creaked after another humid day.

Cuneiform shadows spread over the hardwood floor where moonlight filtered through the lattice screen. The same silvery hues caught on the beveled glass of the two sets of French doors that opened onto the dining room on one side and the parlor on the other. The handsome scholar's desk and traditional yoke-back folding chairs sat huddled in grayness, waiting for Caleb to return. Stretched across the corner by the bay window, a painted screen showed an impressive golden phoenix spreading its wings and flying toward the distant mountains far beyond the mission walls.

Shirley wondered if it would pain her to have that elegant reminder of China, in addition to some of the other, finer antiques she had collected over the past five years, shipped back to her future home in America or if it would be wiser to simply leave it all behind. She would return to America with nothing to show for her time here. No embroidered silk or delicately painted porcelain. No carnelian-colored carved boxes or lacquered picture frames. No objects to touch and call to mind this place and time, as if these years in Cathay had been but a dream with no evidence of their passing. A strange, inexplicable chapter would close forever, leaving only the memory of loss in another land.

Four

The windowpanes rattled, and the brass box on Charles's bedside table fell to the floor. His pocketknife tumbled out and scooted under the bed. He threw off the covers and hurried to the window. Smoke wafted his way from fire in a field not far off, the soil churned up from some sort of grenade or maybe even a bomb. The Japanese had recently paved the road outside the town so that it snaked steadily to the west in a ribbon of dark asphalt. Charles thought it looked normal enough until he squinted and noticed that at a distant bend, a crater of smoldering earth had replaced the smooth surface. The fighting seemed to have come closer to the mission than ever before.

Below his window, the massive doors at the southwest entrance to the mission stood open, and Charles could make out Japanese soldiers marching past. Their boots stirred the yellow dust on the rutted road. Into the mission courtyard below streamed hundreds of Chinese, some limping or injured, many with possessions piled on wooden wheelbarrows or bundled on their backs. But just as many Chinese appeared to be fleeing up the paths that led away from the town. They fanned out in all directions like the ants Charles and Han had set on fire with the help of a magnifying glass and the sun when they were younger boys.

Charles didn't see any damage to the town buildings within his sight except that the American guardhouse appeared to have been attacked, its glass windows shattered, the red, white, and blue wood splintered on the ground. Charles worried about old, blind Mr. Sung, who sat all day on his three-legged stool at the gate. He hoped he had been off tending to his cats when the damage was done. But who, Charles wondered, would want to bombard the entrance to the American compound?

He pulled on his trousers over his pajama bottoms, yanked on his golfing cap, and retrieved his pocketknife from under the bed. He went in search of his mother. She wasn't in her bedroom or in the sewing room, so he started downstairs but stopped short on the landing beside the moon window. The view over the back wall had not changed. On the horizon, the low mountain range shimmered in the morning haze, its blue skirts flowing onto the rosy desert floor. All seemed peaceful in that greater distance, and Charles wondered why the Japanese Imperial Army, or the Chinese military, for that matter, chose to attack one area but not another. It all seemed arbitrary and mysterious.

Into the front hall, swarms of Chinese people poured. Families with small children, older men in coolie hats, a pregnant woman who looked ready to burst, grandfathers hobbling over their canes, and clusters of young men all pressed into their home. Charles's mother stood at the center, an electric look in her eyes, and Lian's shouts rose above it all. She sent some strangers into the dining room, others into the parlor. The handsome French doors had been flung back, glass panes reflecting the many who shuffled in and milled about on the blue carpet with the cherry-blossom design. Charles noticed that the Chinese didn't set down their bags or take a seat on the formal furniture. They hovered about, clearly at a loss for what to do next.

Charles noticed a young man leaning on a friend, with several others surrounding him. He had been shot in the leg and had a tourniquet cinched around his thigh. Down his torn pants, the caked blood had hardened. A frayed rope held his oversized jacket in place, and his cloth shoes were ripped, the sole of the left one flopping loose. Could this kid, who wasn't much older than he, be an actual soldier, even though he wore no uniform? Charles had overheard the servants saying that the Nationalist Army troops had been fighting the Japanese off and on for months in North China and were badly undersupplied and underfed. The injured boy swayed where he balanced between his friends, the perfectly good wicker sofa empty before them.

Charles ran down the stairs and stopped beside his mother. She was leaning over an elderly man crumpled in the middle of the mayhem. With his chin tucked to his chest, the grandfather refused to respond to her entreaties that he move so he wouldn't be trampled by the incoming horde. When she straightened and called for Lian's help, his mother finally noticed Charles and threw her arms around his neck. Then she pushed him away and held him at arm's length. She looked him up and down, searching nonsensically for injuries, then offered a grim and apologetic shake of her head.

"I'm so sorry, my boy. This is an awful mess. Are you all right?"

"I'm fine, Mother." He knew she meant well by her concern, as if it was her duty to make everything right in a world that wasn't one bit right. It made her look tired, Charles thought, her face lined with worry. He shifted away from her now and gestured toward the parlor. "Should I tell them to sit down?"

"What?" she shouted back.

Charles noticed an elderly woman being carried in by two strong grandsons, her bound feet dangling uselessly. A toddler cried, and another child not much older scolded him but then reached down and took his hand. Charles raised his voice, too. "Shall I help them to feel at home?"

"Yes, excellent idea. Thank you, Charles." Her eyes were shining, and she seemed ready to cry. "I'm so proud of you."

"Please don't make a fuss," he said and stepped away, his fists balled at his sides.

In the parlor, he wove past several families and climbed onto his father's leather chair. For balance, he placed one foot on the desk beside the banker's lamp with the green shade. He tried not to notice the abacus that his father had always allowed him to play with, or the letters and ministerial notes covered in his fine, spidery scrawl. Charles reached down and pocketed his father's chop, a two-inch-long piece of marble with a phoenix carved on one end and Chinese characters on the other. The bright-red ink his father had used to stamp his signature smudged on Charles's palm, but he held on to it tightly anyway.

Charles swallowed and then shouted in the local dialect, "Sit!" He gestured to the available chairs. "Make yourselves at home!"

The Chinese stared up at him, and Charles saw only distress and confusion on their faces. Where had they come from, he wondered, and from what were they running? He realized that standing so high above them wasn't helping to put them at ease. He stepped down and began to yank the rocker and other chairs away from the center of the room. He lined them up against the walls, and the Chinese began to drift toward them. "That's right," he tried more patiently. "Put down your things and take a seat."

From his visits to Han's father's quarters at the back of the compound, Charles knew that the Chinese kept their formal furniture around the outside of a room and used it only on special occasions or when an important visitor came. This parlor's usual arrangement of seats clustered before the fireplace and in front of the bay window would seem odd to them, so Charles tried to create his own version of a Chinese setting. As he moved the furniture, Dao-Ming appeared without a sound and began to help him. When they finished, Charles patted her on the head, and she smiled. She always stood a little too close, literally underfoot, but Charles didn't mind having her around. She did whatever he asked, and although Charles tried not to take advantage of her too often, every once in a while he'd say something like "Dao-Ming, sneak me a malt candy stick from the cookie jar where Lian hides them, will you?" And she always would, no questions asked. She had never once betrayed him to his parents or his amah.

He spoke again to the crowded room, bowing first. "My family and I would be most honored if you would permit us the privilege of your taking a seat." He bowed a second time to the most elderly of the gentleman.

The Chinese finally settled in. They sat on the chairs and set blankets on the hearth. More made themselves comfortable along the window seats. But still no one sat on the sofa, which remained in its usual spot on the fine rug. Charles went to the injured young man and gestured for him to lie down on the silk cushions. The injured fellow looked at his friends, then down at his feet. None of them moved. Charles left the room briefly and wove through the crowd. He returned a few moments later and spread one of Lian's rags over the silk pillows on the couch and gestured again. Finally the young man stumbled toward it on his good leg and eased himself down, grimacing apologetically.

The older of his two friends had hollow cheeks and was missing several teeth, but his eyes seemed kind as he adjusted the pillow under the injured boy's leg and crouched down beside him. His other friend had a barrel chest, stocky legs, and forearms as thick around as baseball bats. He swayed side to side and kept a restless, eager watch over his injured friend.

Charles stepped closer to the three men and asked, "So, what happened out there this morning?"

They looked to one another again, and the older man finally nodded. The restless fellow could hardly contain himself as he answered, "Communist guerrillas destroyed a section of the railroad the Japs have been trying to build through the mountains. I heard it was a direct hit!"

"That's a good thing, isn't it?" Charles asked.

"Yes, but they attacked us out on the plains in retaliation! They must have thought we were responsible."

"We don't know if that is the reason," the older man said. "There could be action elsewhere. Or it could still be in response to the Marco Polo Bridge incident in Peking. We must be patient. Word will come."

"But you were attacked near here?" Charles asked. "Where?"

The older man looked at him but didn't answer.

The restless one paced behind the sofa. "If only we had proper weapons and better aircraft, we would stand a chance. Our officers parade around, and the young warlord issues commands from afar." He waved his hand in disgust. "I could run this army better myself."

"Settle down," the older one growled. "And don't forget we did well in the North."

"There's been fighting north of here?" Charles asked.

"They want the coal of this region," the robust fellow said, "and to use the roads through the mountains to get supplies. So far we have not let them. We have been very brave!"

"Control of the mountains is crucial," the older one said, shaking his head.

The injured boy, who had lain quietly until now with his eyes shut, opened them and pushed himself up onto one elbow. "The Reds know the mountains better than anyone. When my leg is healed, I'm joining them."

The robust one patted him on the shoulder. "Do not desert us, my friend, like our traitorous commanders."

The older one muttered a curse.

"What do you mean?" Charles asked. "Your commanders actually left you?"

"They are puppets, nothing more!" the restless one said. Then he leaned closer to the older man and whispered, "I say, let the Imperial Army execute them! I will do the job myself if the Japs don't."

As the injured boy flopped back onto the sofa he said, "There is no such thing as traitors in the Eighth Route Army. No one is conscripted, so there is no reason for desertion."

"You shouldn't believe everything you hear, kid," the restless one said. "Stick with us."

The injured boy let out a soft moan and shut his eyes again. Charles crouched before him and carefully lifted the torn material to see the wound. The other soldiers leaned in closer, too, and seemed unimpressed.

"You will run again in no time," the restless friend said.

The bullet appeared to have only grazed the thigh, but the skin was nonetheless badly torn, and Charles thought he saw bone beneath. If this was considered a slight wound, he hated to think what these men might consider a real injury. He quickly covered the leg again, breathed through his open mouth, and held on to the sofa arm. He tried to focus on the task at hand. He would need to find something to clean the wound, also towels and bandages. But first his head must stop spinning.

"American boy all right?" the older man asked.

"He is afraid of blood," the robust one said and swatted Charles's arm. "You would never make it in my army!"

Charles tried to smile. "I'll get supplies for you," he said to the injured boy.

Light-headed, he gazed around the parlor. Several elders and the pregnant woman sat on the chairs, their families and possessions clustered at their feet. Others crouched on the rug or pushed aside the curtains to look out at the crowded porch and courtyard. What these people hoped for, or what they wanted to see happen next, remained unclear to Charles. What had taken place outside the compound remained equally confusing, despite the explanations from the soldiers.

Charles looked toward the chaotic scene in the front hallway. Each of the Chinese appeared caught in his or her own turmoil, with his mother at the center, trying to make sense of it all. Charles couldn't help laughing a little under his breath. She looked so alive and engaged, her hands gesticulating as she spoke, her head held high, then dipping low to hear the words of a bent elder or small child. With renewed vigor, she appeared to be doing her darnedest to help each and every one of them.

One family, though, sat stonily quiet, asking for nothing and not raising their voices. On the bottom step that led up to the second floor, an older man sat. Two middle-aged women, who must have been his daughters, and several grandchildren crouched around him. Charles recognized the traditional Japanese robes and realized that this grandfather was the town's only fishmonger, a Japanese citizen who had been here at least as long as the Carson family. Charles had always been afraid of the old man, not because he was Japanese but because he was a crotchety bastard who never had a kind word for anyone. The man was quite unreasonable about his prices, but he didn't seem a mortal enemy of the Chinese. Now his hand trembled as he raised it to his brow, and his children and grandchildren hardly lifted their eyes from the floor.

Charles went to his mother's side and whispered in her ear, "Shall I take them upstairs?" He nodded toward the Japanese family. She looked both exhilarated and utterly flummoxed, her mouth hanging open and wisps of hair falling from her bun. Before she had a chance to respond, Charles said, "It's all right, Mother. I'll take care of it."

He slipped away and bowed before the Japanese grandfather and his family, then gestured for them to follow him up to the second floor. At the top of the stairs, he escorted them into his mother's sewing room, a space not much larger than the lavatory, which now felt far smaller with all those people in it. The ladies let out thrilled exclamations at the sight of the Singer machine on its special table with the iron foot pedal underneath. They crowded around and touched it with delicate fingers. One of the grown daughters elbowed the others aside and took the seat in front of it. She read aloud the gold letters written in English script on the side of the black base, and the little girls inched closer and clapped their hands as the woman began to practice on a piece of muslin his mother had used for the curtains downstairs.

Charles joined the Japanese fishmonger, who sat at the end of the iron-framed day bed, his head bent, his palsied hand to his brow again. The old man was so distracted by his worries that he hadn't even noticed the curled body stretched beside him on the pilled bedspread. A tartan throw covered the narrow shoulders, and a lace antimacassar lay over the bald head to keep out the light.

Charles shook Tupan Feng's shoulder. "Rise and shine," he said. "You have visitors!"

The Japanese fishmonger still didn't look up, even when the old warlord's feet in his tattered slippers shifted beside him. Tupan Feng sat up, wiped his eyes with the back of his hand like a child, and blinked several times. He didn't look one bit surprised to find Charles standing over him in the narrow room now packed with strangers.

"Is it time?" he asked.

"Yes, it is," Charles said, though he wasn't sure what the old warlord had in mind.

Tupan Feng's face went red as he pushed himself to stand, one hand on his cane, the other on the handle of his prize sword. "Into battle we must go!"

The Japanese fishmonger finally looked up.

"Whoa, hold on," Charles said and took the old warlord by the arm. He gently eased him back down onto the bed.

The two men sat hunched shoulder to shoulder, neither acknowledging the other. Charles made proper introductions, being sure to sound equally respectful and bowing equally low before each. They nodded imperceptibly and pursed their lips, but neither spoke.

"All right, now, you two should have plenty to talk about," Charles said and tipped his cap. "How about Tokyo, for starters? Old Tupan Feng remembers it, don't you? He was a student there. And you, Honorable Fishmonger, you must have at least visited there before coming to China?"

Both men grimaced. The deep frown lines that sloped down their cheeks acted as perfect mirrors when they turned their heads on their sinewy necks toward one another. If only these two could resolve the war, Charles thought.

At the top of the stairs, he held the newel post and listened to the cacophony of voices all around. After his father's death, the Carson home had felt as chilly as a tomb for weeks. The spring rain had fallen in sheets outside his window and pounded the unyielding ground. The tile roofs had grown slick, and a rush of unceasing water had rumbled down the gutters. Unable to sleep, Charles had crawled out of bed, pushed open the window, and sat with his elbows on the sill, his face splattered by rain. His shirt became quickly soaked, and he shivered but still kept watch. Even in the dark, his eyes stayed on the compound gate. Only when his arms grew numb and his ears filled with the sensation of being lost deep under water in a sea he could not name did Charles realize that he was waiting for his father's mule to come around the corner of the guardhouse and into the mission.

He finally wrenched himself away from the window and paced on the braided rug to keep from crying. Then he threw himself back onto the quilt, and felt the forceful thud of his own heart as it echoed against his ribs. He was alive. He was breathing, even if his father was not. Only there was little pleasure in it.

No joy. Just a pang of guilt and a heartsickness that made every part of him hurt.

If he stayed in bed too late in the morning during those mournful days, Lian would yank back the covers and pull him by the hand down the steps and out onto the front porch, where Han stood waiting. While it embarrassed Charles to have his friend see his red-rimmed eyes, he was grateful to him, too. Lian gave them both a few coins to spend at the market and insisted they bring home fish from the river for supper. Never before had Charles been instructed to go fishing. Lian was also the one who had suggested that Han show Charles the pigeons that Cook had been training up on the compound wall. Charles had enjoyed caring for the birds, even if he didn't know the first thing about them. Mostly he liked being with Han and away from his sorrowful, too-quiet home.

Now, as he went in search of supplies, he considered the possibility that his summer might no longer feel like a lonely nightmare, although he also knew that in more ways than he could fathom, things would never be the same.

Five

A tall Chinese man with silver hair stepped through the crowd on the verandah and crossed the threshold of the Carson home. Shirley had spotted his distinctive profile above the others at the door and noticed the way people shifted out of his way as he moved forward. He stopped before Shirley, bowed first to her and then to Lian.

"Captain Hsu," Lian said out of turn, "what an honor to have you join us."

Shirley looked from Lian to the Chinese gentleman in the threadbare, mismatched jacket and trousers and realized that they seemed to know one another.

"Thank you," he said in clear English. "It is my honor to meet the widow of Reverend Caleb Carson. Your husband was a good and courageous man."

Shirley tried to recall the striking profile but couldn't place it. Surely she'd have remembered the scattering of pockmarks on his cheeks or the pale scar over his right eye.

"You knew my husband?" she asked.

"He was devoted to our cause. He visited our camp up in the hills a number of times. He would be proud of us now, though we still have many battles ahead." He leaned closer and bowed again. "I am Captain Hsu, Eighth Route Army of the Second United Front." He pulled from his pocket a green cap with a red star on it and shifted it between his hands before stuffing it back into his pocket. He then glanced around at the crowded house. "I see that you are like your husband, Mrs. Carson, most generous and brave."

"Not at all, Captain." She glanced around, too, and let out a sigh. "I so wish he were here. He would know what to do. He was far better than I am at dealing with—" She wanted to say "adversity" but felt compelled to admit instead that the trouble she had was with "people."

"Mrs. Carson cannot say no," Lian explained. "I have been telling her we must shut the door. That is all. Simply shut it!"

Outside, the line of Chinese snaked down the porch steps and into the dusty courtyard. Shirley could see similar lines weaving from the other mission homes. The courtyard was packed with Chinese who milled around beside their mules and carts stacked high with bundles.

Captain Hsu offered a nod and said, "I will see what I can do."

He then slipped around the Chinese in the front hall, stepped outside, and stopped on the top step. He clapped his hands. Shirley made her way past the strangers, too, and brushed aside the thick curtain at one of the open dining room windows. The line of people outside grew quiet. Through the open window, she did her best to follow the words of his announcement, but his voice was too quick, though authoritative and resounding. When he finished speaking, the crowd began to disperse right away.

When Captain Hsu returned inside, Lian blushed as she looked up at him.

"What on earth did you say out there?" Shirley asked him.

"I said that you are most generous but that we are Chinese, and we must take care of ourselves. The Eighth Route Army is nearby, and they must sit tight and be patient and join us to create a harmonious and free China. Also, I said that food rations will come to all who wait outside in the courtyard and not in the house."

Lian let out a surprisingly girlish giggle. Shirley wasn't sure why she had felt predisposed to be wary of this captain, but she couldn't help smiling at him now, too.

"And *will* food come?" she asked.

"That is the plan," he said. "But meanwhile, do you need any help here?"

Lian jumped in with a reply. "We need water brought from the river. We have a decent supply of bandages but will soon need more. We have not much rice but plenty of turnips and even a few potatoes."

"Excellent, excellent," Captain Hsu said, and Lian blushed again as she bowed her head.

Was it possible that Caleb had visited the Red Army military camp without her ever having known about it? Shirley wondered. She had often discouraged him from talking about politics, so he must have chosen to spare her his interest in Communism. Although, now that she thought about it, she recognized that his impulse for egalitarianism had grown steadily over recent years. She recalled him using words like "proletariat," "cadre," and "comrade" with striking frequency.

Then it occurred to her that perhaps her husband had never mentioned his interest in Communist ideals because she was of the class the revolution wished to eliminate. With her interest in Chinese furniture and silks, not to mention her love of simple but elegant outfits worn with a strand of pearls at the collarbone—though never anything flashier than the typical ensemble of a tasteful Vassar girl—she would have been labeled bourgeois in a heartbeat. Weren't the Communists all about toppling the current structure and putting well-off people like Shirley and her parents at the very bottom of the heap? She tried to picture her stylish mother as a street sweeper or a chambermaid. Surely Caleb couldn't have hoped for that.

A cry sounded from the parlor just then, and Shirley slipped away from the other two and went in. Charles had correctly placed the wounded young man on the sofa and propped up his leg on pillows covered by a rag, but nothing more had been done for the boy. He bit down on a stick to control the pain as blood oozed through the tourniquet. Shirley noted that the color had gone from his face, and his body sweated profusely.

Shirley returned to the hallway and interrupted Captain Hsu and Lian. "Excuse me, but I will need bandages, Lian. And boiled water, please. Also, retrieve my medical bag from the far back of my bedroom closet. Captain, do you have any iodine or other antiseptic to clean the wound?"

He stared at her blankly and did not reply.

"Something to disinfect a wound?" she repeated. "Your troops must have basic first-aid supplies."

"My troops have nothing. We manage the injured with poultices and other traditional remedies. We know nothing of Western medicine."

Shirley placed her hands on her hips. "But you do know about germs? How infections occur in dirty wounds? More often than not, that is what kills a patient, not the initial injury."

She glanced around at the beleaguered Chinese and straightened her spine. Everyone knew that the average peasant's hygiene left something to be desired, but now, in this fearful time when they had left their homes in great haste and traveled on dusty roads for who knew how long, the bodily smells of the poor around her bloomed with a frightening putridness. "I swear," she muttered as she shook her head, "I sometimes think that I'm living in the Middle Ages. Ignorance and filth abound! Imagine not yet grasping the concept of germs."

The captain straightened up, too. He spoke slowly, his voice quiet and controlled. "Mrs. Carson, you are welcome to teach us new things, but we have our own knowledge, too."

His expression remained dignified as he spoke, and Shirley immediately recognized a familiar pinched feeling that came over her quite often here in China: she had once again been utterly wrong. She let her hands drop to her sides, and her gaze fell to the hardwood floor as she recalled her husband admonishing her at a similar moment. *My darling,* he had said, *the Tsar and Tsarina were executed for behaving in a less imperious manner than you.*

With her head bowed, she said, "I'm sorry, Captain. I apologize for my rudeness. I'm sure that you and your troops are excellent at what you do and know a great deal." She glanced at Lian. "It's just that this is what I do. I am a nurse. At least I was trained as one, though I haven't practiced in years."

"Very good," he said. "And useful."

"I will get the bandages now," Lian said and headed for the stairs. Dao-Ming, who must have been hiding behind Lian's back, scurried along after her.

Shirley didn't know what to say to the captain, nor did he seem to know what to say to her. They stood in the milling crowd in the hall for several endless moments as Shirley began to notice that they were the same height. When she raised her chin, their eyes met on the same plain. She wouldn't have registered such a thing back home, but here in China, where the people were so much shorter, this coincidence felt odd and almost intimate.

"Nurse Carson," he finally said.

No one had called Shirley that since before she had come to China. She wanted to argue with the captain and insist that he call her Mrs. Carson instead, but she simply replied, "Yes?"

"We have injured from this morning's skirmish out on the plains and I assume more to come. I would like to ask for your help."

"I'm terribly sorry," she began, "but I need to be with my son, especially with all this going on." She waved a hand at the chaotic scene around them. "I can't go traipsing off to some military camp up in the hills the way my husband apparently did."

Captain Hsu stepped closer. "We go wherever the fight takes us. As soon as the Japanese Imperial Army leaves this town, which we have reason to believe will be quite soon, I will bring my injured men to you here in your home. You will not have to leave the mission."

"But I have no bandages, no medicines, no beds. Nothing. And I'm not a doctor. I can't be responsible for the care and treatment of an army. That's absurd."

"Do not think of them as an army. With the Japanese here, my men will not come to you in uniform but will look like everyone else. The truth is, they are just country boys, the sons of farmers. None of us has ever seen a doctor before. Whatever you do to help us will be more than we have ever received. We just need care and attention, not complicated medical procedures, though I will see what supplies I can find. A mother's love would be a most generous and needed gift to my boys. I am sure your husband would approve."

Shirley didn't know what to say. She was about to decline the captain's request again when Charles called to her from the second floor.

"Mother, come quick," he shouted.

She did not hesitate but hurried upstairs. "What is it, Charles? Are you all right?" she called.

But when she reached the top step, her son looked perfectly fine. He held a stack of towels and other supplies but managed to grab her hand and pulled her into his bedroom. Lian was there already, standing beside the window with several rolls of bandages limp in her hands. Dao-Ming clung to her side.

Charles stood close beside Shirley at the window; his large, damp hand continued to grip hers. She placed her other palm against the warm windowpane and pressed. When Charles was young, they would sit on the window seat in the parlor on rainy days and together trace raindrops with their fingertips. They'd press their palms to the glass and leave ghostly prints, each trying to catch the other's shadow before it faded. Now, through the glass, her hand felt vibrations.

"See them out there," Charles said. "Aren't they awful?"

The thudding footfalls of Japanese soldiers shook the windowpane as they marched in unison on the dirt road outside the missionary compound. Before them staggered a line of Chinese men, most in tan Nationalist uniforms but some in peasant clothing, all with their hands and feet in iron chains. The Japanese soldiers lined the prisoners beside a ditch at a bend in the road that the Americans passed every time they went to and from market. The Japanese then took their positions, and Shirley couldn't tell which one gave the signal, but suddenly a staggering of sharp retorts sounded as a half-dozen rifles fired in quick succession. The Chinese fell, their bodies splayed in awkward positions on the ground. A cloud of yellow dust rose around them and filtered down onto their bodies, sticking where the blood quickly pooled. Then the Japanese soldiers sauntered forward, no longer in formation, and kicked the Chinese the rest of the way into the ditch.

A high-pitched moan like that of a wounded cat issued from Dao-Ming. Lian patted her back and cooed reassuring words to calm her sorrow. Or perhaps it wasn't sorrow the strange girl expressed but anger, for suddenly Lian had to block her from charging out of the room and down the stairs. Dao-Ming had certainly gotten larger since Shirley had last taken notice and was a more determined creature than she had realized. The girl's pink cheeks became streaked with tears shed from piercing eyes, but a surprising fearlessness caused her arms to flail as her voice mounted into an uncontrolled, vengeful howl.

The Japanese fishmonger's family appeared at the threshold of Charles's room and bowed their heads out of respect. Old Tupan Feng pushed past them, his complexion scarlet and his sword raised.

"We will fight the enemy!" he announced.

"Go back to sleep, Old One," Lian said. "We don't need your help. We need only the skilled and the brave. We need only the good."

Charles squeezed Shirley's fingers harder and muttered, "Can't we do something about this, Mother? Really, we must."

Shirley didn't answer but looked across to Lian in reply.

Six

The needle remained steady in Shirley's hand while Lian's thick, callused fingers on the young man's chest assured the success of the procedure. Very few people would not follow Lian's instructions when she spoke in that firm yet reassuring voice. Shirley was able to concentrate on suturing the wound and left communication with the patient to her maid.

Nursing had never been right for Shirley. Offering solicitous or comforting words didn't come naturally, though she had risen to the occasion when the young Reverend Caleb Carson with a badly broken arm had been wheeled into the hospital where she was working. He had tumbled from a ladder while placing the shiny star atop a massive fir tree on the seminary campus. A more emblematic accident could not have befallen a more charming and handsome gentleman, who quickly became her guardian angel. He had careened into Shirley's life on Christmas Eve, and she had tried to live up to his example of headlong goodness ever since. She tied off the thread now and tried to picture her husband's proud, though queasy, expression. Charles had inherited not only his red hair but also his squeamishness from his father.

"Now we clean it again," Shirley explained to Lian.

The older woman bent closer as Shirley doused the area with Mercurochrome. Charles hovered over his mother's shoulder and seemed as eager and jittery as ever, but to his credit, he had remained quiet while the delicate work was being done and hadn't distracted her.

"Good going, Mother," he said as she stood and wiped blood from her hands onto her apron, causing a tremor of disgust through him. "I had no idea you could do that."

"There's much a son never knows about his mother," Shirley said with a raised eyebrow, unable to hide how pleased she was with herself. "You can handle the bandaging?" she asked Lian.

Her maid, now her Number One Assistant, nodded. Dao-Ming, at her side, helped collect the rags that had sopped up the blood. They would need to reuse them, Shirley realized. Without proper supplies, they would have to be frugal and clever. She decided not to dwell on the difficulties ahead but instead was grateful that this one young man appeared in better shape than when he had hobbled through the front door.

Then she gazed around at the crowded parlor, the packed dining room and front hall, and grasped that each person here needed something—food, water, or medical attention. An ancient grandfather who had been carried in on a stretcher had since died. There must have been three hundred people in her home, each with his or her own story of hardship. Shirley pushed aside the muslin curtain from a front window and guessed that there had to be several thousand more Chinese out in the courtyard.

"Mrs. Carson?" a familiar, tentative voice asked.

Shirley turned to greet Reverend Richard Wells, the head of the mission.

"I wanted to check on how you are doing," he said. "Very good of you to open your doors to all these people."

"Not at all," she said as she tried to contain a curl fallen from her bun.

When Shirley had risen that day, she had decided to finally set aside her mourning garb and instead put on a delicate lace outfit in anticipation of her planned tea with Kathryn. With all the subsequent commotion, the date with her friend was now out of the question, but she was glad nonetheless to have accidentally dressed appropriately to receive the Reverend. Normally she would like to have drawn a comb through her hair or freshened up her lipstick before a visitor arrived, but she was starting to grasp that such concerns were a thing of the past.

The Reverend Wells's owl eyes in his thick glasses blinked several times as he noticed the bloodstains on her apron. "Are you injured, Mrs. Carson?"

"Heavens, no, I'm fine. This is from that wounded fellow over there. I've just finished extracting a bullet from his leg."

Reverend Wells looked across to the young man on the sofa. "I see," he said and smiled politely.

Wells was a nervous man, easily overwhelmed, though an un-natural calm came over him when he rose to the pulpit. Shirley admired his sermons, which were quite erudite. She had often wished that she and Reverend Wells could sit down and parse the Bible, or Chinese culture, or any topic together, but she was relegated to the women's conversations instead. The lady mis-sionaries were a dear bunch, but none of them, except perhaps Kathryn, was a serious thinker.

Wells glanced out at the crowded compound through the screened window. "We've estimated close to five thousand have arrived. Can you imagine? The most we've ever had at Christ-mas service was five hundred. We finally had to shut the gates. I hated to do it, but we had no choice."

"My, I would never have guessed such an enormous number. Whatever will we do with them?"

Wells's lips trembled slightly. Shirley realized the terrible irony for him: for years, he had avoided the missionary trail, preferring to stay in his library rather than go out, as Caleb had, to meet the actual Chinese in town and countryside. But now they had come en masse to him anyway.

"I gather," she offered, "that the Eighth Route Army of the Reds is somewhere about and intends to help as best they can."

"We're not supposed to get involved with the Communists, although they do seem to have a good touch with the local people and better success against the Japanese. But the American board in Boston has sent strict orders for us not to become entangled in Chinese internal politics. That is the policy."

Shirley straightened her spine. "Policy or no, our American board is in America, Reverend. They can't possibly understand the situation here when we can hardly understand it ourselves."

As she spoke, Reverend Wells seemed to duck into his collar, and his face turned a soft and lovely pink. Shirley could imagine her husband whispering frantically in her ear that not everyone was accustomed to what he politely called her *straightforwardness* when what he really meant was her *bossiness*. Ladies, and most especially ministers' wives—in Shirley's opinion an all-too-often simpering and milquetoast bunch—were not meant to speak that way.

She pressed on in a more measured tone. "I just don't think we can follow directives from afar, given the changing circumstances. Don't you agree, Reverend?"

"Yes, of course, you're right. Absolutely right," he said, head bobbing.

Shirley waited for him to continue, but when he did not, she asked, "And so, what *do* you plan to do?"

His eyes darted out the window again. "The Eighth Route Army, you say?"

"I must introduce you to Captain Hsu."

"Why, yes, Captain Hsu," Reverend Wells said, his voice rising in confidence again. "There's an excellent fellow. He used to stop by our Bible study group from time to time."

"Is that so?" she asked. "I was sure the Communists are against religion. Isn't that one of their central tenets?"

"He's not a believer. He came to the study group out of respect for your husband, whom he greatly admired. They developed a friendship of sorts. Caleb was always keen to know the Chinese on their own terms, and he took that experiment to its furthest extent with Hsu. But the captain has a fine mind." Reverend Wells tapped a finger to his thinning hair. "A top-notch intellect. I think Caleb genuinely enjoyed his company. But I'm sure you know all about that."

Shirley nodded pleasantly and did her best to hide her disbelief. How had Caleb developed such a full-blown friendship with someone whom she had never even met? Since his death, she had spent hours and days recollecting the man she had loved. So many moments with him drowning her mind in a ceaseless torrent until she felt there was nothing more to remember, nothing more to know. But now the awkward, though reliable, man before her seemed to suggest a whole chapter of her husband's life about which she knew nothing.

She was about to ask more when Reverend Wells patted her sleeve and gestured for her to follow him into a quieter corner of the front hall. He lowered his voice even further, and she leaned in to listen.

"The other reason I came by, Mrs. Carson, was to tell you that your Lian's family from the country has arrived here at the mission. It appears they want to join my household. I thought you should know."

Shirley stood upright. "How absurd. They should be here with us, of course. If they arrive on your doorstep, send them over to me right away."

"I'm sorry, this is awkward, Mrs. Carson, but Lian visited my wife late last evening and asked our permission." He ducked and hedged again, "Apparently you had not invited them to join your household? I'm sure it was a simple misunderstanding."

Shirley was suddenly aware of Dao-Ming at her side. She shooed the girl away and glanced over at Lian, who chatted with the injured boy and his friends.

"Thank you for coming to tell me, Reverend. I'll take care of it right away," Shirley said. "I seem to have missed the cues Lian offered me last night. I'm not accustomed to the politeness of the Chinese. I was raised to speak up if I wanted something. Simply ask! The business of dropping hints, or even saying the exact opposite of what you want, is entirely lost on me. Caleb was a far more sympathetic soul and better at grasping the subtleties of communication between native and foreigner. I'm abysmal at it."

She started to turn, intending to go immediately to Lian to straighten this out.

"Mrs. Carson," the Reverend said as he took her elbow in a

firm grip, "may I suggest that you let it rest for the moment? After I've gone, offer her family a gracious invitation. You don't want it to seem that you have offered it under duress, do you?"

Shirley looked down at him, and, as Caleb would have advised, she inhaled a long, careful breath. "Quite right. Good of you to remind me, Reverend. I have a hot head and can make terrible messes when I don't control my impulses."

He shuffled from side to side and offered little reassuring noises. "Simple mistake," he said. "We all do it. They are so very different from us."

Shirley made herself smile but understood that the problem was not with the Chinese—though they could be difficult to grasp—but with her own obtuseness. She had never been skilled at picking up social signals of any sort. She withered in the company of well-bred ladies who had been raised to chatter with one another on a different plain, hemming and hawing and never getting to any particular point. Shirley found taking tea with them most aggravating. The topic was always the weather, or their husbands' sartorial habits, and nothing of any interest was ever said outright but only implied. Days later would she learn that factions had formed over the course of dull conversation and cucumber sandwiches.

"Mrs. Carson," Reverend Wells interrupted her thoughts, "do you mind me asking, what you meant earlier by saying that you removed a bullet from that Chinese boy, per se?"

"I meant precisely that. I say what I mean, Reverend, and I mean what I say. I'm simple that way." She let out a sigh. "Perhaps at some point, my husband mentioned to you that I am a trained nurse?"

"Ah," he said as a bewildered look overcame his face and he

shook his head. "So sorry, I don't recall. He very well may have. I am terrible at remembering details about, well, people."

A headache had bloomed over Shirley's right eye. Normally, at this time of day, she would be curled up in her bed, either crying about her lost husband or, before his death, reading. Endlessly engaging with people, which she had done since first thing this morning, struck her as unrelenting torture. Clearly Reverend Wells knew the feeling.

"I realize I have been holed up for weeks," she said, "ever since word came of my husband's death, and before that I kept to myself perhaps more than I should have. I'm sure you've noticed that I have never been an active community member. I'm simply not a joiner, Reverend. I don't enjoy—communication. I know that's criminal, especially for a minister's wife, but you, of all people, can understand that I prefer the company of books and ideas."

The Reverend let out a long sigh, as if he, too, was aching for his library at that very moment.

Shirley gazed out the window again at the shuffling masses in the courtyard. "But I have always found the Chinese fascinating. The variations in their language alone warrant our attention. I would love to study it at university. And such intriguing customs that I barely fathom even after living here for five years. Sadly, though, I never pursued my intellectual interests beyond college. Instead I developed the skills that were expected of me. Like so many girls, I became a nurse, not that it suited me then, or now."

Reverend Wells let out an understanding grunt. He leaned in closer as if they now shared a secret understanding. "Life flows along, doesn't it, dragging us with it? It carries us down unexpected and often less rewarding streams until we are spit out into the ocean and have no way back. The tide pulls us, and there we are—out in the vast blue." He rocked forward onto his toes, a hopeful glow appearing on his face, his voice barely hiding a rising sense of mirth. "Everyone must know," he continued, "that I, of all people, am not meant to be a leader of men, and yet here I am—in charge! That is simply how it is. We must rise to our calling, Mrs. Carson, however ill suited we may feel."

His eyes glistened, and an impish smile appeared. "But how fortunate for us that you are a nurse," he exclaimed. "I will tell the others. Already today, Doc Sturgis has set up the mission infirmary for typhoid inoculations. With the unsanitary conditions and refuse problems, we need that right away."

The Reverend paused and looked at her, waiting, it seemed for her to say something rousing as well. When she didn't, he carried on, his eyes still sparkling behind the thick lenses. "I suggest we relieve Doc Sturgis by setting up another, smaller clinic here in your home. What do you say, Mrs. Carson? It would not be for the worst cases but for more routine problems that suit your nursing skills. We really must take advantage of your training."

Shirley felt distracted by the sight of Lian crossing the hall, a cast-iron pot of bloodied water sloshing in her hands. Dao-Ming followed close behind, her arms laden with used towels.

"I'm sorry, Reverend," she said. "I must go help the others now."

"So here, then? A clinic?" he asked again. "I would offer the Parish Hall, but it is packed to the gills with people already, and I think we'd do better to start small. If word gets out that we're opening an actual hospital here, there will be no end to the Chinese."

Shirley glanced around again at her crowded home, then out at the overrun courtyard, then back to the Reverend, who seemed to be trembling again, but perhaps now with nervous excitement. "There *is* no end to the Chinese, Reverend," she said. "That is the truth of it."

"Yes, and they need our help now more than ever. Your caring and talents can make all the difference."

He was such a sincere little man, Shirley thought, his expression straining with optimism and conviction. She had lacked both of those qualities for so long, she marveled that he could exhibit them so easily. He was a leader of people after all, she thought. Short and with poor eyesight and more dedicated to learning than to life, Reverend Wells appeared to have taken the plunge required of him. In the little boat of his life, he was heading out into the wide and turbulent ocean he had described. There would be no turning back. Shirley supposed that the dizzying feeling that surrounded her now was the tide pulling her out to join him.

"I will need medical supplies," she said. "Have your people bring in as many cots as we can wedge into the parlor and the dining room. Move the table out here in the hall, but leave the piano. Music can soothe a wounded soul."

"Absolutely, Mrs. Carson," he said. "Thank you."

"Let's carry on, then, shall we? Stiff upper lip and all that, as my husband used to say." She finally offered a smile.

Where, she thought, was Caleb? It remained unfathomable to her that he was not at her side any longer. She hoped somehow that he was looking down on her and approving, because she couldn't manage without the thought of him doing so. From now on, she would behave as he would have wished. She would finally rise to the occasion here in China and do some actual good.

Seven

Charles cut across the compound and dodged down the back alley between the Parish Hall and the Chinese Boys' School. He came out in a second courtyard and continued to wind past more clusters of displaced Chinese, some still restless and shuffling about, others sunk listlessly in the sun. He hopped over their bundles of clothing, blackened woks, cast-iron pots, straw baskets of all sizes, bags of grain, and even cooking fires where they had set up camp. Mothers sat on their haunches and chopped vegetables or prepared rice and tea, calling for their children to stay near and not climb too high in the trees. Already patched and tattered clothing and gray undergarments hung from the cherry and ginkgo branches. Shriveled grandmothers in many-layered traditional dresses shouted across the yard to one another as Charles quickly surmised that whole villages, not just individual families, had escaped here together. They had made it out of their ancient pasts and into an uncertain future as one.

The Chinese men congregated and smoked, leaning against the serpentine brick wall dotted with lattice windows. The men didn't look out at the distant plains but instead leaned toward one another and spoke in serious, urgent tones. Grandfathers slept without pillows under their heads in the shadow of the wall as their sons and grandsons whispered over them about what to do next.

These people were not soldiers, Charles realized, and yet they were already irreparably harmed by war. He recalled that some of the Chinese men he had seen executed that morning hadn't worn military uniforms. Chinese citizens, he was starting to grasp, as often as soldiers, were prey to the Japanese Imperial Army.

If only his father were here to explain it all. Caleb Carson knew China better than most foreigners, from his many trips into the countryside and friendships with the people. Charles pulled out his father's marble chop. On one end was carved Fenghuang, the mythical phoenix, with wings partially upraised. His father had taught him that for the Chinese, this bird was a hopeful symbol, suggesting the warmth of the summer sun and the fruitful unification of Yin and Yang. The mysterious creature brought good fortune. For Westerners, the phoenix rising from the ashes had always represented renewal and rebirth. If only his father had carried this good-luck charm with him out on the trail, Charles thought, maybe he wouldn't have perished under the shifting ground.

He pressed the other end of the chop against the back of his hand and was surprised to notice that the bright-red ink made not the Chinese characters for his father's name but the image of a winged phoenix. His father's chop bore that magical symbol, not a written name. Charles lifted his hand into the sunlight and felt a flicker of something—if not hope, then perhaps comfort—as the bird rose. He then let his hand drop again to his side and kept on to the servants' quarters.

In front of Han's shack, he caught his breath. The simple woven bamboo screen that blocked the door remained in place, which struck Charles as odd, given that it was midday. He stepped around it, and when he knocked on the door, it swung open. The single room remained dim even in daylight, but Charles's eyes adjusted, and he could see that no one was inside. No candles flickered in front of the modest altar to the family's ancestors. The sepia-toned, faded photo of Han's grandmother and grandfather in their formal attire wasn't there. The straw sleeping mats that Han and his father usually kept rolled in the corner were missing, too.

Over in the small kitchen area, the storage shelf stood bare, the larder empty. The straw at the back of the cooking stove had been swept clean, and no logs remained stacked ready to be placed inside the oven. The hole where the wok usually sat above the flame was also empty, and the many straw baskets, tin bucket, and wooden water ladle that usually hung beside the stove were all gone, too. The only things left behind were the two ladder-back chairs Charles's mother had given Cook. They remained against the wall, as unused as ever.

Charles turned and left, shutting the door behind him. He strode down the alley, offering a tentative bow to several servants' families, though he didn't recognize most of the faces and they returned his greeting with blank stares. Charles wondered if the ones from deep in the countryside had ever seen a white boy before.

As he approached Lian's quarters, he noticed that the screen had been pulled back and clouds of smoke from the cook fire billowed out the door. Something was wrong with the chimney, he thought. If his father had been alive, he would have attended to it right away. Charles squeezed the cool marble chop in his pocket and remembered his father insisting on the importance of treating others as you wished them to treat you, no matter their station in life. Charles could recall him pressing the point in the pulpit but more often on the streets of the provincial Chinese town, where Charles had stayed close to his side and held on tightly to his hand.

Once, when Charles was seven, his father had bent down and given a coin to a legless beggar and instructed Charles to share one of his dried oatcakes with the man. Charles liked to carry an extra snack tucked in his pocket when they went on outings, but he did as he was told. He tossed the cake onto the ground before the beggar, then turned away from the gruesome sight of the man's stumps. But his father yanked Charles back and insisted that he pick up the oatcake and place it directly into the beggar's filthy hand. In English, he said, *We are not offering food to a dangerous mongrel, my boy, but to a fellow human being.* Then his father stayed and had a conversation with the beggar as he stuffed the food into his toothless mouth.

Only Caleb Carson, Charles had come to realize as he got older, would inflict such an experience on a small child while wearing a smile and repeating the Golden Rule. His knees felt weak as the realization swept over him again that the reliable, wise person of his father was no longer alive. Charles swallowed and tried to focus on the problem at hand. If his father wasn't here, then he could at least summon up what he would think: something must be done about Lian's faulty chimney.

Charles looked away from the roof and noticed an old woman crouched on her haunches outside the door. Beside her, a girl who Charles guessed was around his age sat on the stone bench. The two ate with fast-moving chopsticks from bowls and seemed to be engaged in a heated argument.

He bowed. "Pardon me, esteemed grandmother," he began,

"I am sent from the Carson household, where Lian works. We would be honored to have your company at our home."

The old woman looked up with eyes milky from cataracts. She tipped her head to the side and shouted in a different dialect—one from the countryside that Charles happened to recognize because many of the mission servants spoke it.

"Who is it that speaks so poorly to us?" the grandmother asked the girl. "His voice hurts my ears."

The girl answered her grandmother in the same country dialect. "Hush," the girl said. "He is a white boy. American, I think. He must be the son of that witch Lian works for."

Charles tried not to laugh. He continued in the more formal dialect, which the girl seemed to understand, not wanting to embarrass them by showing that he had grasped their rude comments.

"Lian works for us, and my mother would like to invite you to come with me to stay at our home."

The old woman said, "He sounds like someone caught his tongue in the door."

Charles felt a flame of indignation. No one had ever said he didn't speak well. He would have to ask Han for his honest opinion. The old woman must have cotton in her ears.

"My grandmother thanks you for the kind offer," the girl said, "but we are quite contented here. Lian's home is not large, but there is room for us. She is at her employer's so much of the time, year in and year out, that we rarely see her, but we are quite happy to be here now."

Charles noted the dig she had slipped into her reply. So Lian felt she worked too many hours and days. No doubt, Charles thought. He would speak to his mother about that.

"Are you sure you don't want to come?" he asked again. "We have food and mats for sleeping. Don't you want to be with your Auntie Lian?"

The girl turned to the old woman again and said in the country dialect, "He says they have food and a place to sleep. How about we go?"

"They poison us with their food. I don't trust foreigner devils. How do we know they are any different from the Japanese dogs? They come to rob us. No, we will make our own food. I remember when all we had was stone soup. I remember when the Righteous Harmony Society chased them all out! That was the right idea!"

The girl waved her hand and said, "I've heard your old stories, Grandmother. Maybe I don't want to eat stone soup."

"All right then, go! Leave me here. I will sit like this all day."

As the girl stood, she swayed slightly, light-headed, Charles guessed, from hunger. He wanted to offer her a hand but didn't reach out. The top of the girl's head barely came to his shoulder, her collarbone protruded, and her arms were as thin as young bamboo. But her eyes, dark, iridescent pools, still caught the light. Nothing about her seemed dull to Charles, but clearly she needed more meat on her bones.

"We thank you for the invitation, but my grandmother has been through a lot. It took us days to get here. Lian's food is the first we've had in a while. My grandmother needs to rest before we move anywhere."

"I understand," Charles said, "but I'll drop by again soon to see—" he looked down at the grandmother—"how she is doing."

The girl blushed, and Charles realized that his cheeks were warm, too. He didn't know what to do with his hands, and before he knew it, he had reached out to shake hers. The girl's hand seemed to have no substance to it at all, and he hoped he didn't squeeze too hard. When they let go, she sat down quickly, and he turned away fast.

"Also, I'll bring something to fix the chimney," he shouted over his shoulder as he started down the alley. "It really shouldn't smoke up the room like that. That's not right."

"Yes," she said, "not right," though when he glanced back, she was smiling.

Eight

Charles didn't rush on his way home, and when he emerged from the alley, he saw that the central courtyard remained as crowded as when he had left. He wasn't sure what he had hoped for—perhaps that the Chinese would have all gone back to wherever it was they had come from. It was only the end of the first day since their arrival, and he felt worn out with them already. Charles could hear his father whispering a stern reminder to not be selfish—to think of others, not only himself.

Someone bumped his shoulder, and he stumbled over a stack of straw suitcases held together with a cracked leather belt. More Chinese pushed past, and Charles ducked under the branches of his favorite cherry tree. He reached to grasp the black, slick limbs that he had climbed when he was small. Chinese of every sort surrounded him. Families mostly, with children stumbling along, as burdened as the elders, lugging their own things. The rise and fall of Chinese intonations washed over him in a hot tide, and the shade of the tree did little to cool him. Charles breathed through his mouth to avoid the stench that had started to rise in the courtyard, where latrines had not yet been set up.

He felt certain that he had nothing in common with these desperately poor people who were now victims of war, and yet, as he looked around, he felt an affinity with them. They had all faced their own personal tragedies to arrive here. The Chinese before him huddled so close that their bowed heads practically touched. Charles realized that he and his mother, in the wake of their family's great loss, had lost track of one another. He wanted to be more like these Chinese, he thought, and set off to tell her so.

Charles pushed away from the cherry tree, stepped over and around more people, and went up his porch steps. He slipped into his home, apologizing to those who pressed to follow him inside. He shut the heavy carved door, rested his back against it, and shut his eyes.

A moment later, a woman's voice said, "Had a long day, honey?" His mother's friend, Miss James, leaned against the wall beside him. "You always wanted more to happen around here," she said. "Now you've got it."

He tried to smile.

"I'm sorry your dad's not with us anymore. He'd know how to handle this."

Charles looked down at his shoes, covered in yellow summertime dust. He'd forgotten to stomp his feet before entering. He'd probably forgotten a lot of other normal things, too, because nothing was normal anymore. He wished people wouldn't mention his father so often.

"Your mother's going to be real busy from now on." Miss James nodded toward the dining room, where his mother was instructing several Chinese men on where to place some cots. "If you need anything, kid, you ask me, okay? The single ladies' dorm isn't nearly so overrun as your place. We have a few empty bedrooms with perfectly decent beds. You come over anytime, and I'll sneak you in. This house is going to be crazy now that it's a medical clinic."

"A medical clinic?"

"She says they enlisted her, though I can tell that she loves it. You know how she likes to be in charge."

Miss James seemed to be trying to get a rise out of him, but he wasn't sure why. She always acted as if they were in cahoots, though Charles never knew about what. He supposed it was just her way of showing that she thought of herself as a younger sister to his mother, even though they were close in age.

"But we'll help her out, won't we, Charles? We'll roll up our sleeves together."

He tried to dodge her hand as she reached to pat down his hair.

"You might even become a doctor someday because of all this. That's looking on the bright side."

"I hate the sight of blood," he said.

She wiped something off his cheek with her thumb, and he wriggled away. "Oh, you'll get over that. I can picture you in a white doctor's coat. You'll be quite the catch."

Charles doubted he'd ever get over his squeamishness, and he didn't feel so great about Miss James right now, either. She was his mother's best friend, and he knew that meant he should like her best, but sometimes she acted strange.

"Have you had anything to eat today?" she asked.

Charles shook his head.

"I see how this is going to be. Your mother's still not taking care of you, you poor thing. You need to come over to my place, and I'll feed you. Right now. Let's go." She took him by the wrist.

"I just got back, Miss James. I want to tell Mother something. And I think we have food here. I'm okay. Really, I am."

She patted down his collar and said, "All right, but I've got my eye on you. We can't have you being neglected, can we?" She pointed a long finger at him and offered a flash of white teeth.

Her hand hovered a moment longer, and as if she couldn't help herself, she started to adjust his jacket where it was hitched up wrong on his shoulder.

"Stop it," he finally said and shifted away. "I can take care of myself."

She laughed a little, as if it was funny that he didn't want her pawing at him.

"Remember, now, if you need anything," she said again, "just let me know."

As she reached for the front doorknob, Charles spoke up. "Actually, Miss James," he said, "I'm trying to find my friend Han. You know, our cook's son?"

"Sure, I know Han."

"No one seems to know where he is."

"I'll ask around. But don't worry too much. Everyone's a little out of place right now. And by the by, call me Kathryn. It makes me feel old when you call me Miss James."

As she headed out the front door and negotiated the crowd outside, he heard her apologizing to them for their wait. She wasn't so bad, he realized, just a little peculiar around him for some reason. Charles then went to join his mother, who stood with her hands on her hips in the middle of what used to be their dining room.

"I found Lian's mother, and a girl was with her," he started right in. "Probably her niece. Did you know that Lian has a niece?"

His mother continued to point at the cots and bark orders at the men helping her.

"I forgot to ask her name," Charles continued. "Do you happen to know Lian's niece's name?"

Finally his mother stopped what she was doing and took him by the shoulders. "Charles, thank goodness you're back. I was worried sick." She kissed him hard on the forehead. They stood eye to eye now, and her usual kiss to the crown of his head was no longer possible, so she had substituted this awkward placement. He wished she wouldn't kiss him at all, especially not in front of everyone. He wasn't a little boy anymore.

She let go of his shoulders and said, "We have so much to do, son, it's mind-boggling."

"The thing is," he tried again, circling around and blocking her way, "I couldn't find Han anywhere. Have you seen him?"

"Han? No."

"I have to find him, Mother. He's my friend."

"He'll turn up. Everyone's gone a bit missing right now." She offered a quick smile.

"But what if he doesn't? What if he ends up like those men lined up by the Japanese this morning? We have to do something. We have to find him!"

His mother turned. "Darling, I understand your concern. But I want you to look around and notice. *All* these people need our help, not just one. We have to think about the whole, not just the individual. Captain Hsu was saying something to me this afternoon that resonated so deeply. 'The people, and the people alone, are the motivating force in the making of world history,' he said. Isn't that a simple, yet staggering, thought? These people, Charles, these people right here are the makers of world history. We need to face that extraordinary fact and help as many of them as we can."

Color had come back into his mother's cheeks, and her forehead glistened under her fallen wisps of hair. He could barely follow what she was talking about but thought that at least she wasn't as miserable as she had been. His mother—lost for so many weeks and gone over to the ghosts—was now replaced by this manic person before him.

"Whatever you say, Mother. That's swell. But I'm going to find Han. I'll see you later."

Before she could object, he had turned on his heel and left the house again.

In the ruins of the splintered guardhouse, Charles found Mr. Sung, the blind self-appointed watchman. With his three-legged stool nowhere in sight, the man crouched on his haunches, his can beside him, as always. The high ping of his betel juice hitting the tin was the most recognizable sound outside the mission.

"Esteemed Mr. Sung, are you all right?"

The old man stopped chewing and cocked his head. "American boy?"

"I didn't expect to find you, grandfather."

"I am here," the old man said matter-of-factly.

Charles looked beyond the dirt road to the ditch, where some of the bodies of the Chinese men had still not been collected.

"Do you want to come inside the compound, sir?" Charles asked. "It would be safer."

"I must not leave my spot," the old man said. "It is my duty."

Charles pressed his forearm against his eyes. "All right, then," he said, mustering a voice as much like his father's as he could. "Carry on! Keep up the good work! Fight the foe!"

The old man gave a blackened grin and saluted.

As Charles headed up the rutted road toward town, he tried

not to stare at the dead bodies. Contorted in the worst possible ways, they lay in pools of blood, slick and iridescent as tar. Flies lit and swarmed. Charles yanked his gaze away and watched the millet swaying in the fields, golden in the sun. He tried to fathom how such a fine summer day could continue unchanged.

The town consisted of only several shops on one side of the main street. Across the way, the flimsy cardboard and splintered wooden stalls of the farmers' market displayed meager root vegetables and fruit. The fishmonger also sold his catch there, if he had any. The Chinese usually had very little money, so commerce tended to be irregular at best. Still, Charles hoped to find his friend. He skirted piles of rubble, broken boards, and clods of soil where the land had been ripped open, Charles guessed by grenades. Hand-to-hand combat must have taken place here, but he saw no Japanese soldiers now. Instead, an eeriness filled the quiet town in the aftermath of that morning's skirmish.

At the entrance to the market, several more Chinese soldiers lay dead. One boy had been bayoneted through the ribs and left to die beside another with his head tipped back unnaturally, his throat slit. Charles stared for too long and had to race to a gully to vomit. When he opened his eyes again, he saw that the churned-up soil before him had also run with blood. He knew he should turn back. He had no business being outside the mission. He had never seen anything like this, and he knew his mother wouldn't want him to see it. She had tried to shield him for so long, but how could she here in China, where, even before this Japanese attack, illness, starvation, and other deprivations abounded? Charles thought his father had been right to introduce him to the legless beggar years before.

Look him in the eye, he had said, *even if his eyes are crusted over and he cannot see you. Search, my boy, for the human soul inside the suffering.*

But Charles wondered if even his father would have felt this was too much evil to witness. He wiped his mouth on his rumpled sleeve, then tore off his jacket altogether and, with shaking hands, placed it over the head and torso of the young soldier whose throat had been cut. Charles continued deeper into what remained of the market, searching for at least one open booth or anyone who looked familiar. He wanted to shout Han's name but didn't dare expose him. Although Charles still had not seen any Japanese soldiers, he worried that they could be anywhere, hidden in doorways or behind toppled carts. Farther down the destroyed row of stalls, Charles noticed that the Japanese fishmonger's place had been burned to the ground. Sheets of paper stamped with the Japanese flag hung on what remained.

He finally stumbled on a stall that appeared open, two meager piles of shriveled turnips and potatoes displayed before the owner, who sat on a low stool. Charles bowed, but the woman's dull eyes showed no recognition.

"Madam Chen, I'm Charles Carson. Remember me, from Sunday school? Your son and I, we played together years ago?" When he mentioned her son, Charles thought a flash of recognition passed over the woman's face.

"Fifty thousand," she said.

"Pardon me?"

"No less."

"For turnips?"

She scoffed and looked away.

"Have you seen Han, by any chance?" Charles tried. "You

know, the cook's boy? He was in Sunday school with your son and me."

"Do not mention my noble son," she said, glaring now. "The boys are gone. No more boys. You go now, too." She brushed him off as if he were an annoying fly.

As Charles thought about it, he realized she was right. On his walk through town, he had seen only elders and young children. A few mothers but no fathers, and certainly no young men who weren't already soldiers in uniform.

"Where is everyone?" he asked. "Where are my friends?"

She spat on the ground. "They are not your friends. They were never your friends."

Charles staggered back and took off running, dodging the craters in the road and the few remaining Chinese who walked with bundles on their backs or pushing cumbersome wheelbarrows piled high with junk. He passed more Chinese soldiers fallen by the roadside and didn't want to look but made himself, to make sure they were not Han.

At the Buddhist temple, Charles bent double and put his hands on his knees. As he caught his breath, he noticed that the grand spreading cedar tree had been struck and had lost a few limbs. He ran up the low steps and saw light streaming in through gaping holes in the damaged roof. Normally it was so dark and smoky from incense inside the temple that you could hardly see anything, but now the slanting sun revealed that the idols had been badly chipped and shattered by mortar fire. Only one of the standing Buddhas remained intact. Around it, someone had placed fresh flowers, newly lit candles, and incense.

Charles wondered who would even consider coming here on such a hellish day to light candles. He wanted to shout that people lay dying in the streets, and any strength should be saved for them, not for one's ancestors, or the Buddha, or for that matter Jesus Christ. Back at the mission, additional services had been scheduled for every afternoon, not just Sundays. Charles couldn't imagine why people would waste time praying instead of trying to stop the nightmare that was taking place around them. He wondered if he could ever make himself go to church again, knowing what God had allowed on this day. His father would tell him otherwise, but his father had not seen what Charles had seen.

Outside again on the dirt road, he kept his eyes down and started spotting small treasures—ammunition clips, cartridge cases, a canteen, and hundreds of pieces of paper with the Japanese flag printed on them. He scooped these items up and stuffed them into his pockets alongside his father's phoenix chop and his penknife—all for what purpose he didn't know. From the ground, he lifted a Chinese Army cap with the blue-and-white Kuomintang insignia and twelve-pointed sun. He slapped it against his leg, and yellow dust scattered. As he put it on, Charles wished he could show Han, but he was starting to suspect that his friend might already have one of his own.

With the mission compound in sight just up the road, two Japanese soldiers shouted in Chinese for Charles to halt. Before he knew it, the tip of a bayonet had knocked his new cap off his head.

"We could have shot you, America," a young Japanese soldier shouted. "Foolish boy, do not wear Chinese Army cap."

Charles realized it was the kid who had swept their back steps. "Hey, how's it going? How come you're still here?" Charles asked. "Looks like the rest of your company's moved on."

"Do not ask questions," the older soldier said. Then he turned to the younger soldier and asked, "Who is this kid?"

"This is no-good, spoiled American," the younger soldier explained.

The older Japanese soldier pressed Charles's shoulder with the sharp tip of his bayonet.

"Hey, now," Charles said, "I'm not the enemy."

"America is weak, worthless country."

Charles tried to think fast, tried to think at all with the bayonet blade so near his neck. "Say, you fellows ever hear of Jean Harlow, the movie actress?"

Their eyes remained unflinching.

"You know about Hollywood, right?"

The older soldier may have nodded.

"Then you know that Hollywood's biggest star is Jean Harlow." Charles was surprised by the jauntiness of his own voice. "She's my girlfriend. That's the truth of it. She and I been going steady for a while now."

The older soldier cocked his head, and the younger one leaned forward almost imperceptibly.

"I need to get going," Charles said as he started to back away. "My girlfriend's waiting for me. Jean Harlow. Remember that name. You see her on the screen someday, and you'll know, she's my girl. See you around, fellas." Charles offered a little wave, turned, and started to stride off.

"Halt, America!" the older one shouted.

Charles's frantic pulse whooshed in his ears, and he worried that he might faint, but he swallowed and turned back. "What now?" he asked. "My girlfriend's going to be mad if I'm late."

"You no Hollywood," the younger one said.

"You bet I am!" Charles said. "I'm Hollywood all over!"

The soldiers glanced at one another, and in that instant, Charles snatched up the Chinese Nationalist cap from the ground and took off running.

"American devil!" they shouted after him.

Charles pulled the cap onto his head and felt like himself for the first time that day.

Nine

Over the following days and weeks, the injured continued to arrive from the countryside. Shirley's brief nursing experience, which had begun in the emergency room at Cleveland General, then shifted to daytime hours in the pediatric ward, had done little to prepare her for this. Chinese came, leaning on one another and on sticks, some carried in on homemade stretchers. All of them, Captain Hsu insisted, were civilians, although it seemed obvious to her that his men had simply disguised themselves. They exchanged their uniforms for peasant clothing or turned their shabby jackets inside out and stuffed their red-starred caps into their pockets. Despite Reverend Wells's warnings against getting tangled up in the conflict, Shirley thought that even if the young men had been wearing proper uniforms, she wouldn't have turned them away. Many weren't much older than her son, and all were badly in need of care.

Every day, Hsu stood by the front door and determined who would be seen and who would be denied care. Shirley's feverish hope to help them all was impossible. She knew that. Her job was difficult, but when she glanced over and saw the captain shake his head at some beleaguered person, she understood that his task was even worse.

When sporadic fighting erupted in the countryside at river and railroad crossings, or on roads that led to crucial mountain passes, more disguised soldiers arrived, along with hapless peasants of all ages who had been caught in the crossfire. Some engagements involved heavy artillery, though Shirley surmised that hand-to-hand combat also often occurred. The knife wounds alarmed her almost more than injuries caused by bullets. The Japanese seemed expert at slicing the bodies of their enemies, leaving them without fingers, hands or eyes. Shirley began to think that those hit by grenades or mortar fire were the luckiest because they would die the quickest.

And then the Chinese women started to arrive, and Shirley thought that what they had survived was worse. Although the bulk of the Japanese Imperial Army had departed for the front to the north, several units remained in town and went on rampages, seeking food and the spoils of war. Chinese women stumbled into the clinic, barely able to walk. Some could no longer speak, their minds having left the shells of their flesh behind. The young girls were the most tragic, but several grandmothers had born the same treatment.

Shirley couldn't imagine that Doc Sturgis over at the infirmary was encountering anything worse. Reverend Wells had promised that she would receive the less challenging cases, but she soon realized that Captain Hsu, who seemed to have a network of Chinese throughout the mission, the town, and the region, either orchestrated, or was at least aware of, everything that went on. He could answer any question or see to any request, and Shirley had quickly come to rely on him, as did many others. It was also becoming clear to her that the Red Army's infiltration of the province over the previous months had made it a target for the Japanese in the first place. The Red soldiers bore the brunt of the ongoing nightly air raids on the plains out beyond the town, yet Shirley couldn't help but blame them for the trouble and wish they would move on to another province altogether.

One evening, she sat at the bedside of a young soldier who appeared to have survived an attempted beheading. She had chosen not to wrap this poor boy's head because she couldn't risk having bandages stick to the horrific wound. The truth was that she would need them shortly for the next patient. The youth sat up with a dazed and distant expression, his skull essentially sliced open. She estimated that he would die within a half hour of arriving, and as he did, she held his hand until the end. He never spoke. And she, with all her expertise in the Chinese dialects of the region, did not say a word, either. She felt herself soften as she gently squeezed his hand. As he breathed his last halting breaths, she said a prayer in his language, not about Jesus but about finding rest and peace elsewhere and with his ancestors, his family far from here. When she finally stepped away from the bed, she did not cry. She felt more useless than ever but also knew that she had done her best under the circumstances.

Captain Hsu appeared at her side and asked, as he often did, if she needed anything. Shirley raised her eyes and stared into the man's lined face. She considered that his pockmarks and the scar over his right brow could have made him appear sinister and yet didn't. Instead, he seemed serious but kind. That his eyes were even with hers came as a relief after this long day. She was tired of looking down into the faces of people she could not possibly save. They had stared up at her with hope, even when there was no reason for hope.

"I could use a smoke," she said.

He reached into his jacket breast pocket and pulled out a tin case of hand-rolled Chinese cigarettes.

"This will make me even dizzier than I already am."

"Did you eat, Nurse Carson?"

She took a cigarette and wandered toward the screen door, where a slight evening breeze seeped over the threshold. No one waited in line any longer, but several families had bedded down for the night on the wide verandah. She stepped outside, and Captain Hsu followed. He lit her cigarette with a match struck on the side of the brick house. Shirley stood on the top step and smoked.

"You did well today," he said.

"I did all right. But, luckily for me, the revolution is not about a single person, but the whole."

He smiled. "I think you have only a partial understanding of what I've been saying to you."

"I'm teasing," she said and sent a stream of smoke into the night.

"You are the one who continues to ask me questions," he reminded her. "I am happy to work alongside you without philosophizing."

"I enjoy our conversations, Captain."

Through the open windows came the moans of her patients. The town itself was quiet now that the Japanese Imperial Army had moved on to different parts. But far beyond the compound, periodic mortar fire struck the earth. Several weeks before, Japanese aircraft had hummed loudly and low over the foothills. The distant echo of their bombs had surprisingly caused the bottles of medicine on the shelves to tremble. According to Captain Hsu, the fighting had returned to the ground again soon after, as the young warlord's troops confronted the enemy to the east, and other factions fought to the north. The captain would mention these areas of engagement casually, in passing, and never with any explanation. Shirley's overall impression of the military actions taking place in the province around her was like that of a picnicker hearing the buzzing of bees in nearby flowerbeds but never quite seeing them.

Still, although a dull sense of menace hung over her days and a feeling of futility overwhelmed her at times, Shirley shook out her arms now and was oddly grateful for the sensation that shot through her with something like vitality. Though surrounded by the dying, she felt inexorably alive.

"Now that you mention it, I am hungry," she said and rose on her toes and stretched. "How about you?"

"Famished."

"Shall we go into the kitchen and make something?"

"Nurse Carson knows how to cook? I did not think American women knew how."

"We do. We just don't cook here in China."

"And why is that?"

"It isn't done. We have cooks instead."

Captain Hsu nodded.

"You don't happen to know my cook, do you? He disappeared some weeks ago."

"Yes, I know him."

"Oh," she said and wondered if there was anything—besides modern germ theory and some Western notions—that Captain Hsu did not know. "Will you tell me where he is?"

The captain took his cap from his pocket, ran his fingers over the brim, and appeared ill at ease for the first time since they had met. "I can tell you that he is all right," he said.

"But you can't share with me where he is?"

"I think it is better this way."

"What way?"

"For an American woman to make her own food for now, since she is good at it."

She took another puff and studied him. The red star on the cap in his hands caught the light before he tucked it back into his pocket. She would get nothing more from him this evening.

"I'm not sure how it got like this, foreigners having cooks," she said, "but that's the expectation. I couldn't exactly go to market and haggle with farmers and the fishmonger myself, could I?"

He lifted an eyebrow.

"You would have me do that, wouldn't you? But we have servants to do that for us. We employ the Chinese fairly here at the mission. We pay well, and we don't take advantage of them."

She thought the corners of his mouth rose slightly.

"If you didn't have the upper classes, whether foreign or Chinese, to employ people, the whole business would collapse," she said. "But I forgot, that's what you want, isn't it?"

He finally chuckled. "Nurse Carson, you think this?"

"Yes, I think this."

"Then yes is my answer, too. The whole business would collapse."

Shirley flicked her cigarette over the side of the porch. She didn't like being teased, but she realized she was naive about politics and vulnerable to sounding foolish. It seemed such a harebrained idea to upend everything, though in China there was no question that the peasant class lived more wretchedly than any people she had ever known. The Russian serfs had no doubt had it bad, but who could say in 1937 if life was better for them under Communism? And now the poor Russians were dealing with

Hitler, so none of it mattered, anyway, as they tried to simply stay alive. Still, Shirley had to guess that if Communism was ever to work, it might work here in China, where poverty, ignorance, and illiteracy kept the people in the Dark Ages—though now, in this war with Japan, there were other, more pressing concerns.

"That's enough of that," she said. "Let's have supper." She started toward the door.

"Thank you, but no." Captain Hsu bowed. "I have my men to attend to. You enjoy your meal."

"But you haven't eaten all day, either, and they must be asleep already, your men, whoever, and wherever, they are."

"I have told you about my men, Nurse Carson. They are country boys. You have met a few of them yourself. And they are hungry, too. So I will go now. Please excuse me."

"Oh, for heaven's sake, are you suggesting that I feed them, also?" She crossed her arms over her chest.

Captain Hsu did not reply.

"I haven't *mien* for them all."

Again he did not answer.

"And my son, wherever he is, must be hungry, too. I'm sure he'll be home any minute. I can't just give away the last of what's in my larder. Who knows how long this siege or whatever it is will go on?"

Her head was pounding, and whatever exhilaration and ca-maraderie she had felt before were now being extinguished by exhaustion. She wished she could blink and have the whole lot of them disappear. Blink and have Caleb at her side again. But the best she could do was retreat inside and try to put out of her mind the captain's stern and quizzical gaze.

"Good night, Captain Hsu," she said and started in.

"Good night, Nurse Carson. I will be back again at dawn."

Shirley let out a slight groan, stepped over the threshold, and skirted around the Chinese asleep in her front hall. The kitchen, located in a small dependency off the back of the house, was dominated by a mud-encased brick *kang* that Cook normally kept fired with logs or coal. It stood cold now, and the low-timbered room remained dark. The truth was, Shirley hadn't cooked here, not even once, and had only visited the kitchen a few times. That seemed a sorry thing to admit, but there it was: she didn't know the first thing about how to make a meal in China.

She lit a kerosene lantern that hung from a hook by the stove. There appeared to be no electricity in this shadowy hut—quite unfortunate, given that a kitchen was precisely where you needed the best light. She wished Caleb were here to correct the situation but realized that now all such problems fell to her. Over the past few weeks of running the clinic and making her home function as efficiently as possible, she had started to sense that her husband had neglected a great many things around the house because of being occupied elsewhere. She had come to realize there was much she didn't know about him—about his friends like Captain Hsu, what he truly believed politically, and no doubt other things as well. And wasn't it odd, she wondered now, that she had been so little aware of the workings of the household while her husband was alive? She had to wonder what else had gone on under their roof without her knowing it.

With one hand, she held aloft the lantern, and with the other, she searched around on an open shelf, shifting heavy bags of grain in search of something to cook. She found several iron pots—or rather one pot and one frying pan with edges that sloped up more like a bowl, a Chinese invention, that wok thing she had heard about. Then she reached for a parcel wrapped with string that she hoped held noodles. She picked it up off the shelf, and a rat scampered out. Shirley caught herself before the scream escaped her mouth but trembled from head to toe.

"Dear Lord," she said. "Vermin, too!"

She sensed someone behind her, lifted the large frying pan in her hand, and turned. "Keep back!" she shouted.

Standing before her was the little Japanese grandfather who ran the only fish market in town. He bowed low. Shirley let the pan fall to her side as she, too, bowed low. He bowed even lower. She bowed lower. He was starting to bow for a third time when she banged the pan on the stove, and said, "Konnichiwa, grandfather."

"Konbanwa," he replied with a nod, correcting her with "good evening," not "good day," in Japanese. Behind him appeared his two grown daughters and several granddaughters, all in traditional Japanese dress. Continuing in the local Chinese dialect, he said, "My family is here to serve you."

"Excuse me?" Shirley asked.

"My daughter and her daughters will serve you. You give us roof, we serve you."

"They will serve me what?"

"Supper. We cook food for you. Help with patients in medical rooms, too," he said and pointed toward the front of the house.

"Very kind of you to offer. I don't think the Chinese would cotton to a Japanese nurse, but we can ask Captain Hsu in the morning."

"My family and I have been here thirty years," the fishmonger continued. "We do not approve of war." He made a face. "Japanese soldiers behave very badly."

"I'm very glad to hear that you are not like them and thank you for offering to help in the clinic, but many of the wounded Chinese are not from here. And even the ones who *do* come from our own town may not like you very much—not because you are a barbarian but because your prices were always too high." She added with a slight smile, "You can't deny it."

The fishmonger studied her face for a long moment before he got the joke and laughed. "Ah, yes," he said, "prices too high! Very good! Very true!"

Shirley handed him the pan. "You may cook for me and my son until our own cook returns. Thank you again for offering."

She left the kitchen and wondered how she was going to explain this to Captain Hsu. Not only could she not cook for herself, but she seemed to have engaged the enemy in doing so for her. She was too tired to even consider the problem. When she reached the front hall, she sat down on the piano bench and let her head droop onto her folded arms as they rested on the keyboard. A moment later, she opened her eyes again and looked past her lap and recognized the pair of size eleven Jack Purcell sneakers covered in yellow dust. She bolted upright and threw her arms around her son. For once, he didn't flinch or pull away but let her hold him there, his head tipped onto her shoulder.

"Oh, Mother."

"I know," she said. "It's all so terrible." She wanted to hold him and rock him to sleep as she had when he was small. Reluctantly she let him slip out of her arms but kept hold of his hand. "Supper will be ready soon," she said and caressed his thick red hair. "You must be starved."

Charles nodded but then started to pull her after him across the front hall.

"Where are you taking me?" she asked. "Be careful, now, step around these people." She had no choice but to follow as Charles maneuvered through the sleeping Chinese. "What is it, darling?" she whispered. "Is something bothering you?"

He stopped midstride and looked back at her. "Yes, Mother," he said with a smirk, "something is bothering me."

She felt strangely grateful for his quintessential teenaged tone. "Sorry, silly question," she said. "It has been such a day in such a week."

As they rounded the corner to the former dining room, Dao-Ming popped out and scampered away. Shirley let out a gasp and whispered to Charles, "That girl is constantly underfoot and everywhere at once. Whenever I come upon her, my heart skips a beat. It can't be good for my health."

"Oh, Mother, of all the things to complain about," he said. "That's the least of our problems. Now, follow me." He continued to weave through the cots. "I was down in the cellar earlier today, looking for that special sweeping tool Father used on our chimney last fall."

"What tool?"

"A long broom with lots of bristles at the end. I need it to fix something."

"What on earth are you up to?" she asked and stopped at the center of the clinic. "Come, now, Charles, that's enough for one night. Can't this wait until morning?"

"No, it can't."

As stubborn as he had been as a toddler, she thought as she untied her filthy apron, took it off, and balled it up. But since no laundry would be washed anytime soon, she carried it to the coat tree beside the front door. She tried not to notice her husband's crumpled fedora tipped jauntily on a brass hook. If she did, she might start to weep.

Charles opened the cellar door, took the kerosene lamp off its hook at the top of the steps, and lit it. As with the kitchen, Shirley had been downstairs only once or twice. From Lian, she had heard that snakes enjoyed the cool damp down there, but she wasn't going to mention that now. The steps creaked, and when they reached the bottom, Charles started across the mud floor, his footsteps squishing loudly.

"Dinner will be ready any minute," Shirley said as she ducked under the stairwell and followed Charles. "Aren't you starved for a bowl of *mien*? I never thought I'd say that with such relish, but here we are, aren't we?"

She knew she was prattling on. If Caleb had been here, he'd have turned and kissed her on the lips to get her to shut up. Her husband would have known she was frightened. But she couldn't show that to her son, who seemed oblivious to the dangers all around.

Charles stopped and lifted the lamp. Before them was a small door held closed by a rusted metal hook. "Have you ever noticed this cabinet?" he asked her.

Shirley shook her head and let out a high, worried sound. She couldn't bear another tragedy, especially if it involved her precious boy. But instead of a bed of snakes, a Japanese soldier in waiting, or another dead and bloodied body, when Charles raised the hook and opened the door, Shirley saw before them Caleb's ham-operated radio transmitter. The clumsy old thing sat on a tidy little shelf. Headphones hung beside it from a nail. The inked image of a Chinese mystical phoenix had been stamped in red on the wall, a signature of sorts, Shirley guessed. And a microphone was positioned in front of a single stool on which sat a rosy pink pillow with lovely embroidered chrysanthemums. At least a year before, the pillow had gone missing from the wicker sofa in the parlor, and Shirley had accused a day laborer of taking it. But here it was, no worse for wear. Upon it, to Shirley's amazement, sat her husband's driving cap. She would have recognized Caleb's cap anywhere, and apparently so had her son.

"Father, must have—" Charles began.

But she hushed him. "Not a word," she whispered and pressed a finger to her lips. Then she gestured for him to close the door and return upstairs. She took her boy firmly by the wrist and pulled him after her. When they reached the steps, Shirley pushed Charles before her, and up he went. She stepped lightly after him, trying to make as little noise as possible.

Part Two

Ten

The Reverend Caleb Carson gazed up at the scudding clouds and counted his blessings in seeing another day. He had always thought of himself as a man of simple pleasures, and one of them was to be out-of-doors on a fine summer morning like this one. To breathe in crisp mountain air that reminded him of his boyhood in New Hampshire, though little else about this rugged setting was the same. The cedar trees here were spindlier, the scrub brush more spiked, the rocks more jagged than those in the mountains of his youth.

Even when he had crossed this range in North China as a healthy man, he had felt it blanket his spirit with barrenness and gloom. At dangerous bends in the trail, the Chinese had placed simple altars to their ancestors and gods. Over his five years of expeditions to the outlying churches, Caleb had come to understand that stopping to pray in any fashion was entirely the right idea. Otherwise the setting felt altogether too godless and the poor traveler abandoned to his fate.

Yet the sky overhead now on this summer morning struck him as promising. With some effort, he turned his head to his good side and gazed over the cliff toward the long valley below and the town too far in the distance to see. That he suspected he would die before ever returning to his home in that distance caused a literal dull ache in his heart, while the rest of his body was shot through with a simpler, more searing pain.

Eight weeks before, during a break in the spring rains, the clouds had lifted and sunlight had caught on every shining pale green bud. Caleb's heart had felt as it always did in springtime: as if the Lord himself had scrubbed clean the earth, and he, too, needed ablution. A garbled message arrived just then on his two-way radio. American marines on a reconnaissance mission were cornered in the North. Now was the moment, he thought, to purify his heart and his goals by assisting in the communication between the brilliant, though somewhat naive and isolated, Communist leaders and the outside world.

Caleb told his wife he must visit the outlying churches. It was a matter of urgency, he said, and as he expected, she did not inquire further, preoccupied as she was with her own affairs. He left at dawn, before Shirley and their son awoke. He took Cook with him, since the older man had proven himself an excellent companion on previous trips. Captain Hsu tried to dissuade them from departing by reporting that the road was more dangerous than ever—slick underfoot and overrun with not just the usual bandits hoping to make up for profits lost during the rains but the Japanese invaders as well. Caleb would hear nothing of it.

They left the mission in chilly darkness, but by the time they reached the foothills, the path reflected pink sunrise. As they rose up into the mountains, switchback after switchback, all seemed vivid and hopeful. Until, at a point where the trail narrowed because of a rockslide farther up the mountain, Caleb's mule refused to go on. As he assessed the situation, he wondered if perhaps the animal was of the correct opinion. But his mission was imperative, so he tried coaxing the beast with words, then with his heels to its sides. He even climbed down off the animal and tried to yank it forward. Cook's mule seemed prepared to cross the dangerous pass, but Caleb felt he should be the first to try terrain so extensively drenched and unstable.

As is so often described, the more he pulled, the more his mule dug in. Finally Caleb gave up and turned away, and in that moment, the contrary animal took one step forward—one fateful step that set off a series of mishaps. Still holding the reins, Caleb lost his balance and stumbled backward. The animal lurched forward, and their combined weight caused the ground beneath to give way. Down they fell into a rocky crevasse on a slide of mud.

The earth was the color of the purest honey, and Caleb had come to know it well. Yellow dust from the Gobi turned to paste in springtime and coated every surface. As he fell, he swam through it, slipping with increasing speed on its thick and sticky consistency. In retrospect, the descent took an awfully long time. Slowly he tumbled, aware of the animal rolling beside him. Tree limbs and rocks tore into him, inflicting punctures and lacerations. Even at the time, there was an endless quality to the incident, long enough for him to think over the error of his decision to force the animal where it did not want to go.

His fall came to an abrupt end, and Caleb found that he was covered in mud and unable to move. He passed out for a short time, and when he came to again, he tried to wriggle his arm, but the pain was too much. He shifted a single finger, and although that pain was also penetrating, he managed to create a pocket of air near his lips. He sputtered out foul dirt and realized that with each inhale, he was sucking it back in again. He heard muffled voices and sensed movement nearby. Before he blacked out for a second time, he heard his cook's voice shouting and thought that if there was ever a man good enough to rescue him, Cook was that man.

Cook fashioned a stretcher from branches and green vines and dragged Caleb out of the crevasse. Passing Red Army soldiers then carried him the rest of the way to the their camp over exceedingly treacherous terrain. How Cook and the soldiers had managed it was a miracle of the type that only the Chinese can achieve, Caleb thought. A more industrious and ingenious people did not exist on the planet. Being in the care of such routinely heroic types gave him hope that he might survive to see his family again.

Since the morning of the accident, he had been on his back on a military cot in the cave at night; in the day, they brought him outside to take the air. His lungs were still lined with mud, and his breathing was badly impaired by internal ruptures. No doctor had seen him, but he had no complaints about his care.

"Reverend hungry?" Cook asked in his faulty English.

Out of courtesy, the good man had kindly switched over to a language he had never mastered. Since the accident, Caleb had been unable to understand the local dialect. He couldn't even have managed the more refined Mandarin, not that Cook spoke it, either. Caleb's mind simply did not work well enough any longer to accomplish it. He let out a slight sound in reply.

Words, English or otherwise, had become too great a challenge for him, although he knew he needed to keep trying. That was the thing—he had come to realize that life was one long series of tries. A nice summation, he thought, worthy of a sermon. Caleb wished he could dictate his ideas to someone for future lessons. He had never been a deep thinker, never the wise minister he had hoped to someday become. His mother's brother, whom he had never met but had heard of as a boy, had come to North China over thirty years before, and the elders here still spoke of him in mythic terms, as someone not only comfortable with the natives but inspiring from the pulpit as well. Caleb, by contrast, simply helped people by seeing that tasks were accomplished in the name of the Lord. He was a minister of the trail and of duty, not of words.

The irony was that he had finally achieved the proper distance on life to be able to sum it up, and yet he could no longer speak. He had become the sage that the collar he wore was meant to suggest, and yet he had lost the words to convey his thoughts. And wasn't that a lesson in and of itself, he thought: the maddening lesson known as life?

He let Cook lift his head so he might sip mild broth. Caleb suspected it was nothing more than stone soup, but he relished the taste. The turnip added a bittersweet tang to the water that, had he been healthy, he would hardly have noticed. So much in life is overlooked, he thought, while our minds are busy on other things. Under normal circumstances, he would have spit out this thin concoction and not noticed how even its smell suggested life itself—the rock-hard reality, the mineral quality, the very soil to which we all must return in time.

His mind tended to go down the path toward death with almost every thought now. After too many weeks in pain, he let it. At first, he had tried to rally. He had hopes that he would soon return home to see his wife and son. He would walk again. He would sit up. All grand ambitions, as it turned out. In reality, his energy was better spent on the simple acts of clearing his breathing passages and using his nostrils to their fullest extent. Air was what mattered. The taking in of air.

Cook set Caleb's head back on the hard pillow. That the Chinese had not discovered feather pillows seemed a surprising oversight. Historically they had chosen instead lacquered blocks in the finer homes, but out here on the trail, it was a pile of pine needles pressed together and wrapped with string. Caleb shivered uncontrollably, and the wretched wool blanket was placed over him again. The damned thing was a curse that chafed the skin under his chin, but he did not complain. And wasn't that how life revealed itself to us, with every ounce of comfort overshadowed by accompanying irritation? The miracle of the Lord on the cross was not as Caleb had once thought it to be, not only a higher lesson in salvation but also one of simple survival through everyday trials. The poor savior's palms and feet where the nails had been stuck must have not just ached but also itched terribly.

When Caleb awoke again, he heard voices and commotion over at the heart of the Communist camp. He thought he detected Captain Hsu's sincere and gravelly tones. Never so fine a man as that one, Caleb had come to realize. And the fellow had no higher education to speak of. No advanced degrees except those given out by life. That distinction, Caleb realized, was fodder for at least one Sunday morning's lesson. How life's school was all around us, there for the taking, if we only opened our eyes, which he accomplished now with some effort.

The missionaries here in China could stand to be reminded of that, Caleb thought, not to mention certain parishioners back home who were overly preoccupied with the credentials of their minister and treated him like a boyish puppet. He had gone to great lengths at seminary to stand out, to be deemed as having promise. He had been rewarded with a small, established parish, where, unfortunately, perhaps because he was still so young, the stout ladies and bent deacons had continued to assess and hover and criticize until the Chinese hinterlands had sung to him of freedom. Tales of his uncle's adventures in this distant land had risen to the surface of Caleb's memory, and although that story had not ended well, he felt certain the world had changed sufficiently with modern times for him and his family to have a more successful outcome. But where had his newfound freedom taken him? he asked himself now. As far from civilization as imaginable and longing for a potluck supper of casseroles and Jell-O compotes under his congregants' watchful eyes.

Caleb wished now that he had not learned so assiduously from books nor labored so painstakingly over the complexities of human foibles but had gathered wisdom instead only from the woods. Thoreau had had it right. Although, Caleb recalled, while at Walden Pond, the philosopher had lived just down the street from his dear mother, who continued to take in his laundry every week. Wouldn't Shirley have gotten a kick out of that? Caleb thought. Then he promptly reminded himself not to let his mind wander to his beloved wife. It only made his body hurt more radiantly when he considered his brilliant, complicated, and often vexing partner. Hers were the human foibles he had tried most to parse, often without success. His son was a much simpler creature, but recalling him was entirely out of the question. For as many hours of the day as Caleb could manage, he kept his mind on anything but his boy.

Nighttime was another matter. During sleepless hours in the damp cave, his family haunted Caleb and caused him to cry as he hadn't since he was a boy. He had always been a proponent of the school of life that believed in slogans such as *Stiff upper lip! Pull up your socks! Carry on!*—words that were now seared through with irony and even despair. How could one possibly have a stiff lip and dry eyes in a world so fraught with misery? How could one keep the chin tucked and the back stiff when it was literally broken?

Caleb let the tears come now. He swallowed them down, and his lungs, which were already dangerously compromised, filled again, which led to another choking fit. Each time this happened, Cook appeared at his side. The old fellow was at a loss to soothe him. Caleb wished his Chinese servant would no longer rescue him but, instead, that the earth would rise up and drown him in a sea of sorrowful memories—sorrowful precisely because they were so happy. More and more often, Caleb could imagine the dreadful satisfaction of choking to death on one's own tears.

Eleven

Shirley and Captain Hsu stood at the bedside of a young lady, a girl, really, who had been raped who could guess how many times and remained unconscious. They whispered, though it was unclear whether the patient could even hear them.

"We must be prepared for more wounded from the countryside. We will need this bed for my men. Please see to it, Nurse Carson."

"What would you have me do with her? I can't toss her out into the courtyard as if she was bathwater."

"If you are unable to do this," Captain Hsu said, "I will take care of it."

She had noticed over their weeks of working side by side that the captain wasn't a callous man, just straightforward and no-nonsense. But she also recalled that in China, the birth of a daughter was sometimes met with condolences; it wasn't unheard of for baby girls to be drowned or left to die. Shirley felt determined to protect this damaged girl, even from the captain, because in all likelihood she had never been protected before.

"No," she said, "leave it to me." Then she called over a pair of young men she assumed to be soldiers whom Captain Hsu had assigned to help her. "Please carry this young lady upstairs to my bedroom," she told them. "Be very careful with her. Do you understand?"

She looked about for Lian and found her across the hall, bandaging a broken arm. Lian had proved indispensable in the clinic and had taught Shirley a trick or two from her country ways: simple though surprising treatments such as how to create poultices for burns out of rhubarb, herbs, and dung, something Shirley had never dreamed of before. Shirley then noticed Dao-Ming seated cross-legged in the corner, rocking over a pad of paper and scribbling with the nib of pencil she must have found in Charles's school things. The poor creature, she thought.

"Dao-Ming," she called.

The girl did not look up. Shirley took off her apron, hung it on the coat stand, went over, and gazed down at her. Her chubby feet were covered in crusted yellow mud. Her hands appeared to be rubbed raw, the fingernails and cuticles bitten to the nibs. She had nasty-looking bites up and down her arms, no doubt from fleas. Dao-Ming continued to rock, now with her eyes shut, and let out an occasionally hoarse and phlegmy cough.

"Dao-Ming?" she asked again in a calm voice so as not to startle her.

Nevertheless, it did. The girl scrambled clumsily to her feet, pawing at the air. She scampered into the corner with her thick arms up over her eyes.

"It's all right," Shirley said. "I'm not going to hurt you."

Dao-Ming panted, and her brow furrowed into anxious ridges. Shirley glanced around for Lian again, and when she turned back, she saw that Dao-Ming had been looking for her, too.

"Lian is busy, but we'll be all right without her, won't we?"

The girl whimpered.

Shirley crouched so they were eye to eye. Dao-Ming's black, straight hair fell in ragged bangs over her eyes. When Shirley brushed them aside, the girl flinched. Her breathing sounded troubled, a fraught wheezing. In addition to her other challenges in life, Shirley realized, she must have asthma.

"Do you see that young lady over there?" Shirley pointed to the unconscious girl. "She needs someone to take care of her, to sit beside her bed, stroke her hand, and speak to her."

Dao-Ming's narrow eyes narrowed further.

"Or," Shirley corrected herself, "if not actually speak to her, then communicate. You may squeeze her hand or comb her hair. Do you think you can do that?"

Dao-Ming nodded, and her bangs flung forward and back.

"Grand," Shirley said and stood again. "Go along, then, and help the young men get her settled in my bedroom."

Shirley started to step away, but Dao-Ming tugged on her skirt. "What is it?"

Dao-Ming pointed upstairs with a worried expression.

"I know, I don't usually allow strangers onto the second floor, but this will be our little secret, all right?"

Dao-Ming mouthed the word as if she had heard it before and relished the sounds.

Shirley stepped outside for a smoke. On the verandah, Tupan Feng reclined in one of the rocking chairs, his eyes half closed. Since the arrival of the Chinese into her home, Shirley had seen the old warlord shuffling about more often, using his cane to point their visitors in the proper direction and telling them what to do. He seemed to enjoy his new role, although it appeared to have also exhausted him.

At the bottom of the steps, Captain Hsu was conferring with several men. When they left, he joined Shirley on the top step as she lit up.

"I don't know how you manage so much," she said to him. "Yet you never seem hurried. It's as if you had all the time in the world."

"Time is not an issue if you believe in what you do."

Shirley dusted a stray thread of tobacco from her lip and wondered if that was true. She had certainly never experienced it. She hitched herself up to sit on the railing and inhaled slowly. "You'd be surprised how many Americans race about, forever feeling they don't have enough time."

"They lack conviction," he said matter-of-factly. "That is their problem."

She let out a long stream of smoke.

"What did you do in America, Mrs. Carson?"

Her life back home seemed strangely distant and faded now, especially compared with the vivid, all-consuming days in the clinic. "I was a student, of course, and good at it. I might have liked to go on and study further."

"A society needs its scholars," the captain said as he started to pace before her. "But for most, being a student is just a phase. We must step forward into life. Your decision to become a nurse is for the good of society. A wise choice."

"I suppose so," she said. "But I dropped it as quickly as I could when I married Caleb. I didn't feel like working anymore."

Captain Hsu stopped and stared at her. Shirley thought he could have done better at hiding his disappointment. Perhaps his frankness was a sign of their deepening friendship, though she suspected it was more an indication that he was starting to fray at the edges from working so hard.

"Captain," she said, "why don't you have a seat here beside me? Rest a moment."

"I must get back to my duties," he said. "I don't have time to discuss decadent American lives."

She let out a laugh. "Is that what I was describing, my decadent life?" She flicked her dying cigarette onto the hard soil.

"You felt like quitting as a nurse, so you did—just like that." He snapped his fingers in the air.

He must be joking, she thought, but when she looked at him, his stern expression startled her. His knuckles whitened around his leather belt, and he said, "I think I will leave the Eighth Route Army today because I feel like it. Yes, that is what is best for me. I quit!"

"Oh, come, now, Captain."

He pressed on, his face reddening. "Capitalism convinces you that you are lucky to make this choice. You call it freedom. But think of the waste of human potential!" He slapped the railing with his palm. "All those American lives with no purpose. We fight for a new China to free not only ourselves but our brothers, too, from poverty and lives like yours of no purpose. We do not choose to sit on the sidelines because it is more comfortable to do so. We do not quit because we feel like it!" He pushed off from the railing and headed to the steps. "I can't understand how you and your people are not ashamed of yourselves."

He bowed abruptly and wished her good day. Before Shirley had a chance to stop him, Captain Hsu was making his way through the crowds camped on the grounds. A high, light cackle came from the seat behind her, and Shirley turned to see Tupan Feng's shoulders shaking.

"What are you laughing at?" she asked.

"Captain is correct," Tupan Feng said. "Americans are lazy!" He shifted in the rocker and tipped too far forward, then scrambled to right himself. "But so are the people of my province. Hsu thinks they will work hard for the good of the country. They will not work hard for anything! Believe me, I tried to make them work." He started to cough and couldn't stop.

"Don't get yourself too riled up," she said and patted his back.

As his coughing fit subsided, he sputtered, "Revolution is all well and good, but they should keep the old system in place, too. Bring back the warlords, I say!" He swung his cane in the air, and Shirley sidestepped it. "I will lead their revolution!"

"There's an idea," she said. "Why don't you suggest that the next time you see Captain Hsu?"

Tupan Feng set down the cane. She lifted the tartan throw from where it had fallen at his feet and tucked it around his neck. As she headed into the clinic again, the captain's words settled slowly over her, coating her thoughts like the dust that slipped under closed doors and changed every surface in summer in North China. She watched the dozen Chinese nursing assistants busy at their patients' bedsides or cleaning and restocking the storage shelves. They knew the tasks required of them and coordinated their efforts well. She wondered if she had ever felt more purposeful than now, working alongside these women and men. Perhaps the captain was right: she had had to leave America behind and come all this way to a distant outpost in a foreign land to fully experience a genuine sense of conviction.

She tied on her apron and went to the nursing station to check the patients' charts, and just as she was choosing the next bed to visit, Kathryn appeared at her elbow. Shirley set down the rough-hewn clipboard and offered her friend a hug. Kathryn responded with limp arms and stepped away quickly.

"How do you like it?" Shirley asked.

Kathryn studied her up and down.

"No, not me," Shirley said, spreading her arms toward the clinic. "The setup here. Look at all we've done since you were last here. We're going full guns. A total of thirty beds and various other triage spots around the house. My assistants are remarkable. Very quick learners, the Chinese. And Captain Hsu says we're making a genuine difference. Our patients leave with their bodies at least somewhat restored and their morale boosted. Isn't that something?"

Kathryn peeled back the white kid gloves that she usually saved for Sunday service or visiting Chinese matrons. She adjusted her little cloche hat, also usually reserved for special occasions. Was Kathryn trying to impress her with her stylish appearance? Shirley patted down her own hair and couldn't recall if she had brushed it that day.

"You are something," Kathryn said.

"Oh, it isn't me. I've never met such resilient, hardworking, decent people. Caleb used to say as much, but I hardly listened to him. The truth is, they deserve better than the lousy hands they've been dealt in life. I just wish we could do more."

"Who do you mean by 'we'?" Kathryn asked.

"Captain Hsu and I and the others."

Kathryn did not smile.

"You're welcome to join us anytime. I would love to be comrades with you."

Kathryn bristled at the suggestion.

"I didn't mean 'comrades,'" Shirley said. "I just meant—"

"I think the good captain has been filling your head with propaganda," Kathryn said.

Shirley could feel her face going hot.

"You know we're not supposed to be supporting the Reds. It isn't policy. It's fine that you've been helping the injured, but I think you should consider closing up shop here and joining Doc Sturgis and the other Americans at the infirmary. I've been assisting over there, and he's really quite crackerjack at what he does."

"That's wonderful, but I've been doing perfectly well over here, too."

"He's a doctor, Shirley. Have you forgotten that you're not?"

Shirley let out a shocked laugh, but Kathryn continued. "I know he would love to have a real nurse at his side and not poor imitations like me. The two of you would make an excellent team. *That's* the team you should be crowing about."

"I've trained a fine staff of Chinese to assist me."

Kathryn gestured to the crowded rooms. "So I see. Chinese everywhere you look."

"Shouldn't there be Chinese everywhere? It is *their* country, after all."

"But this is *our* mission. This is neutral territory. We are not at war with the Japanese. We are Americans, not Chinese. We need to remain in charge."

"I am in charge!" Shirley threw up her hands.

"Clearly," Kathryn said, as she yanked back on her gloves, "you have chosen to work with the Chinese precisely so you can be in charge. Over at the infirmary, you'd have to give that up. You'd have to play second fiddle."

"I don't think that's the issue at all. I'm doing what Captain Hsu has asked of me. I'm joining the cause like everyone else."

"Well, hurrah for the revolution and all that!"

Shirley took a step back. "Kathryn, you're not making any sense. First you accuse me of only doing this so that I can be at the top of the heap. And then you seem to worry that I'm joining in with the ranks of the masses. You can't have it both ways, my dear."

Kathryn bowed her head. Her shoulders rose and fell as she gathered her breath. Then she reached out and took Shirley's hands. "I'm just so worried about you. I don't know what you're up to, and it makes me nervous." She squeezed Shirley's fingers for emphasis.

"Just before you arrived, I was thinking that I've never felt more purposeful in my life. But of course, I miss you terribly. I can't offer you tea in the parlor any longer." She gave a weary smile as she glanced at the changed room. "But you are always welcome. I mean it."

Kathryn slipped her hands from Shirley's and started to step away.

"Give my best to Doc Sturgis," Shirley added.

Kathryn flung open the screen door and marched down the porch steps.

Shirley stood in the center of her front hallway and looked about. Kathryn was right: Chinese surrounded her. She wished she'd spoken up to her friend and said, "Why, yes, you're right, hurrah for the revolution!" She wanted to shout it now.

Instead, she headed for the piano, which had stood untouched for weeks. She pushed open the cover, sat heavily on the bench, and, after a long pause, threw herself into playing. The dark, romantic riffs soothed her and stirred her and reminded her of the universality of life's tragedies. She played with as much vigor as her sleep-deprived and hungry self could muster. She swayed and shut her eyes and tried to block out everything else. When she opened her eyes again, Dao-Ming was at her side, and for once, the girl didn't startle Shirley. Instead, her thick, sweaty palm on Shirley's forearm gave a sense that they were all in this together. The music had brought the unfortunate Dao-Ming to her, and Shirley could offer these chords as a gift in return.

Then the child pinched her with those dirty little fingernails, and Shirley stopped playing. "Damn it, child," she said in English. "Don't do that!"

Shirley had not cursed in a long time. Caleb couldn't abide it, and so she had changed her habits years ago, but it felt awfully good now. Then she noticed Dao-Ming's eyes filling up. She patted the girl's back and tried to soothe her.

"I'm so sorry, love," she said. "I didn't mean to frighten you. Was the music too much for you?"

Dao-Ming nodded.

"I hope I didn't bother the patient upstairs? How is she doing?"

Dao-Ming mouthed a word. They all knew that the girl understood language but seemed unable to use it either for physical or emotional reasons—Shirley had never bothered to consider the cause. But now she leaned forward and put her ear to the girl's lips. Sound began to issue forth surprisingly smoothly, perhaps coaxed out of her by the inspiring music. Shirley hoped that was the case. She listened with great concentration, not wanting to misunderstand the Chinese syllables. But Dao-Ming spoke without trouble, and the word she said was "Dead."

Twelve

Charles thrust the broom into the chimney pipe, and soot bloomed everywhere. His khakis and button-down shirt were streaked with ashes, his face and hands gone gray. He pushed back the Chinese Army cap, and his hair became dusted with it, too. He knew he had no business being up on the patched and splintered bamboo roof. But he plunged the chimney one more time, then made his way back down the ladder, whistling as he went. That he'd brought his own ladder seemed to him a heroic gesture, but the girl had hardly acknowledged it when he'd come up the alley with it teetering on his shoulder. He hopped from the bottom rung, and the billowing ash made him sneeze. She finally looked up from where she sat on the stone bench and giggled. Charles wiped his nose, which only seemed to amuse her more.

"You're funny," she said.

That wasn't his intention, but he tried to make the best of it. At least her grandmother wasn't around to spoil things with her sour tongue. The old woman's snores floated out from the shack, offering a rather lousy soundtrack, Charles thought. In the movies, the leading man nonchalantly leans against something and looks down at the girl, who gazes up at him with adoring eyes while romantic music swells. Charles leaned against the wall of the mud shack now and looked down at this girl, who in turn looked down at her lap. He joined her on the bench and asked her name.

"Li Juan."

"That means beautiful," he said.

She remained unsmiling, her head bent with strands of dark hair draped over her sallow cheeks. He knew he should say her name was perfect for her, but he couldn't make himself form the compliment. "You seem sad. Are you missing someone?" he asked.

She appeared startled by the question but then nodded.

"Did you lose someone?"

She nodded again.

"A parent?"

"My mother has been gone from me."

Charles swallowed hard. The Chinese had strange ways of saying things without coming out and saying them, but he supposed she meant that her mother had died. "I'm sorry."

"My grandmother and I must leave again soon," she said.

"But you just got here. It's too dangerous to go back to where you came from."

She shrugged.

Charles stood and said, "You need to stay with us. If Lian doesn't want you in her quarters, come to the big house with me. My mother's got the whole Red Army in there, so she won't even notice."

"The Red Army is at your house?"

"Just some injured soldiers disguised as peasants." He sat down again, closer to her this time. "I should be whispering about that, shouldn't I? I'm lousy at this."

She smiled, and he wondered if he could reach over and take

her thin hand in his again. He remembered how it had felt. But then he glanced down the alley and noticed Lian headed toward them at a rapid clip. As always, she took small steps but managed to move very fast. She was bent with a braided straw basket on her back, held in place by a strap around her forehead. Such baskets were used by laborers or farmers during harvest; bow-legged men who came up from the coal mines, misshapen by the weight of the rocks in similar baskets on their shoulders.

"Here, Lian, let me help you with that," he said and went to take it off her.

She shooed him away and set it down on the packed ground. She wheezed, the humid, sunny day clearly getting to her. The basket was filled with clothing and towels torn into strips and used as bandages, now covered in dried blood.

"What are you doing here, Charles-Boy?" she asked.

"I saw that your chimney needed fixing," he said and pointed to the ladder.

Her eyes shifted from Charles to Li Juan and back. "You are man of the house now, I see. You carry on Father's duties. Very good. Soon you study for pulpit and join other ministers and visit parishes that Father love so much. Excellent, Charles! Mother will be most proud. Off you go. Time to study Good Book!"

"Esteemed Lian," he said, and kicked a pebble up the alley, "you of all people know that life's not for me."

Li Juan sprang from the bench then, raced forward, and threw her arms around Lian. She pressed her cheek against the older woman's plentiful chest and cried out, "Ma-ma," as if she could hold back the word no longer. Charles wondered if he'd heard right, but then she said it again.

Lian patted her on the head. "Sit down, little niece. Sit, tired one. She is exhausted from many travels," she explained to Charles. "She does not know what she says."

The old grandmother's screeching voice came from inside the shack. "Is that my daughter I hear? Is that my Lian? I hope you brought us warm buns to eat and a delicious feast of duck and dumplings, but I suspect you did not. No matter. Come to Mother so I tell you all the things your daughter did wrong today. She is sullen girl and of no help to me."

Li Juan shouted at the open door in the country dialect, "I'm worn out with you, Grandmother. Who wouldn't be with all your complaining?"

Lian's hand shot out and swatted Li Juan's backside, but the girl was quick and escaped a second hit. She hid behind Charles's back, and her small, powerful fingers wrung his arm.

"I thought you said your mother was dead," he said.

"My mother is not dead!" she said. "She is here, with you and your mother, but never with me! She is gone from me all the time." Tears welled in her eyes and tumbled down her cheeks.

"Madam Lian," Charles asked, "is this true? We thought you didn't have children."

"Do not bother me, Charles-Boy." Lian looked down into the basket of dirty laundry and shook her head. "I have work to do. Out of my way, you bothersome children."

Charles turned to Li Juan. "Lian is your mother?"

"And Dao-Ming is my little sister," she said.

"We thought Dao-Ming was an orphan. Why didn't you tell us, Lian?"

She reached into the basket and grabbed a handful of rags as if she intended to wash them right there in the dusty alley. "I needed a job. I say I am from town and have no family or they do not hire me. But it is no matter now."

"So Li Juan has lived without a mother for many years, and you without your child?"

"*You* are my child, Charles-Boy. That was how it is. Li Juan knows this."

He tried to keep hold of Li Juan's hand, but she pulled it away.

"I wish you'd told us. I'm so sorry we didn't understand." Charles looked to Li Juan, but she continued to glare at her mother. "I think you've done enough for today, Lian," he offered. "You should stay here and be with your family. We can manage without you."

Lian squinted up at him. "Maybe you are man of house now, after all. You have grown up. You are like son to me. I have no real children of my own. I might as well be barren."

"You are not barren!" Li Jung shouted. "I am your daughter. You have two daughters!" She turned to Charles and said, "You see, she does this. She convinces herself she has no children. It makes no sense. I used to think she did it so she wouldn't miss me so much, but now I think she does it because she doesn't want me. "

Lian shook her head. "Sad truth, I have no boys. I must do all the work myself. I am cursed. I have Dao-Ming, who is like small animal. But Li Juan, you are strong. You must do your part for the family. That is what girls are for. Otherwise they are useless. You must get along with your grandmother!"

Lian lunged at her daughter for the second time, and the girl skittered around behind Charles again. He couldn't imagine such a thing. In his household, his parents hardly ever raised their voices and certainly never a hand to him.

"Mother," Li Juan said, "things can change. I can live with you now. This young American says it's okay."

Charles made himself stand taller in the way his mother did when she wanted to assert her authority. "I wish to invite you and your family to stay at our house, where you will be safe and where we can share our food and supplies. And best of all, where both of your daughters can join you."

Lian's expression remained stony, but Charles thought he saw a faint glimmer in her eyes. "Mrs. Carson does not need more mouths to feed," she said. "I already have one child underfoot who eats all the time. They said Dao-Ming would die young, but she is sturdy as water buffalo and looks like one, too."

"Mother!" Li Juan said. "That's not nice. My sister can't help it. I will keep her happy and out of the way so you can do your work. And I hardly eat a thing." She inched closer to Lian and continued, "I am very good at cooking and at doing chores in the house. I am strong. Feel this!" She held up her thin arm, and Lian squeezed it like a melon at the market.

"With Cook gone, I suppose I could use some help," Lian said.

"I can do it for you!" Li Juan said. "You will see."

As Li Juan tried to convince her mother, Charles recognized the look in his amah's eyes: she was secretly pleased with her daughter. She did not offer a reassuring smile but sternly assessed the young lady before her and approved. Li Juan took Lian's hand now and led her to the stone bench. She sat her down and knelt before her and began to massage her red and swollen hands.

"I will do laundry for you to start with," Li Juan said. "I am good at laundry."

Lian leaned back against the mud wall and shut her eyes. Li Juan looked up at Charles in a way that was finally a little bit like the girls in the movies. But now, he couldn't imagine how she'd ever really like him, knowing that he had stolen her mother away from her for all those years. He would try to make it up to her, although he knew that nothing could fill the hole a missing parent made in a child's heart.

Charles gathered up the ladder and headed back toward home through the crowded mission compound. It worried him that the Chinese seemed to have erected more established lean-tos out of wood, cardboard, and tin. Their cooking fires burned incessantly, carrying sharp, charred odors that seeped into every corner of the mission. They appeared to be here to stay.

The massive red doors of the chapel stood open, and a line of coolies rose up the steps and into the darkened chamber. Charles doubted they were lined up to attend service; they were probably waiting instead for rations of rice and millet. At the entrance, the diminutive Reverend Wells looked lost amid the barefoot crowd in tattered clothing. The rickshaw drivers, who usually hung about outside the gates of the mission, ready to pounce on any potential customers with boasts and bravado about their services, had pulled their carts up to the chapel steps, where they waited for food with everyone else. They were always the thinnest and wiriest of men, and Charles wondered how they had been managing on even less food than usual. One of them listlessly lifted his head and called out to Charles. The man's concave chest was bare, and every rib pressed against his skin, giving it a bluish, almost bruised tint.

"Here," Charles said and reached into his pocket. "It's not much."

The man's hand shot out and snatched the oatcake from Charles's palm. The snacks always tasted like straw, but he still carried one or two with him whenever he went out. The rickshaw driver clearly didn't mind its dryness. The man wore a burlap bag with holes cut in it for his legs and tied with a frayed rope. Charles stood beside the shoeless skeleton as he gulped down the last of the crumbs.

"I give you ride!" the rickshaw man shouted. "I take you to your home like prince! Best ride in town! Smooth and fast! Faster than all others!"

Several other rickshaw drivers growled their usual denunciations and curses about their competitor's abilities to do the job as described.

"I've got a ladder," Charles said.

"I carry it for you!" the driver shouted.

Charles couldn't imagine how the man mustered such enthusiasm. "No, you'll lose your place in line if you do."

The man gazed up the steps to where the rations were being dispensed. The poor guy was probably starving, Charles thought. "You can take my mother and me to market sometime soon," he offered.

"Excellent!" The man bowed. "I give you best ride in town!"

Charles moved on. When he came to the stone steps that led to the top of the wall surrounding the compound, he set down the ladder. It had never been risky to leave anything lying about in the mission. You could return days later and still find whatever you had left. But now, as he glanced at the many strangers passing by, he decided it was worth the risk of losing the ladder. He took the steps two at a time, came out above the compound, and hurried to the corner where he and Han had built the pigeon coop. The anxious sounds made by the abandoned birds made his chest tighten. He had forgotten to feed them for he wasn't sure how many days. He wondered if he should let them go free now. He didn't want it on his head if they died of starvation in their cages, though if he let them go, they would be eaten in no time. Either way, the poor things were making a racket and seemed not long for this world.

But when he reached the coop, he saw that their tray of food had been filled and their water replenished. They were making all that noise as they gorged themselves. Charles took off his Nationalist Army cap and watched them eat. Who was taking care of them? he wondered. Maybe it was Han? He missed his friend so badly in that moment that he walked over to the side of the wall and shouted.

"Han!" he yelled. "Where the devil are you?"

Charles studied the gray tile rooftops of the modest town. Little had been done to clear the rubble from the original Japanese attack that had woken him that morning weeks before. Several homes on the outskirts had collapsed into their courtyards, their private rooms exposed to the street. From what he could see, the market remained derelict, but that was often the case by this time of year, when summer drought left the farmers with nothing to sell. Piles of debris and earth blocked the central road to the west, requiring a more circuitous route. The townspeople had been inconvenienced by the summer's military incursions and remained wary of troops of any sort, even their own. But since the bulk of the Japanese Imperial Army had departed, they no longer felt in imminent danger. Shopkeepers opened each morning by sweeping yellow dust from their steps but kept their windows boarded, just in case. Fewer Chinese families fled on paths leading into the plains, where the fields of hemp shimmered golden brown in the heat. The countryside needed rain, but that was to be expected in high summer. All in all, Charles thought, things seemed as ordinarily dismal as ever.

The few Japanese soldiers who remained behind behaved as they had during the earlier occupation before the fighting began, milling about and generally ignoring the Chinese. Two younger ones stood directly below the mission wall, and Charles tried to see if he recognized them. With their caps on, it was hard to tell. An officer finished speaking to them, then turned and marched away. Charles squinted and thought he recognized the Japanese boy who'd swept their back steps.

"Hey," he shouted down in the local dialect, "how's it going out there? It's me, Hollywood!"

Charles wasn't sure what he meant by calling out to them. Later he tried to think it through, but the truth was, he didn't mean much. He just missed Han and figured the other fellows who were about his age weren't so bad to talk to. At the sound of his voice, the two young soldiers scurried across the dirt road and ducked behind a barricade made from the destroyed guardhouse. Charles could see the barrels of their guns pointing outward, searching, he assumed, for the source of the voice that had shouted at them.

"Whoa, guys," he called again, "take it easy. It's just me, Hollywood. I'm not the enemy."

One of the soldiers tipped back his cap, and Charles could see his familiar face. He was about to tease the kid about Jean Harlow again when he heard a sharp retort. Charles felt the bullet go past so close it whistled in his ear, just like in the movies—shrill and piercing and far too near. He ducked down fast and slumped against the side of the wall, his heart going wild in his chest. The dumb Japanese kid, he thought. Charles would report him to his commanding officer. He would tell his mother. As a neutral American on American soil, Charles had been shot at by the Japanese.

But then he yanked the Chinese Nationalist cap off his head and twisted it between his hands. As his breathing calmed, he wanted to shout to the kid that this wasn't a game, but clearly the Japanese soldier knew that already. Charles was the one slow to understand. He should never have worn the cap. He had almost gotten himself killed. He told himself he had to face things as they truly were. He was alone now, without his best friend or his father.

He cleared his throat and tried to think what his father would want him to do. He sat up straighter and remembered something so obvious it startled him. Every time his father had left the compound on one of his tours to the outlying parishes, he would say, "Take care of your mother, my boy." He had said it even when Charles was small. The request had always mystified him, since clearly it was the other way around: his mother had taken excellent care of him, perhaps too good care, fussing over him and seeing that he got anything he wanted. Yet his father had asked him to take care of her. Charles had no idea how to do that when Nurse Carson was more headstrong than ever, but he knew he must try.

But first he needed to find Han. He could do nothing to get his father back, but at least he could make an effort with his friend. He stayed low as he made his way back to the pigeon coop. The plumpest and handsomest of the kit had been Han's favorite. Charles unlatched the cage of that bird now.

"You miss him, too, don't you, Hsiao P'angtze?" he asked, calling their best bird by the nickname that they had given him: Little Fat Boy. Charles stroked him all the way down his sturdy back. The pigeon cocked his head to the side and seemed to be listening.

When Charles was young, his father would sit on the edge of his bed before sleep and use his hands to make shadows in the lamplight against the wall. He had shaped his fingers to become bunny ears and a round tail. His thumb and forefinger would part to resemble the mouth of a barking dog or a howling wolf. But Charles's favorite by far was when the hands wove together and flapped, mimicking the wings of a phoenix rising up into the flickering light. Charles could still see the magical bird taking off, courageous and free.

Lian had taught him that the phoenix Fenghuang was also known as the August Rooster. Contained within it were all birds, and other brave creatures, too, representing the full range of Yin and Yang in life. It appeared in auspicious times and brought goodness, virtue, and grace. From high in the K'un-lun Shan Mountains nearby in North China, where it lived, it would someday swoop down and bring everyone below good luck. Lian had boasted that those in the North were most likely to profit from such auspiciousness, which seemed to Charles a feeble perk given the many hardships of living in the region. Still, when she told him to keep watch for the Chinese phoenix as it circled the sky above the compound, he did. At any moment, the bird might descend, she said, spreading immortality and happiness. Charles looked about him now and longed to see its shadow.

"Find Han!" he whispered, pressing his mouth to Little Fat Boy's feathers.

He could feel the fast-beating heart as the bird's small system quivered, eager to take off. Charles raised the pigeon above his head and flung it out and over the wall until it disappeared into the cloudless sky.

Thirteen

Please, Mother, get in. Don't make a scene."

"Humans are not meant to be beasts of burden. I hate to encourage it."

"It's the man's job."

"I'm fastest in town!" exclaimed the rickshaw driver.

"Let's go now," Charles pleaded with her, "so the other drivers leave us alone."

She slid in beside him, and the rickshaw bolted forward, throwing them both against the straw seat. Though he wore no shoes, the coolie ran swiftly as he navigated the deeply rutted road that led away from the mission compound and into the town. When they were young, Charles and Han had raced barefoot on the hard-packed dirt to the river, and he knew how the pebbles cut into you.

"We need to find him," he said, more to himself than to his mother.

She patted his knee briskly. "We *will* find your friend," she said. "We *will*."

Her rising determination almost made Charles imagine she could see to it. Since opening the medical station in their home, she had been behaving as if she could accomplish whatever she set her mind to. He had to wonder if her confidence rose in inverse proportion to how hopeless their situation had become.

On the narrow main street, only a few shops appeared open. Young women dressed in high-cut, tight-fitting *cheongsam* strutted in front and called out to any men passing by. From the doorsteps of deserted buildings, grandfathers in traditional robes smoked thin pipes and gestured with long pinkie nails coated in white powder. Stocky, unshaven Russians in Western-style black suits and fedoras even in the summer heat hissed prices at Charles and his mother as they hurried past.

When the rickshaw reached the farmers' market, they climbed out. The driver set down the bamboo poles and doubled over with hacking. When he finally stood straight again, Charles saw blood on his lips. His mother was about to pay, but Charles snatched the coins from her and slapped them down on the straw seat. The driver pocketed the change quickly and was gone in an instant.

"That driver was not only sick," his mother said, "but utterly lackluster and exhibiting very strange behaviors. All that twitching and the way his arms shook. Did you notice? I suspect he has several illnesses at once in addition to being malnourished."

Charles wondered how it was possible that his mother had lived in China for five years and still couldn't tell an opium addict when she saw one. The rickshaw driver with his scabbed arms and rheumy, darting eyes looked like every man who ever stumbled out of a den after a binge. Charles had never been inside one of the smoky rooms down the back alleys but had peered in as he passed and seen the sickly-looking customers lolling about on couches, their heads thrown back onto threadbare pillows in some sort of unpleasant ecstasy. His mother had always said that she loved the Chinese people, their language and history, but as far as Charles could tell, she had rarely left the mission before now and certainly had never wound through the passageways and side lanes the way he had with Han. The Chinese people must have remained abstract to her—more the idea of a people than the real thing.

But on this warm afternoon, she strode into what was left of the marketplace, a straw basket swinging on her arm, as if fully expecting to find the makings for supper. Charles did a quick two-step to keep up with her as she pressed on past the destroyed stalls, many of which had been converted into makeshift homes with laundry hanging across their fronts instead of awnings. Someone tossed a tub of bathwater onto the path, and his mother simply skirted it. She even kept her balance when a pack of wild dogs raced by and knocked against her legs. None of it seemed to bother her.

When they reached the one open stall, his mother stepped up but didn't seem to recognize Mrs. Chen, who looked even more bedraggled then the last time, her clothing torn and her hands scabbed and encrusted with dirt.

"How much for these root vegetables?" his mother inquired in the local dialect. Charles was afraid she might touch a shrunken beet, but luckily she seemed to know that wasn't done.

Mrs. Chen continued to repair a filthy and tattered straw basket and barked an unreasonable price. Charles's mother laughed outright, placed her hands on her hips, and exclaimed, "Why, that's robbery! No one has that kind of money any longer. These vegetables shall rot before you find a willing customer." She then glanced around at the peasants who rummaged through what was left of the market. "Good woman," she said, "have you no feeling for your compatriots? You don't need to sell your precious produce to me, but at least offer a better price to your comrades."

"She's not going to budge," Charles whispered. "Let's go."

His mother rose taller, leaned over the stall, and said, "Your fellow citizens are starving, madam. If you have food, then it is only right that you share it. Your generosity will come back to you. Captain Hsu will see to it that you are given a portion of the millet we have at the mission."

The woman finally looked up. "Captain Hsu?" Beetle nut juice fell slowly and deliberately from her bottom lip onto the dusty ground. "That man is dog and traitor. The Reds are responsible for this." She spread her bony arms. "If he and his sons of bitches, turtle-egg, festering dog-bitch men had not come here, the Japs would have left us alone." She snarled quite a bit like a dog herself, Charles thought.

"He is none of those things," his mother persisted. "He fights for the country and its people. He's against capitalist greed, which I can plainly see you remain in favor of."

"Mother," Charles tugged at her arm, "please don't get involved."

She turned suddenly to him and said in English, "But I am involved. I'm deeply involved, and you should be, too."

Then she turned back to Mrs. Chen and continued, "Captain Hsu and his compatriots think about the whole, not just those at the top. China is far too destitute a country to have the marketplace rule. I see that now. The Communists intend for the vast majority of your people to be literate and fed. Isn't that marvelous? Other countries may have higher goals, but here that is what's needed. But everyone must get on board. I think you should join them."

Mrs. Chen's three-legged stool fell over as she stood abruptly and hobbled off. "American woman is Communist," she muttered. "Now I have seen everything!"

Charles finally pulled his mother away. "You can't get tangled up in this. We have to leave."

"Yes, you're right, it's time we got back to the mission. Hopefully we'll still come upon something for supper on the way."

"I don't mean leave the market," Charles said. "I mean leave the province, leave China. It isn't safe here any longer. I want to go back to America."

His mother stared at him for a long moment, and her face did not soften, even when she should have noticed his eyes filling and his bottom lip quivering almost imperceptibly. He didn't intend to cry, but the beginnings of tears were there, and she should have sensed them. When he was younger, his mother had always known when he was injured or sad or had gotten his feelings hurt by friends. She had called him sensitive—which he knew meant overly sensitive. But, while that was true, it was also true that she had been overly sensitive to him. Alert to his every pain, his mother had known how he felt almost before he did. But apparently not any longer.

"I'm surprised you don't understand that we are still needed here, Charles."

"All right, I wasn't going to tell you this," he said, pulling the Nationalist Army cap from his back pocket and using it to fan his face, "but it will change your mind. A Japanese soldier shot at me today."

His mother's eyes narrowed. She didn't throw her arms around him, as he had expected she might. She didn't invite stares with her exclamations of fear for his life or gratitude for his safety.

"I wonder," she said after a long moment, "if we need weapons."

"Mother!"

"Now, hear me out," she continued. "Perhaps we would be wise to have more protection than we have."

He had assumed that once she heard of his narrow brush with death, they would start packing their bags. She would understand that the safe and idyllic mission compound of his childhood was now no different from the occupied town, and while things might have calmed down somewhat for the time being, the whole province was basically lawless and fraught with danger. In the hinterlands of Northwestern China, far from international scrutiny, the Japanese could do anything they liked. The wild bullet that had grazed his head had taught Charles that.

But his mother carried on, "Every one of these Chinese boys has a mother. Some have died in my arms when they should have been home, helping in their family field. I feel we owe it to them and to their mothers to not just traipse off when the going gets tough. One can't leave an army on a whim, Charles."

He looked down at his dusty sneakers and felt dizzy. He wanted to sink right there on the dirt path and let the stream of people continue around him. Perhaps she was braver than he. Perhaps he remained a coddled boy after all. He wished his father were here to sort it out.

"Son," his mother continued as she held on to his shoulders with two strong hands, "I'm afraid I have to ask, but where were you when this incident took place? Were you outside the mission? Were you wearing that cap?" She gestured to the Nationalist Army hat, which he hurriedly stuffed back into his pocket. "Charles, were you asking for trouble in some way?"

"You think it's my fault that I got shot at?"

"Sometimes your judgment isn't the best."

"You think I deserved it?" he shouted.

"Of course not! But, perhaps it was just an instance of mistaken identity, or you weren't as cautious as we need to be. If we stay within the compound and are protected by Captain Hsu and his men—"

"Mother, Captain Hsu can't protect us. The Geneva Convention can't protect us from the Japs if they choose to attack."

"We don't call them 'Japs,' Charles. We call them 'Japanese.' And Captain Hsu is not an inferior commander. He is very wise. You could learn something from him."

She loved it, he thought, the chaos all around. "I can't listen to you. I have to go." He turned and started to push through the crowds.

"Charles, get back here!"

But he kept on, weaving through the Chinese—each selling something, wanting something, when he wanted nothing except to leave.

"Young man," his mother gave one last shout, "come back here this instant!"

Charles turned down an alley, and another, and finally a third, until there was no way her voice could still reach him. He hoped more than anything that he might come around a bend and bump into Han. Charles pressed on, following his Jack Purcells, which he had tried to keep clean instead of covered in ugly yellow silt because he thought that was how the boys back home in America wore them. The truth was, he didn't know how the boys back home did anything. *Life* magazine arrived six months late, when it arrived at all. The last movie shown in the Parish Hall was over a year old. For all he knew, Jean Harlow had been replaced several times over by younger leading ladies.

He came out of an alley onto a crowded road. People hurried

past, intent on repairing their homes and shops, refilling tin buckets, carrying loads, scavenging or trading scraps of food. They knocked into him where he stopped, but he didn't care. Charles kicked clods of torn-up dirt, soiling his sneakers even more. He would buy a new pair when he got out of here. Because, he made a promise to himself, he was going home to America, no matter what his mother said or did.

"Hey, good-looking," a skinny, sickly girl called to him from the door of a boarded-up shop. She wore a tight dress with slits to the tops of her thighs, her thin arms also exposed, unlike a proper Chinese woman. She beckoned him with long, red-tipped fingernails. "Come on over," she purred. Smoke and the voices of men drifted out onto the street from inside, along with the rattle of dice and the percussive slap of mah-jongg tiles.

"Thanks, anyway," he said and added, "I'm an American."

The moment he said it, he realized it was irrelevant to her trade. She cackled, and he couldn't blame her.

"And I'm a beautiful flower. You want to pluck a beautiful flower?"

An older woman in a flowing, large-sleeved gown appeared from the shadowed doorway and stepped into the harsh afternoon light. Elaborate decorations floated from a bun high on her head. Her face was painted white like the actors in Chinese opera Charles had seen in the provincial capital. Black lines representing eyebrows curved upward in a maniacal way as the grande dame towered over the sickly girl, who shrank beside her.

"Back inside to customers!"

"But I found this delicacy," the girl said as she tossed another beckoning glance at Charles.

The madam looked him up and down and hissed, "He is not

for you. Now, go!" She swatted the girl's backside in the tight dress.

Charles knew he should move but remained stuck in the same spot, transfixed by the elaborate costume and makeup. The madam was far too tall to be a Chinese woman, he thought, and only later considered whether she might not have been a woman at all. Beads of sweat stood out on her painted forehead, and the whiskers on her chin had been powered white as well, like one of the characters in Lian's terrifying bedtime tales.

"You America?" the madam asked as she stepped closer.

He nodded.

"Get lost, America! You don't belong here."

Her sudden rudeness woke him from his spell. "All right, I'm going," he said, but still he didn't budge.

"What is it now, boy?" she asked, changing her tone. "You want to come inside? Don't just look. Touch. But first," she held out a hand with the long pinkie nail, "give all your coins to me!"

Charles remained transfixed by her unnatural appearance and voice. The words seeped out of her in a high singsong that grated on the ear but was also strangely enticing. She gave him the creeps, but he couldn't take his eyes off her.

"No, you see," he began, "I just wanted to say that we're not the enemy. We're on your side. Look," he pulled out the Chinese Nationalist cap and placed it on his head. "I even have this."

She careened down off the wooden steps in her silk skippers and scurried toward him. With a high-pitched cry, she lifted her arm in the elaborate robe, waved a folded fan in his face, and used it to knock the cap off his head. "Take that off!" she shouted. "Only our soldiers wear that!"

Charles snatched the cap from the dusty ground.

"Go back to Christian church and pray for us." She swatted his shoulders with the fan. "Go, America! Go home and pray!"

Charles jumped away from the crazy woman, turned, and hurried off. When he reached the mission compound, he couldn't bring himself to go in through the open gate but instead scrambled up the stone steps to the top of the wall. He needed to see the countryside. The madam was right, he thought. He and his mother and the other missionaries should go back to America and pray, though he knew his days of praying were over. He'd never kneel again, or whisper into the folds of his hands before bed. Even his father's advice seemed wrong now. He didn't need to care for his mother. She was stronger than he was and had a will of her own. What he needed to do was take care of himself and get the hell out of there.

The cooing of the birds reached Charles as he reached the top. At least he was keeping his promise to them. Dusk meant feeding time. But when he turned the corner, he saw that the cage was already open. The birds fluttered about as their seeds were scattered before them on the brick walkway.

"Han!" Charles shouted as he ran toward his old friend and hugged him. "Dear Lord," he said, "you're a sight for sore eyes."

Han nodded enthusiastically, his face bright and open.

"Where on earth have you been?" Charles asked.

Han smiled and nodded, though more shyly. "I'm with the Eighth Route Army," Han said. "The best army in all of China. We have tens of thousands of recruits now!"

Charles stood back and looked his friend up and down. Han stood straighter and seemed taller. He wore a pale blue jacket and matching pants, thin cloth shoes—a real uniform, including a belt that cinched his narrow waist with a buckle bearing the Communist star. He even had on a Red Army cap.

"You look good," Charles said.

"We don't have much food, but we manage. And all the soldiers take lessons in reading and writing. I help teach them. It's good, Charles. The country is changing. For the first time, the people are in charge. No more warlords and, no offense, no more greedy foreign influences. Not you, but, well, you know—"

Charles didn't know, but he wasn't going to ask Han to explain it to him now.

"Because of my experience here in the mission," Han continued, "I will serve as a translator for our top leaders. Some are the sons of peasants and laborers, but very smart men. I've never known such intelligent men, and brave, too."

Charles had never heard Han speak for so long or so eloquently about anything before.

"But how are you?" Han asked. "I see our birds are plump. You have done a good job caring for them."

"Not really," Charles said.

"It is good to see you." Han reached up and clapped Charles on the shoulder. "But," Han said, stepping back, "where did you get that Nationalist Army cap?"

Charles pulled it off and tossed it onto the bricks as if it was on fire. "I found it by the side of the road. I don't mean anything by wearing it. I'm not in favor of them. I don't really know who I'm in favor of, except you, of course. If you want me to burn it, I will. We could burn it together!"

Han laughed. "You are so dramatic, my friend. No need to burn it. Just don't wear it. It's not safe. And also not right."

"Of course, absolutely."

"Would you like my Red Army cap instead?" Han asked.

Charles could hardly believe it. "That's too generous."

"I shouldn't wear my uniform in town, anyway, even with only a few Japs around. I would be honored for you to have it."

Han handed him the green cap with the red star, and Charles bowed. "I'm the one who is honored."

"You are my friend," Han said.

Charles wanted to mention how much he'd missed Han and how he hoped they could talk things through like they always had. But instead, the two boys watched the birds as they milled about on the wall, pecking at the last of their food.

After a few moments, Charles asked, "Can you tell me where you've been?"

"For now, we are at a camp in the caves. I can't say more."

"I see," Charles said. "Up in the mountains."

Han stepped closer and asked, "But I wonder, do you know what you and your mother are going to do?"

Charles let out a long breath. "I want to leave, but she's gotten tangled up with that fellow Captain Hsu. I think he wants her to stay and keep running the medical clinic in our house. Seems like a crazy idea to me."

"Hsu is an excellent leader, and I heard about your mother. She is known in many provinces as a very brave woman."

"I suppose," Charles said.

"But you feel it is time for you to leave?" Han asked, his expression more serious than ever.

He looked like a soldier, Charles realized. He looked like a man.

"So, where will you go?" Han asked. "Peking?"

"No," Charles said. "It's time for us to return to America."

Han nodded. "I am sure your father would want that."

Charles let out a relieved chuckle. "How did you know that I keep wondering what he would want? You're such a good buddy to me, Han."

Han smiled, too. "I feel quite certain he would want you to leave China. Yes, I feel this is true."

Charles wondered for a moment why his friend seemed so convinced. He dug a hand deeper into his pocket and ran his fingers over his father's marble chop, his confidence growing as he touched the familiar worn shape of the carved phoenix. "You're right," Charles said. "I'll tell Mother. I'll positively insist on it. Would you like to join us for supper?" he asked. "We haven't much, but I bet it's better than army food."

"Army food is not great, but I must be getting back. I came to see Hsia P'angtze. He knows me, you know?"

"Sure, I know. I assumed he found you and that's why you're here. I sent him."

"*You* sent him?" Han asked.

"Well, who else would have sent him?"

Han looked quickly again at the birds. "It doesn't matter. I am here. That's what matters."

Charles wanted to ask more about Little Fat Boy and where Han had been and what he was going to do next, but he had to let it go. Han was a soldier, with all the knowledge and secrets that entailed. Han hustled the last of the pigeons back into the coop. He kept Hsia P'angtze out, took a small strip of paper from his jacket pocket, and attached it to the bird's leg with a thin black thread. Then he raised the creature up into the air and, with a flourish, let him go.

"I don't know what you're up to, Han," Charles said. "But I assume it's for the good."

"Yes," Han said, "it is."

He closed the door of the coop, turned back to Charles, and bowed. Charles bowed, too, and when he stood straight again, Han was striding toward the stairs. Charles rushed to look over the edge of the wall, but his friend was already gone, somehow blending in with the many other Chinese passing on foot and in carts. Charles put Han's cap onto his head and looked out at the fields that burned red in the late day with the sun going down.

Fourteen

From all the way across the courtyard, Shirley could see Japanese soldiers standing at attention in front of her home: the young one who had swept her back steps and a second one who also looked familiar. Major Hattori paced the verandah, his hands clasped behind his back. During her afternoon expedition into town, she had been surprised to find few signs of the Japanese Imperial Army. Weeks before, they had swarmed in, worse than locusts descending on an already weak harvest, and attacked and ravaged the town before swiftly moving on, she hoped, to the next province. And yet, here were three of them in the mission compound. She wanted to stomp up her front steps and give the major a piece of her mind. But instead, she clenched her fists as she wove through the Chinese camps beneath the fruit trees. Their cooking smells soothed her now in a familiar way, but she was not to be calmed. She spat on the ground as the Chinese did to clear ill humors, knowing it was fury she must expel. She stepped through the moon gate, skimmed the steps, stopped before the stone-faced officer, and offered a crisp, perfunctory nod.

"Good evening, Major Hattori. It's awfully late in the day to be paying a visit."

He gave an abrupt bow. "I wait for you, Mrs. Carson."

"I'm sorry to keep you waiting, but I'm not available at the moment. My head is spinning, and I haven't eaten all day. My son has taken a wrong turn, and I have many mouths to feed. I must get on with my evening plans."

"We will meet now," he said. "We know you have Chinese under roof. We suspect some are soldiers. You offer them not only food but medical help, too. Our general is aware of all this. You should be punished. But that is not why I am here."

"Oh, really?" she said nonchalantly, trying to hide her alarm.

"Also, I am not surprised you lose your son. You are very bad mother."

Shirley let out a gasp. "You do seem to have theories on many topics, Major. And in addition to everything else I've been through today, you seem interested in chastising me. Are you a parent yourself? If not, I suggest you hold your tongue."

The major's grip tightened around the holster at his hip.

"Please," she tried again, "let's speak tomorrow. I'll be much more civilized then. Are you available to come for tea? Let's say four o'clock. Now, good evening, Major Hattori."

Before he had a chance to reply, Shirley spun around, opened the heavy door, slipped across the threshold, and shut it behind her. As she pushed the iron bolt into place, her heart beat so loudly in her chest she worried he could hear it on the other side. She was certain he would start pounding at any moment, but as she stood with her ear to the carved rosewood, his boots retreated down the porch steps, leaving her surprised by her easy victory.

Shirley took off her sunbonnet and headed to the coat rack. The nurses huddled together in the front hall had overheard her conversation with the Japanese major. They watched her in both awe and horror. One of them, a Chinese girl with close-cropped hair and the trousers worn by the Communist women, said, "Japanese dogs! Yellow Army dwarf bandit sons of whores. I say we invite them inside and kill them! If you offer tea," she hissed at Shirley, "I poison his cup!"

Several of the more sensible young ladies looked appropriately shocked at this idea, but at least as many appeared to seriously consider the suggestion. Who could blame them, Shirley thought, after what they had seen the Japanese inflict on their compatriots, soldiers and citizens alike?

"The Japanese Army has been absolutely barbaric," Shirley said, "but you must remember that our American compound remains neutral territory. We are safe here. There is no rule against us running a clinic to help Chinese citizens if we choose. We've done that for years, offering inoculations and various treatments. But we must behave in as civilized a manner as we can in this tense climate in order to remind them that America is not their enemy. Otherwise we will risk losing our clinic and will be unable to assist anyone. Now," she said, as she handed the empty food basket to one of the women, "tell me, dear ladies, did any of our patients pass over to the other side while I was gone?"

The young Communist woman said, "I say, fight them here and now and get it over with!"

"My dear, you are far too young to instigate such action," Shirley said. "You must leave the military strategizing to men like Captain Hsu."

The Communist woman put her finger up to her lips and squeezed Shirley's arm. The other young ladies crowded closer, their faces wild with concern, their heads shaking from side to side. They all seemed to be trying to tell her something, but before she had a chance to inquire further, Kathryn rose from the piano bench. Shirley hadn't noticed her there and was startled to see her but grateful for the familiar face on this most wretched of days.

"Kathryn, my dear," she said and reached out with open arms, "I have missed you so. How are you? I hope you've had a better day than I. I can't crawl into bed fast enough."

Kathryn took a last drag on a cigarette and dropped it onto the polished wooden floorboards of the front hall. Shirley was shocked but tried not to show it. That Kathryn would smoke so openly wasn't terribly surprising given the tense circumstances, or even that she would do so inside a missionary home. But Shirley did not appreciate that her friend now treated her house like a pool hall. However, when she saw her friend's cool expression, she decided to let it go. She stepped closer and let her arms drift to her sides again. There would be no hugging.

"I'm so sorry," Shirley said, "I've been remiss and haven't paid a call in I don't know how long. I've hardly seen anyone for days."

"You seem to have seen many people," Kathryn said, looking around at the medical helpers and the beds occupied by patients. "Just not the usual ones."

"That's true, isn't it?" Shirley said, offering a smile. "And I see you've taken up smoking publicly. Whatever will the other ladies think?" She let out a friendly titter, which Kathryn did not echo.

"The other ladies are more understanding than we knew them to be. They have each risen to the situation in their own way and are not as petty as we once thought. I've come to like them quite a bit, actually."

Shirley found that hard to imagine but did not contradict her friend. "How nice," she said.

"I came by to tell you about the meeting last night."

"Oh, the meeting! I knew I forgot something. Yes, do tell."

"The entire congregation met. Reverend Wells did an excellent job. He has stepped up to the plate better than anyone could have expected."

"No longer the rumpled little bookworm that he used to be?" Shirley tried again with a smile.

"No," Kathryn said with an arched eyebrow and an accusing look in her eye. "No one is who they once were."

Shirley nodded. "I suppose not."

"A vote was taken, and plans have been made. We are all leaving."

Shirley went to the piano and settled on the bench, her elbows accidentally hitting several deep and discordant notes.

"We will take the train to Peking and from there to Shanghai, where we will make passage."

"Passage?"

"To America," Kathryn said. "I assumed you knew that."

"No," Shirley offered softly, "I didn't know."

"Orders have come from the American legation in Peking. All American women and children must leave the country immediately," Kathryn said. "Foreigners are being kicked out. It isn't safe for us any longer."

Her stoniness was as jarring as the news itself. But then Kathryn surprised Shirley by kneeling down before her and taking her hands from her lap.

"You've been wonderful and heroic, but you really must stop now. It's time to go home."

Kathryn pressed her cheek into Shirley's hands, and Shirley instinctively stroked her charming bobbed hair. She was such an enthusiastic, large-hearted girl. It was good she was returning to America. She would find a new life there. The man who had not materialized for her here in China would find her on the ship going back. Shirley could picture it: Kathryn would lean against the ship's railing, the wind blowing her hair around her pretty face, when an impressive fellow with an eye for finer things and a mind expanded by his years in the Orient would step forward to light her cigarette, and together they would commence a new life. Just like that. Such things did happen. All the time. To other people.

"Thank you, my dear, dear friend," Shirley said. "You are so kind to have come to tell me this important news."

Kathryn raised her head. "So you will pack up and leave with us? We have a few days to prepare, but no more, perhaps less, depending on how the arrangements are fulfilled. As it turns out, Reverend Wells is excellent at this, too. Who would have guessed it?"

Kathryn finally smiled as Shirley lifted her up and they stood. She held her friend's hands in hers. "Yes, I will discuss it with Charles right away, and we will make a sound decision."

"But there is no decision to be made. You must simply do it," Kathryn said. "This is not something to *discuss* with a teenaged boy. You are his mother. You must tell him what to do."

"I'm sure you're right," Shirley said and turned toward the young nurses. "I'll be with you in a moment, good ladies," she called to them.

"I see," Kathryn said and removed her hand. "Well, I can't say that I didn't try."

"No," Shirley said, "you did more than that. You have convinced me."

"I have?" Kathryn asked.

"There are just a few things that I must put in order first."

Kathryn appeared skeptical but said, "Well, I'll be damned."

Shirley adjusted her friend's adorable pillbox hat. "Wherever do you find such perfect accessories?" Shirley asked as she escorted her to the door.

Kathryn beamed, her good nature bringing color back into her cheeks. "You know how my mother loves to shop. When we get back home, she wants to take us both out for a rousing expedition to F. R. Lazarus. We really will be rising from the dead then, won't we?"

Shirley loved a good pun and laughed, then bade her friend good-night. She opened the door quickly for Kathryn, glanced around, and felt relieved to confirm that the major and his soldiers were gone. When the door shut again, Shirley made a beeline for the waiting helpers and was just reaching for a patient's chart when she felt something tug at her linen skirt.

Dao-Ming appeared before her, stranger than ever, her cheeks flushed, her eyes practically swollen shut, her socks mismatched, and her rotund body wrapped in several layers of dirty Chinese robes. Shirley noticed a new item that weighed her down: a thick, heavy belt with the Red Army star on it. But then Shirley spotted something even more peculiar: the girl appeared to be wearing Caleb's driving cap.

"Where did you get that?" Shirley asked, forgetting momentarily that the child could barely speak, or chose not to.

"Did Charles give it to you?" she tried again.

Dao-Ming shook her head.

"You found it yourself downstairs?"

Dao-Ming nodded.

Shirley stepped away from the other ladies and took Dao-Ming by the hand. She hustled her over to the stairs that rose to the upstairs quarters. With some effort, she lifted the child onto the second step so that they might speak eye to eye.

"Where is Lian?" she asked.

Dao-Ming pointed down the hallway toward the kitchen dependency.

"I see. Is she is helping to prepare food?"

Dao-Ming nodded, and then, as if speaking had never been a problem, Dao-Ming whispered the words, "Hsu down."

"You mean Captain Hsu?"

The girl nodded.

"What do you mean by 'down'?" Shirley asked.

Several loud and insistent knocks sounded on the front door just then. Dao-Ming's eyes widened.

"It's all right," Shirley said.

But the girl's head shook frantically as she whispered, "Jap devils."

"Lian," Shirley called down the hallway, "would you mind answering the door for me, please?"

Lian came swiftly from the kitchen, followed by the young woman, Li-Juan, who had recently come to help. Behind them were the Japanese grandfather and his daughters. And after them hobbled Tupan Feng, body bent over his cane and sword swaying with each halting step. What they were all doing in the kitchen with hardly any ingredients for supper was a mystery to Shirley.

On her way to the door, Lian whispered harshly to Dao-Ming, "You took him?"

Dao-Ming nodded, panic making her limbs stiff and more awkward than ever.

"So," Shirley asked, "Captain Hsu is hiding in our basement? Is that it?"

Lian wheeled around and hissed at Shirley as Dao-Ming shook her head madly, tears starting to stream down her face. "Great man must be kept safe," Lian whispered.

"Absolutely," Shirley said, standing straighter. "I will not let them touch a hair on his head. I promise."

She hurried to Lian's side and reached the door just in time to open it herself. "What is it now?" she asked Major Hattori and his two soldiers. "I believe I said I wasn't available this evening."

They stormed past her and into her home. Shirley leaned out and took a quick glance at the dark courtyard for her son. It wasn't like him to stay out this late. "Charles is upset with me," she whispered to Lian. "We need to keep an eye out for him."

Lian did not reply, but her expression only made Shirley more anxious. She turned to join the others in the front hall and asked, "Now, Major, what can I do for you?"

As she spoke, she pulled back her shoulders and offered a calm, even serene visage. They had barged into her home, but she intended to behave like a lady of sound intelligence, a Vassar graduate with a good head on her shoulders, and not someone to be trifled with. She thought of her husband's handy phrase, *stiff upper lip*.

"Mrs. Carson," Major Hattori said in English, "you, madam, are under arrest."

Shirley let out a high, alarmed laugh, which was quickly stifled by the two soldiers, who snatched her wrists in a firm grasp. Lian stepped forward and tried to wrench the soldiers off her.

"That's all right, Lian," Shirley said. "You mustn't upset your heart. I'm all right."

Li Juan began weeping, her arms wrapped around Dao-Ming, who positively wailed. Lian tried to stop the men for a second time by planting her considerable body in front of the open doorway. The soldiers simply pushed the older woman aside. She stumbled and sprawled on the wood floor.

Old Tupan Feng doddered forward and, with some effort, pulled his long, ornamental Japanese sword from its lacquered sheath, almost toppling as he raised it up toward the ceiling. "Halt," he said. "Unhand Mrs. Carson."

Major Hattori had been standing back with his hands on his hips, but he now strode toward the old Chinese man and laughed. "Where did you get that saber, grandfather?" he asked.

Tupan Feng blinked several times and brought the sword back down to his side. "Tupan Feng Number One Student at Tokyo Military Academy. Top of class. Excellent training." He bowed.

"That's right," the major said without bowing as he took it from Tupan Feng's trembling hand. "I recognize this as one of ours." He held the sword out before him in his open palms. The silver blade shone handsomely in the dim light of the front hall. "You have taken good care of it."

Tupan Feng raised his chin as high as he could. "We were taught many important things. Discipline and virtue above all. I tried to bring this superior Japanese standard to my people here in my province. But they were lazy and would not obey."

"Of course." Major Hattori chuckled. "They are Chinese. What did you expect?"

"But," the old warlord continued, his voice growing stronger than Shirley had ever heard it before, "they were never cruel, evil, or heartless. They are not barbarians like you!"

The major swiped the saber in the air, and the others skittered back, but Tupan Feng stuck out his chest and kept his firm gaze forward. "If you must take a prisoner," he said, "I volunteer. I am highest ranking of these people. I am the only military here. They are civilians. We do not attack civilians. We are civilized."

The major signaled his men. As they pushed Shirley out onto the porch, she called over her shoulder, "Please find Charles and reassure him that his mother will be all right." Once out on the porch, she planted her feet on the red-painted floorboards and shouted, "Let go of me! I am perfectly capable of walking without assistance. Major, tell your men to release me."

The major nodded to his men, and they let go of her arms. Shirley straightened her skirt and blouse and looked down upon them with fiery eyes. "My riding coat, gentlemen. I never go out in the evening without proper outerwear." Lian instructed Li Juan to bring the coat. After it was placed over Shirley's shoulders, she said, "Do get word to Reverend Wells, though I hate to bother him in the evening when he likes to read."

"Enough instruction," the major shouted. He motioned to his men, and one of them prodded her forward with the butt of his rifle to her shoulder blade.

"That is completely unnecessary," Shirley said as she started down the steps. But then she stopped: there he was, tromping up them, looking as bedraggled as a boy his age could. "Charles," she asked, "are you all right?"

It took Charles a moment to come out of his haze, but then he looked up and saw Japanese soldiers standing behind his mother, their rifles pointed at her. He clutched the railing and stepped out of their way. "Mother! What's going on? Where are they taking you?"

"Don't panic, darling," she said. "It's just a misunderstanding.

We'll get it straightened out. *Steady hand and cool heart*, as Father used to say."

Charles then surprised her, and perhaps himself, by speaking directly to the Japanese officer as he passed. "This is a clear violation of the Geneva Convention. The legation in Peking will hear about it. We'll get the American forces involved if we have to! Don't even think of hurting her, and I mean it!"

The soldiers nudged Shirley onto the mission grounds. Lian threw her arms around Li Juan, who held on to Dao-Ming. The major gestured for Shirley to move, and she set off. Fear swirled and tangled her thoughts and made her legs weak and heavy, but her heart was calm.

Fifteen

Cook set Caleb's head down on the straw pillow and wiped watery porridge from his chin. "Sun out today. Reverend feel better," he said.

Caleb tried to smile.

"Han-Boy brings news."

Caleb frowned, which for some reason was easier to accomplish than a smile.

"No worry," Cook said. "He not tell others. Family does not follow. They carry on without Reverend. Very good!"

Cook's upbeat voice echoed against the damp cave walls. Caleb's eyes shifted to the opening, where the sky hung like a perfect blue cutout made by a child.

"American Mrs. Carson joins Red cause."

Caleb raised an eyebrow.

"You do not believe?" Cook asked with a chuckle. "I not believe, either. But very sorry," he shook his head, "Reverend cannot see to believe."

Caleb looked up into the man's lined, yet cheery, face.

"Do not trouble self." Cook set down the bowl of porridge and clapped the dust from his hands. "You prepare instead for the other side."

Cook's friendly-sounding words descended over Caleb, as heavy and uncomfortable as the wool blanket that weighed him down. Cook, of all people, grasped that he had outstayed his welcome in this life. He was but skin and bones, and many of those broken. But his mind would not stop. It had the tenacity of his old mule, which had miraculously survived the fall. But luckily for the animal, it had been shot in the head soon afterward and finally set free. We only reserve such kindness for animals, Caleb thought. His eyes grew moist again as he realized that the mule's release was what he longed for, too.

Cook stepped away to allow him privacy, thoughtful as always. Caleb could rest now. But then the young man came near, Cook's son and his son's friend. Caleb couldn't recall the young man's name as he pulled up the stool to sit beside the cot. He heard whispered Chinese words. Then the boy leaned in closer and placed his round, handsome face in Caleb's line of sight.

"Esteemed Reverend," he said in quite good English and bowed his head.

Caleb wished with all his heart he could reach out and touch the black hair and fine, though already creased, forehead. The children of this country grew up far too early, Caleb thought, and faced hardships far worse than those endured by most adults back home. Chinese boys did not tromp into the mountains in springtime in search of small game and mild adventure. They did not discover through play a boundless sense of themselves, as Caleb had with his older brothers. A spasm of pain shot down his spine at the thought, and he scolded himself for remembering.

"I have seen your son," the boy said.

Caleb grimaced.

"No, it is all right, Reverend. He is well."

Caleb bit his bottom lip as the pain suddenly returned. He

didn't want to frighten the young fellow, but he sensed an uncontrollable scream rising up inside him.

"Charles has come to the decision to leave. Not just our town and province but China."

With great effort, Caleb fought back the urge to moan or exclaim. He even tried to make the corners of his mouth rise into a smile.

"That is what you wanted, yes?" the boy asked. "I told him so."

Caleb couldn't help the moan that finally seeped out of him.

"Please do not worry," the boy said and laid a gentle palm on his chest. "I did not tell him you are alive, or that I see you. But I said to him that I am certain you want him and his mother to leave the country and be safe."

Cook came over, touched the boy on the shoulder, and said something to him in Chinese. The young man bowed his head again.

"I must go," he said. "You are greatly missed, Reverend. Charles-Boy loves you very much."

Caleb could feel his eyes brimming over, and he no longer cared. The boy wiped his own eyes with his sleeve, and that was fine with Caleb, too.

Cook remained dry-eyed as always as he said, "Enough. Reverend sleep now."

Caleb lifted his finger, but the boy was gone. Caleb hated for him to go and wished with all his heart that he could have asked questions about his family. But his thoughts were coming slowly today, staying deep within. The boy had said that his son was all right. That was what mattered. There was no need for words beyond that.

As sleep started to slip over Caleb again, a clear, powerful thought struck him, and he was suddenly wide awake. Like his wife and son, he, too, must move on to the next stage. He must leave this life behind. His stubborn body had refused to release him, but Caleb knew a way around that. Every soldier in the camp carried a weapon—a rifle, pistol, knife, or bow. These young men had been raised on farms around livestock and understood that an animal with a broken back was done. He would ask the best of them, the one with the keenest intellect and deepest sympathies. When he awoke, Caleb would ask Captain Hsu to kill him.

Some hours later, he awoke again and was alone on his cot at the mouth of the cave. Midday sunlight drenched the leaves, but the cool, moist air from inside the mountain felt refreshing. On fine, clear summer days like this one, Caleb recalled, he and his brothers had tromped out into sunlight, brushed through high, wild grass, and taken the paths up the mountainside. They knew the trails by the rocks and trees that marked each bend. In mid-August in the White Mountains, berries weighed the branches low, tempting the boys. They knew it was still too early but couldn't resist and popped them into their mouths only to spit them back out again. "You have to learn to wait," his oldest brother would say as they washed their stained hands in an icy brook and pressed on toward the peak.

Caleb understood now that those familiar mountains had been his testing ground for this mountain in China. So far away from where he had begun, and yet he knew the feel of the damp walls and the pebbled floor that surrounded him. For hadn't he and his brothers taken shelter in caves many times? When the wind whipped up and sudden bouts of rain came careening across the open sky, first darkening the mountainside across the way, then releasing torrents, the boys would duck into a cave to wait it out. That was all he needed to do now, Caleb told himself: wait it out.

As he and his brothers waited, they watched the rainfall and told stories. His oldest brother was the best at creating an entertaining chill in the younger ones. Rumors and tall tales circulated among the country folk and in the mountain villages. Certain stories caught hold and couldn't be shaken for generations. Once a group of boys—not Caleb and his brothers but boys of his grandfather's era—had lifted their lantern to see down a defunct mining shaft and spotted with their own eyes the bones of a man, his clothing stripped away and the whiteness of his skeleton shining as if lit from within. The boys raced home, but when they returned to the woods with their fathers, the skeleton was gone. Ever after, it was said that the ghost of that fallen miner roamed the hills.

Caleb tried to chuckle at how that story had kept him awake many nights until he was almost his son's age now. Never a brave or stoical child, Caleb had been unable to banish it from his mind, especially before sleep. It had haunted him the way Lian's bedtime stories bothered Charles until Caleb had finally forbidden their amah to tell them. But the damage had been done: Charles, like his father, had a too-active imagination. It tortured him, even when every rational explanation offered by grown-ups insisted otherwise. He and his son were weak in that way, Caleb knew, and susceptible to worry. But he loved Charles for it, for he equated a fanciful mind with a generous heart.

Caleb could no longer pretend to maintain a self-imposed stricture on memory. Grasping that he would not live much longer, especially if he enlisted Captain Hsu's help, Caleb decided that he might as well let the stories from his past cascade over him as readily as the tears that he let fall willy-nilly. During the endless hours when he lay half awake and half asleep in the cave, he would allow himself to recall and invent and dream, his mind roaming—in search of what, he wasn't sure.

Another story his brother had once told wove its way into his thoughts. A hiker had wandered off the Appalachian Trail as an early winter squall rumbled down from Mount Washington. The young man took cover in a cave, where, wet and cold, he shivered and ate the last of his food. Snow quickly burdened the pine boughs and obscured the shapes of rocks and cliff sides. If he ventured out again into the rising drifts, he might take a misstep and tumble over the edge. So the hiker stayed in the cold of the cave. As the sun went down behind the hills, the world outside became as blank and forbidding as a sheet of paper in a platen, its purpose not yet known to the writer. Night fell, and the young hiker pulled leaves around himself to try to keep warm, but he knew it would be impossible. He would not survive to see dawn paint the whiteness with a gentle, rosy glow.

But the young hiker did awake the next morning. He stumbled out of the icy cave and found the trail not far away. At the general store in the nearest village, he drank black coffee with trembling hands. The owner's wife, old Mrs. Knox, didn't look up from her crossword puzzle as she asked, "Bear save you, did he?" The young man nodded into his cup, realizing she must be right and no longer amazed by anything. He would spend the rest of days searching for an embrace as warm and miraculous as the one that had surrounded him in that cave.

Caleb shivered, and Cook appeared and added a second blanket to the weight that already bore down on him. He shut his eyes and wished for the warmth of that surprising creature, though the summer was full and dry outside, and to anyone else, the air was mild. By mid-August back home, the birch leaves would have begun to flip like coins in a pool of golden light, registering the coming season long before anyone else sensed it. Faint, glowing, upright friends, those white birches had been like family to Caleb. His grandfather, eyeglasses catching the sun, trousers creased sharply, and his minister's collar worn tight. All the men on that side, including Caleb himself, were as thin as young birches, their tall, sturdy New England bodies bending into the wind.

Like the poet, Caleb had seen birches arched by snow, limbs caught under a crust of ice. He had freed them more than once, though he never chose to ride one, as Frost and Caleb's more adventurous brothers had. He was too young when they had wrapped their skinny legs around the trunks to make a winsome whip. Caleb had watched instead, snow frozen inside his woolen mittens and up his sleeves, the cuffs chafing him with the red wrists of winter. Scrawny and made mostly of bone, he was often sick as a child and easily scarred by the elements, drawn on like the birches by shadowy lines that he understood now had foretold his end. He was a lone birch, too pale in a forest of pines, weaker than his sturdier relatives.

What he wanted now more than anything was to be amid that glade of white birches on the trail toward home. He longed to see them now—his brothers, his family, and those shimmering branches a little farther ahead.

When he next awoke, night had fallen. He did not move his head but let the sounds of Chinese voices wash over him. Cook and another man spoke rapidly in the local dialect. Caleb had stopped trying to understand that foreign tongue, and perhaps because he no longer made an effort, the Chinese cadences wormed their way into his mind. After a few moments, he surprised himself by recognizing a phrase or two.

The Japanese had taken his wife into custody. He heard Cook and the other man discussing it. He wanted to call Cook over and ask for further explanation. By the urgency of the men's voices, he could tell that this news had just arrived and that action was being taken. Captain Hsu was no doubt already doing his best to correct the situation through his many channels with the elders of the town. And Reverend Wells, never the most competent at dealing with others, would also rise to the occasion. Caleb assumed that some mistake had been made. The Japanese couldn't possibly want to hold his wife for long. She was an American, after all, and a woman, for heaven's sake.

But not just any woman, he thought with a smile. She was his Shirley: sturdy and unbendable in ways that he was not. Shirley Carson was not to be trifled with. If anything, she would see to her own release and not leave it to the others. With this confident thought, Caleb drifted off again, aware that he must stay alive a little while longer, at least until word came that she had returned safely to the mission compound.

Sixteen

Shirley was willing to bow, but not low, or at least not as low as the Japanese general would have liked.

"Thank you for joining me this evening, Mrs. Carson," he began as he poured tea for them into fine porcelain cups.

She had certainly not joined him freely but had been forced by the Japanese soldiers through the mission, out the gate, and down the empty town streets until she and her entourage arrived at this municipal building, formerly the center for tax collection under both Tupan Feng and then his warlord nephew. She had visited here with Caleb some years before when he wanted to express his outrage at the practice of excessive levies and bribes. He had felt hopeful that he could help change the historically corrupt system. As she noticed the Nambu pistol in its holster on the Japanese general's hip and the fiery shine of his shoes, she found herself longing for those old days, when the warlord was greedy, unprincipled, and vulgar, but at least had a patrician sense of responsibility to his people and province.

"Won't you have a cup of tea?" the Japanese general asked in impeccable English.

She had refused to look him straight in the eye but did so now. "You realize it is past midnight."

The general spoke to his soldiers, who turned and withdrew, leaving Shirley alone with him. He approached with the teacup, and she took it. Short and rotund, he appeared tidier and cleaner than anyone she had seen in weeks. The stars and medals on his chest shone, and the creases in his pant legs were sharp. He wore thick, black-rimmed round glasses, and his thinning hair was slicked back and greased with something pungent and familiar.

"Please, make yourself comfortable. Have a seat." He gestured to a wicker chair in the middle of the room. She had been surprised to see the Western-style furniture in this office, a large teak desk and banker's chair, not the tatami mat, stools, or low tables that the Japanese usually preferred.

"I believe the majority of Americans today do not drink tea," he said. "They prefer Chock Full o' Nuts or Nehi soda pop. But Mrs. Carson, I am sure you do not care for such a low-class drink, even if I could get it for you." He offered a good-natured laugh.

Shirley eased into the wicker seat as he leaned against the desk before her, his legs crossed at the ankles.

"I was always partial to Coca-Cola myself," he continued, his voice confident and friendly. "Delicious drink. If they ever sell it in Japan, the tea tradition will be over forever. But I will never forget the hot toddies at football games. What a grand custom of your people! I still carry a flask with me." He patted his breast pocket. "During final-examination period, we drank black coffee late into the night. Were you Vassar girls allowed to do that? At Princeton, no one watched over us. The young men were untamed. Nothing could have prepared me for the wildness of American boys." He leaned forward, his voice dropping lower. "I understand you have a teenaged son. I do not envy you." He shook his head. "In Japan, we know how to handle boys. We are much better at this. You Americans could learn from us."

Shirley calmly lifted the cup to her lips, unwilling to betray her surprise at everything he said. But as she drank the bitter tea, one crucial thing occurred to her: this general was trying to impress her.

He set down his cup and offered his hand. "General Hayato Shiga, Princeton class of '15."

His plump and clammy palm repulsed her.

"Everyone called me 'Hal.' I doubt you remember me, but I remember you. I saw you at Vassar's final spring dance our senior year. You stood out even in that company of lovely young ladies."

He pushed off from the desk, strode to the window, and gazed out. A flash of acid orange light appeared far off, briefly bathing the horizon in a sudden, astonishing glare.

"You Vassar girls were regal," he continued. "I was not allowed to dance or date because I was engaged to be married back home. But that was all right. I was terribly shy. I admired you American girls from afar. Such thoroughbreds, isn't that the term? Highborn women. Women of the royal court. Princesses, every one of you."

"Not exactly," she said. "My stepfather owned shoe stores. I was no princess."

His insistent smile suggested that he was not to be dissuaded.

Shirley took another slow, deliberate sip to gain courage before speaking. "We are here now in North China, General Shiga. Times have changed. But I am so glad that our two countries remain on good terms. Yet, as friendly as we are, I cannot be bribed with a cup of tea." She set hers on the desk and raised her chin. "I was taken by force from my home this evening, was marched across this unfortunate town, and am being kept here against my will. I know with great certainty that you have violated any number of international laws by treating me this way."

Behind the thick glasses, his eyes grew sharper. "I brought you here, Mrs. Carson, in the hope that we could ignite camaraderie, even friendship. We have a shared past. But you are hardheaded. I should have expected it from an American woman."

Shirley straightened her spine. "Why don't you tell me the real reason you brought me here, General?"

He strode behind his desk. "I have heard that you are a nurse. You care for the Chinese citizens who seek temporary shelter at your mission compound. Your Reverend Wells and I have discussed this, and I agreed that under our current rules of engagement, American civilians may assist the population. But my primary concern is my officers. They are in need of medical attention. They suffer from maladies, private medical conditions."

"War wounds?" she asked.

"None of them have been injured."

"So they do not suffer like the Chinese who have been bayoneted and left to die by the road? From our window, my son and I witnessed the execution of not only military but also civilians. They were shot and tossed into a ditch. Has a similar fate met your soldiers?" As Shirley spoke, she rose from her seat, her voice growing stronger. "Or perhaps they have been attacked like the Chinese women I saw in the marketplace, their bodies ruined for any future life, their very souls flayed from them."

"Come, now, Mrs. Carson," he said with exaggerated patience. "You are an innocent. It is not your fault that you are a sheltered, spoiled woman who has never seen such things before. What you have witnessed is typical of war, nothing more." He waved a hand toward the window, where another flash of light illuminated beyond the farthest edge of town. "My request of you is nothing so horrific. I would not presume to burden you with real injuries. I don't think you could handle them."

Shirley squeezed her hands together to control herself. She longed to tell him all she had done to oversee the care of the badly wounded Chinese, but instead, she simply said, "Good of you, General."

"Our complaints are more rudimentary. One of my officers needs dental help, and another has such bad hemorrhoids that he can no longer sit down. They have bunions from marching. Indigestion from rancid Chinese food. Coughing, most likely from TB give to us by the unsanitary Chinese. Basic ailments for which we need your help, Nurse Carson. I request that you attend to my officers. In exchange, I will see that you are fed and kept safe. My protection is worth all the money in this lousy country. And if you serve us for even a short time, I will see that you and your son are escorted out of the province to safety. I think that is a fair offer."

Face the foe, her husband had always said, half in jest, but Shirley knew he would not be joking now. She pulled back her shoulders and said, "I wish to be escorted back to my home, General Shiga. I must decline your offer, but I thank you for considering me for these tasks." She meant to continue in this vein, civilized and in control of her feelings, but could not. "I'm flattered that you trust me with bunions and hemorrhoids and other insignificant complaints."

A growl began deep in the general's chest and erupted loudly. He stroked his slick hair and spun away from her. He called out to his men, who came and grabbed her by the wrists, but Shirley yanked free.

"I will not tolerate such rudeness, General. If I were to help you, it would have to be on civilized terms."

"Then you will still consider my offer?" he asked.

"It must be after 1 in the morning, and my son will be worried sick. Please, I need to get home."

"You may go," he said. "My soldiers will escort you. But do not dismiss my offer, Mrs. Carson. As you Americans say, sleep on it, all right? I hope to hear from you soon." He bowed.

She bowed, too, but before turning to go, she added, "I do remember you, Hal. You were one of two Asian boys who attended the dances. You and a good-looking one would huddle in the corner by the band. What was his name, I wonder?"

The general seemed to flinch behind the heavy lenses. "Chen," he said. "Harvey Chen."

"That's right. You two seemed to be such good friends. Thick as thieves."

The general barely nodded.

"I think I heard that he married a Vassar girl. They live out in sunny California now. My, my, isn't he the lucky one?"

The general may have blanched but turned his back quickly and did not answer.

Outside, Shirley leaned against the side of the building and let the thick night air embrace her. Beads of sweat rolled down her ribs, and she realized she was shaking. From around her neck, she untied a silk scarf that Caleb had given to her. On it, a colorful phoenix spread its wings and dove across a royal-blue sky. In the dim light cascading from the municipal building, the magical bird looked fierce and free. From her study of Chinese antiques, she knew that Fenghuang bestowed on all who saw it not only grace and good luck but also immortality. She patted the powerful image of the bird against her lips now and then pressed it to her damp breastbone above the buttons of her blouse, hoping for strength.

Shirley started off through the quiet town, two Japanese soldiers escorting her. They held their rifles cocked, and she suspected that Chinese watched from inside darkened doorways and through the cracks in boarded-up windows. At a corner, she almost stumbled into the bent back of a coolie who was rummaging through a pile of garbage. The soot-stained man appeared haggard but unfazed and purposeful. The fear Shirley had held at bay with the general rose up, and her stomach turned. She raced to the side of the road and retched into a gully. A second wave of nausea overtook her, but she had nothing left inside. When she raised her head and noticed the desolate scene around her, she felt panicked that she had behaved in such a headstrong way with the general. She had always been like that: cocky in the face of trouble, her instinct never to flee but to stride directly toward whatever frightened her. But that was foolishness now, she thought, hubris of the first order.

As she straightened up, one of the soldiers stepped closer and addressed her in Japanese. Shirley couldn't understand the words but looked down into the young man's worried face.

"I'm all right," she said in the local Chinese dialect.

The young man appeared baffled by her words, too, but bowed. Shirley bowed in return. The second soldier eyed them warily, and Shirley wondered if the compassionate younger soldier would be reprimanded. He was a boy, just a boy. So like her son. At the gates of the mission compound, she bowed again before leaving the Japanese soldiers and hurried inside. She needed to get back to Charles.

At the sight of her home and the stone gate bathed in moonlight, Shirley lifted her skirt and ran. She dashed up the steps and flung open the ornamental screen, but the iron handle on the thick front door did not turn. In peaceful times, Caleb had insisted it never be locked. She ran her fingers over a colorful bas-relief statue of a door god that he had nailed to the door frame, the ferocious warrior figure put there to protect the family inside from evil spirits.

Shirley was about to pound on the door when the thick handle turned and it swung open. Dao-Ming stepped back as Shirley entered her home. She glanced around at the peaceful sight of the patients stretched out on their beds and the nurses curled on pallets on the floor. Charles sat sprawled in the wicker rocking chair, his long legs stretched onto the stained coral blossoms in the blue carpet. He had no doubt waited up for her as long as he could, but then sleep had overtaken him as he reclined where she used to rock him as a boy.

Dao-Ming appeared to have been weeping, although her eyes were always pink-rimmed. Shirley took the girl's chin into her hands and lifted her sorry face toward the light. Dao-Ming trembled all over, and Shirley realized that was part of her condition, too. She brought the girl closer and wrapped her arms around her thick, curved back. Dao-Ming did not reciprocate at first but merely stood like a lump of plentiful flesh. Then the full weight of her pressed against Shirley, and Shirley did not push her away. Instead, she held on and whispered into the girl's ear, "It's all right. I'm back now. I'm here."

As she felt the distinct pressure of Dao-Ming's breasts hidden under her many layers of clothing, Shirley realized that the girl was more mature than she had previously understood. Dao-

Ming might even be Charles's age. Though short of stature, she was a substantial person, a young lady, in fact—a person to be fully considered and no longer ignored. Dao-Ming drew back and stared up at Shirley with serious, knowing eyes.

At that moment, Shirley recalled Caleb's words spoken from the pulpit: *We have no one if not each other. We are united in our humanity. We are one.* He had meant that we are all citizens of the world, brothers and sisters, grown from one family tree. As hard as it had been to fathom previously, Shirley thought now, this strange young woman standing before her in this strange land was of the same blood. *And we must keep watch over one another,* Caleb had said. *We are our brother's keepers.*

"Yes, love," Shirley whispered aloud in English, "that's right. We *are* our brother's keepers."

Dao-Ming smiled quite genuinely at that moment, as if understanding the words Shirley had just spoken.

"Mama Shirley no leave?" Dao-Ming asked. "Mama Shirley stay!"

Shirley stared into those dark, narrow eyes that seemed bottomless and saturated in unreserved hope just when there should have been none.

"That's right," she said. "Mama Shirley stay."

Seventeen

Charles stepped into the too-bright morning to meet Reverend Wells as he came up the porch steps. The older man's hair had turned white in the weeks since the fighting had begun, and he had developed a limp. Always an odd bird, the Reverend appeared even more so in the Chinese coolie hat he wore to keep off the sun. Kathryn lagged a few paces behind him, her own stylish hat worn low and lopsided on her head. They both looked beleaguered and worse for wear.

"Thanks so much for coming, sir," Charles said and pumped the Reverend's hand. "But everything's all right. Mother's back now. She got home late last night and is still asleep upstairs."

The Reverend took Charles's hands between his and patted them. "My poor boy," he said, "do not consider yourself abandoned. That's good news about your mother. I was prepared to visit the Japanese headquarters myself this morning to insist on her release."

Charles gently pulled his hands away. "I haven't seen her yet, but I gather she wasn't harmed at all. They just wanted to talk to her. And Lian's found *mien* at the market this morning, and we're planning a feast for later today. Not a feast, exactly, but, you know, a farewell dinner. No need to worry about us. We're all quite keen."

The Reverend glanced at Kathryn.

"I'm glad your mother's safe," she said, "but Reverend Wells and I wanted to talk to you, Charles, about your situation. Remember when I told you that you can always count on me, kiddo? It's true, you know." She reached across and straightened his collar. "You've grown up a lot this summer, but we want to make sure you understand the danger you're in. I'm worried that you haven't been given a full picture of things."

Charles nodded warily.

"We don't want anyone confusing you about what you should do next," Kathryn said. "You must be prepared to leave at a moment's notice. As soon as we receive word that passage has been secured on a ship out of Shanghai, we go. Are you ready to do that, Charles?"

"My bag is packed."

"You will have only one chance, my boy," the Reverend insisted. "Nothing, and no one, must get in your way."

"All right, I get it," Charles said, his voice rising. "I won't let her change my mind."

At that moment, he noticed the shadow of his mother in her white dressing gown standing at the screen door. Through the metal mesh, she looked like a ghost. Her face appeared unchanged for a long moment, and he felt frightened that while her body had returned home the night before, her spirit remained elsewhere.

"Mother!" he shouted and flung the screen open. He took her hand and led her out onto the porch. He hugged her, and she seemed sturdy enough in his arms, which gave Charles courage again. But then she turned to Reverend Wells and Kathryn, and her warm smile disappeared.

"I'm glad that you and the others know your plans," she said to them, "but please don't presume to tell my family what to do."

Kathryn threw her hands up and said, "But Shirley, you've already told me you're coming with us."

The Reverend reached for Shirley's hands and said, "I'm so relieved you're all right, my dear. I was terribly worried."

Shirley slipped free of him and stepped back.

"Mother, Reverend Wells and Miss Kathryn are only trying to help," Charles offered.

His mother's expression remained stern.

"I know you are aware, Mrs. Carson," the Reverend said, "that I'm officially in charge of everyone here in the mission. I have orders from the Missionary Board in Boston as well as the American legation in Peking that I must see us all returned home to U.S. soil."

Charles moved closer to his mother's side.

"I owe it to the memory of your husband to see that Charles is safe," the Reverend continued. "We all know how much Caleb loved the boy."

His mother finally lowered her chin.

"And I must insist that you leave with us, too, Mrs. Carson. Those are my orders."

She crossed her arms over her chest and stood very still. Charles had seen that expression on her face more times than he cared to remember. When his mother was backed into a corner, there was no telling what she might say or do. He stepped forward and put his arm around her waist. He had never done that before. He took her by the hand as if he intended to escort her out onto the dance floor for a little spin.

"Mother, here's the thing," he said. "I'm ready to go back to America. I'll miss it here, but it's time. I think Father would agree, don't you?" His mother's gaze drifted toward the crowded courtyard. How, he wondered, could she look out there and not grasp that they must go? "Shall we pack your bags, too, Mother? Lian is planning a farewell dinner tonight. We'll say our good-byes and be ready to leave whenever we get word. America," he added, in case she had missed his enthusiasm, "here we come!"

Reverend Wells rocked forward onto his toes and back onto his heels. But Charles's mother remained mesmerized by the sea of Chinese before them.

"Thanks a lot for dropping by," Charles said as he escorted the Reverend and Kathryn toward the porch steps. "We appreciate it." Then he leaned closer and whispered, "She's a little stunned at the thought of leaving. Just keep us posted. We'll be ready."

"You're a sound young man, Charles," Reverend Wells said, shaking his hand. "Your father would be proud." He tipped his Chinese straw hat and said, "Good day to you both."

He and Kathryn went down the steps, conferring with one another as they left.

Charles stood beside his mother at the porch railing. "Thank goodness you're all right. The Japs didn't hurt you, did they?"

"No, Charles, I'm fine."

Her voice sounded far off, and he worried that she might not be telling the truth. He wanted to know what had happened to her. He wanted to take care of her. But he also somehow didn't want to know. He couldn't bear it if she had been harmed.

She finally looked away from the busy courtyard. "Reverend Wells is right. This is no place for a child. No place for you, Charles. But I can't imagine leaving just yet. My patients still need me."

He studied the lines around her eyes and her hollow cheeks.

She had lost weight since his father's death, and now she appeared almost frail. He had never seen her looking so sallow and drawn. "You don't look well, Mother. Are you sick?"

"No, not at all," she said and touched a cool palm to his cheek. "I feel quite well. Perhaps better than ever." She brushed hair from his forehead and let her hand settle lightly on his shoulder. "I will join you. That's what I'll do. It can be arranged."

"What do you mean?" he asked.

"I want you to go ahead with the American women and children. I will come along soon after, perhaps with the men, or some other way."

He flicked red paint from the porch railing and then held on to it. He wasn't dizzy, exactly, but felt mild vertigo. For days, he had let himself consider the possibility of leaving China without his mother, and now she was saying that that was how it would be.

"I need to check on my patients now, darling. You'll be all right," she said and stood on her toes to plant a kiss on his forehead. "Reverend Wells is correct in saying that your father would be terribly proud of you—as am I."

She turned and left him on the porch, looking out at the Chinese who went about their business in what had been his front yard. Charles wanted to hate them. They were the reason his mother wasn't leaving with him. They needed her more than he did. Charles spat onto the dusty ground below.

"Damn," he said loudly in English. "Damn this damn country."

Charles headed off to where he always went when he got riled up inside. He took the stone steps to the top of the wall. He needed air and the view across the rooftops to the millet fields and the purple, shadowed mountains. His father had been lost in that great distance. He spat again—not down at Japanese soldiers on sentry duty below but instead beside his own dusty sneakers on the brick path.

When he looked up, he noticed that one of the pigeon cages was open, and he went to close it. As he rounded the corner, the full coop came into view, and Dao-Ming stood before it. She had a feedbag at her feet and was sweeping the open cage with a handmade whiskbroom.

"Hey," Charles said, "what do you think you're doing?"

Dao-Ming didn't look up from her task.

He stepped nearer and changed his tone. "Did Han ask you to do that for him while he's away?"

Dao-Ming nodded.

Charles reached for one of the pigeons that was strutting about and stroked it. "I always did whatever Han told me to do with the birds. He knows everything about pigeons."

"I know more," she said in a high, crackly voice, and in English, too.

Charles nearly dropped the bird. "Since when can you talk?"

She offered an odd smile.

"And what do you know about pigeons?"

"I know we use them to help cause."

Why had she kept quiet for so long? he wondered. He cocked his head to the side and looked her up and down. "What cause?" he asked.

Dao-Ming laughed. "The cause your father work for, silly."

"Now, wait a minute—" Charles began.

She held up a pudgy finger and shushed him. "With radio and supplies."

Charles took off the Red Army cap, slapped it against his leg, and suddenly noticed that she was wearing his father's wool driving cap.

"Where'd you get that thing on your head?" he asked. "That's mine. Give it to me."

"Not yours. Reverend leave it behind."

"I know. I saw it down in the cellar, but I tell you it's mine."

Dao-Ming went back to cleaning the cages and even hummed to herself as Charles tried to fathom that she had known his father in a way that he never would.

"All I want is his ugly old cap. It's all I've got left of him." He could feel tears starting down inside, though he didn't cry anymore.

Dao-Ming finally looked up from her work and tossed it his way. He snatched it from the walkway and put it on his head. Then he looked at the Red Army cap in his hand and sensed her watching him with her small, dark eyes. He walked over and placed Han's army cap on her head.

"Here," he said. "You're the Red, not me."

Dao-Ming gave a big grin, a front tooth missing and eyes crinkled shut. He suddenly worried she might think he had given her the grungy cap because he wanted to go steady.

"I better get going," he said and started to stride away.

"Han here," Dao-Ming shouted after him.

Charles stopped and went back. "What on earth do you mean by that?"

Just then, Han stepped out from behind the corner tower. He no longer wore a Red Army uniform but still appeared strong and sure of himself.

"Jesus," Charles said, "you gave me a fright."

Han bowed, but Charles wasn't having it. He strode to his

friend and lifted him up in a big bear hug. Han laughed, and Charles did, too.

As Charles set him down, Han said, "Charles-Boy is in good spirits. You are going home soon."

"I'm happy, all right," Charles said, "but, sad, too, if you know what I mean."

"It is sad we must say good-bye. You and your family are good people. May many happinesses come to you in your own country."

Charles was at a loss for words, but he sputtered out, "You, too, Han. You be safe, now."

Charles realized how ridiculous that sounded. He might be excited about his own future, but Han had nothing to look forward to except more fighting, and Charles couldn't imagine how his friend could be happy about that.

"My country will be great someday. Our dream will become a reality," Han said. "The people will no longer suffer. You will see. There is no better satisfaction than that."

Charles nodded and wanted to understand but knew the time was past for that. Soon he would start the long journey back across the ocean to the America of his dreams. How could he possibly explain the joy in that to Han? Instead, Charles reached out, and they shook hands like men.

Eighteen

As the others lined up outside the kitchen for their supper, Shirley slipped past them on her way up to her bedroom. She found a clean linen blouse in the back of her closet and a lace skirt she had usually saved for Sunday service. She dragged her hairbrush through her knotted curls and applied lipstick for the first time since her husband's death. In the intricately carved mirror above her dressing table, she saw a changed woman: older, more haggard and thin, but flushed with life.

Once back downstairs, Shirley received a bowl half filled with noodles from Lian.

"For you, Mrs. Carson," Lian said. "Sit on piano bench and eat."

"I can't imagine what you went through to find food for all these people," Shirley said as she sat. "You have done well by us in so many ways."

The young woman named Li Juan came up then, bowed, and handed Shirley a plate with meat swimming in a red, gelatinous sauce. Shirley suspected she was the only one to be given this delicacy. She would share it with one of her patients who needed the protein, or with her son, who was still growing and hungry all the time.

"Thank you, kind and esteemed Mrs. Carson," Li Juan said, "for allowing me to live here."

"My pleasure."

As Shirley raised her chopsticks, she noticed the helpers crouched on their haunches in the hallway or seated on the edges of cots in the clinic, each digging into their bowls of noodle soup. The elderly Japanese fishmonger huddled on the bottom step as he had on the day he had first arrived at the mission. Only now Tupan Feng sat beside him. The two appeared to be having a debate about the correct use of discipline in child rearing. The old Chinese warlord insisted the rules should be the same in the home as in the military, while the fishmonger felt that a softer touch was needed. Though combative, they seemed to be enjoying one another.

So little joy had surrounded them all for too long, making this brief moment of peace all the more precious. Shirley cleared her throat, rose again, and in her best imitation of a minister's resonant oratory addressed the small band of friends. "I want to thank each of you for your fine efforts. I have great confidence that you will continue to run the clinic beautifully when I depart soon with my son. It has been an honor to work beside you."

The nurses' aides bowed their heads and accepted the praise.

"I would like to especially offer my gratitude to Lian for her forbearance and skill in all she does."

Lian's arthritic fingers twisted the rag that hung from her belt. She pulled back her shoulders as if Shirley's words were stones pelted her way. Charles, who must have sneaked in from his usual roaming about, leaned against the door frame, a lanky young man who, Shirley was surprised to realize, might even be mistaken for someone rather suave. He addressed the assembled group like the man of the household he had become.

"Madam Lian," he said, "you have been a second mother to me, often more reliable than my first, if I do say so."

Lian hissed, "Do not be rude to Mother, Charles-Boy."

"But really," Charles continued, "I wouldn't be the fellow I am today without your help. I learned so much from you, especially from those crazy bedtime stories you told. Frightened the devil out of me and made me want to grow up faster. Anything to escape those witches and spirits in the night!" He bowed. "Thank you, esteemed and patient Madam Lian."

Lian dabbed at the corners of her eyes with the rag and hurried off toward the kitchen. The others returned to their soup and shared memories of the terrorizing fairy tales of their own childhoods. Shirley patted the piano bench, and Charles strolled over to sit beside her.

"Well said, Charles. Now, help yourself to this plate Lian made for me. I was afraid to ask the type of meat, but I think you're so hungry you won't care."

"Mother, I don't understand you," Charles said as he started in with his chopsticks. "Did I hear right? You just told everyone that you're leaving with me. The last I recall, you were staying behind and planned to join us later, however that might work."

She studied his handsome profile and piercing blue eyes, his large hands as they expertly used the sticks, and the overall heft of him. To look at her son, anyone would assume he could manage just fine on his own. It was true, he didn't need her any longer. But she had come to realize that she needed him.

"I've changed my mind," she said. "My assistants have learned to run the clinic quite well. They'll do fine without me. Also, I don't want to be like Lian, separated from my child for the wrong reasons. That just seems too pitiful. So I intend to go with you."

"All right, then," he said.

"But I've promised Captain Hsu that I would accompany him on a brief visit to his camp on the plains to the east of here. It's quite nearby. They've set up a medical clinic like this one."

Charles set down the empty plate and pulled one of his father's handkerchiefs from his pocket. "When?" he asked.

"Tonight. I'll be back by morning. I'm ready to leave with you whenever the word comes."

"I don't know. That doesn't sound like such a good idea to me," he said as he wiped his lips. "What if we have to leave tonight?"

She took the handkerchief and dabbed a spot of red sauce from his cheek. "It's already 9 o'clock and dark outside, son. They couldn't possibly mobilize us to depart this evening. And besides, I already agreed to go with the captain. We've put it off for days. He's coming back to pick me up shortly. But don't worry, you and I will still leave the mission together. I promise. Doesn't that make you happy?"

He stood and stretched but didn't reply.

"Well, it makes me happy," she said. "But will you agree to a haircut when we get to Shanghai? I've never seen such a disgraceful mop."

He planted a quick kiss on her forehead.

"Where are you going?"

"To say good-bye to Li Juan."

"Ah, I thought so," she said with a teasing smile.

But he hadn't heard, or didn't care, and was already stepping away.

Nineteen

The Reverend Caleb Carson felt the stirring of the trees on all sides and listened as the wind picked up. He heard the beginnings of rain before it arrived. Leaves began to fall, and twigs whipped past his cot on the cliffside. He would have liked to reach out and catch some but could not move his arms fast enough. He simply shut his eyes and felt himself becoming a part of the maelstrom. Flimsy and insubstantial, he welcomed the sensation of being sucked into it.

But then Cook was at his side. As always, dear Cook. And his son, Charles's friend, whose name Caleb now remembered: Han. He recognized in their voices the timbre of concern and perhaps something like love. They had been unerringly kind. The sudden drops of rain struck Caleb like small punishments, punches from God down the length of his prostrate body, bestowed upon him for his foolishness.

Days before, word had come that his able and forceful wife had returned to the mission after being briefly detained by the Japanese. Apparently she continued to perform her good works at the small medical clinic now set up in their home. Her will was strong, Caleb thought, while his had always been weak. Ever since his accident, he had asked himself how and why he had gotten into this wretched position. The only answer he could muster was that he was pitifully human.

But there was no time for such sad reflections now, with the rain falling fast. The father and son leaned over him and raised the cot to return Caleb to the cave, leaving the rain to pelt the rocky ground. Their backs—one young and narrow, the other crooked and wide—grew wet in a matter of moments. Both so healthy, it might even have felt good to them after the dryness and heat. But to Caleb, the rain came like another irrefutable curse.

They lifted his cot and carried him over the rough earth. He heard their shoes slosh in sudden puddles and worried that they didn't have proper footwear. He would have liked to give them his fine leather boots, but those had been lost to the mudslide many weeks before. Since then, he had had no need for them, but he hoped he might need them eventually. He had made it through the summer and seemed to be improving, or at least holding on. He could lift his head now. And as he did, he saw great torrents fall outside the mouth of the cave.

Han began to laugh at the rain, which made Caleb smile, too. It rolled over the cave door like a waterfall, and they were inside it. Yes, Caleb thought, that had always been a fine sight. He and his older brothers would hike miles up the trails near their home, and after a final steep bend in the path, they would come upon their favorite hidden gem: a waterfall that seemed to him, even at a young age, ancient and profound. In August, when other streams were dried up, white water churned over the rocks at this falls, fed by snow melting deep in the bowl beneath Mt. Washington.

The boys would throw off their clothes and scramble across the slippery rocks and dare one another with its icy touch. They sensed the danger and knew never to mention it to their mother, who would have forbidden them if she had known. A fall from that height at that distance from home would never permit rescue. If one of them fell, each brother would blame himself for the rest of his life, and so all four would be sacrificed to the failed expedition. They owed it to one another to never let that happen.

Caleb, being the youngest, was always the last to make the ledge. For years, his legs were not quite long enough to step over. While his brothers waited, he had to jump the final expanse across to the other side. They stood trembling inside the waterfall, their shivering backs pressed against the dry rock, while Caleb remained on the outside looking in at their wild and joyous faces. The frothing water poured down like a veil between them as they waited for him to take the last leap, which their shouts encouraged him to do. He would never forget the instant when he hung between rock and rock and waited for the firm grip of his brother's hand as it reached out through the falling water to bring him across to safety.

Caleb felt the tears roll down his cheeks before he realized he had shed them. Such was his new state of being: more fluid than solid. He reached a trembling hand up and swiped away the wetness. Outside, the rain carried the sky downward with it. The peak of the mountain over his head, Caleb could imagine, becoming one with the wet sky.

The Chinese youth beside him danced a boyish dance, and Caleb wished he could join him. Caleb recalled Charles performing a similar rain dance in fresh puddles when he was younger. Without words, Han was reminding Caleb that the rain was not a curse against him but merely the changing of the seasons, proof that life carried on, and they with it. He had never believed he would make it this long with his broken back, but he had, and the boy's excitement gave him hope that he might just make it through to the next season, and even the next. He did not want to die. He wanted to rise up and rejoin the living. He wanted to dance with his boy again.

Han hovered over his bed as Cook massaged the blood back into Caleb's feet. He thought he might even walk today. He might sit up, as he had several times, and actually walk.

"Reverend," Han said, "I have news from the mission."

Caleb smiled at the young man. "You look well, Han."

"Thank you, Reverend. You look better, too."

"You are happy?" Caleb asked.

"Yes, very happy. Shall I tell you about your family?"

Caleb looked out at the rain and wondered if he could bear to hear it. Any news of his family both fueled his recovery and pained him. He nodded carefully, his neck finally repaired enough to allow him to do so. He longed to show Shirley his progress.

"An order has come from the American legation in Peking. They are all leaving, sir."

"What's that?" Caleb asked, though he had heard the boy.

"Your family and the others will start their journey back to America today," Han shouted to be heard above the sound of the rain. "They will travel by train across the north to Peking, then down to Shanghai, where they will leave on a Swedish ship, the *Gripsholm*. They are fortunate to have booked passage. Some foreigners are not so lucky."

The rain continued, loud and insistent and pure. Caleb wished he could listen to it and keep daydreaming. He had imagined a reunion at the mission, his family amazed by the miracle of his return. But now his family was leaving China for good without him. Han had brought word.

"Ah," Caleb finally said.

"You are not surprised by this news, are you?" Han asked. "This is what you wanted, isn't it?"

"Yes, it is. Of course."

"The Japanese front continues to expand, but we are ready. Our leaders say the whole country must fight against them together."

"That's a good plan."

But Han did not appear convinced by Caleb's reply and repeated, "Your family, Reverend, must leave quickly to escape. No one will be spared. You understand?"

"So it must be."

But in his heart, Caleb longed for more time. For the rains to have held off longer. For his legs to have regained more strength. For the searing pain in his back to not cripple every part of him, even his mind. He understood it would be impossible for him to join them after they had left the mission. He would never make it to Shanghai to board the same ship. Later though, he would travel alone across dangerous territory and eventually make his own passage to America. But he could not possibly make that journey by himself, when still so fragile and the conditions so harrowing. His mind went white with confusion and doubt as he realized he would never get home.

"Thank you for telling me," he made himself say. "I pray they make it out without incident. With all my heart, I pray for that."

Caleb felt tears leave his eyes again and roll down his cheeks. He could not bear his own selfishness. That any part of him wished they would stay for his sake was wrong, and he knew it. He cried at his feebleness of spirit. He was a flawed man who had given up caring that he opened like a faucet, the tears pouring from him as naturally as the rain outside. He could not bear his own company any longer.

He began a prayer in his mind that his beloved wife and son be escorted away from him and into a new life. They must leave this hard and disastrous land and return to America, where everything was easier. They deserved to be free of China and of his tired, broken bones. How could he have imagined burdening them with his wounded self? If they were to make it out alive, they did not need to be toting along a cripple who would only impede their progress. They needed to go on without him. That was only right.

"It is good," he said more firmly.

The boy crouched closer and nodded. "Yes, very good."

Then Han stood and bowed and left Caleb's side.

Part Three

Twenty

Captain Hsu had brought only one mule, not an ancient one but not a sprightly one, either. He climbed on first, then offered a hand up to Shirley. She pulled herself onto the animal's back, more awkwardly than she had hoped, her skirt and linen riding coat tangling in her legs before she finally settled into position.

"You will fall sitting that way," he said.

"This is how we do it at Vassar. We call it sidesaddle."

"Traditional Chinese ladies sit that way, too. You need trousers instead. How can a woman carry a pistol in her belt or hop onto a horse at a moment's notice in such a frilly outfit?"

"My outfit isn't frilly," she said and smoothed her skirt. "And besides, I hope to never do such things."

"In China, everyone should have these skills."

He kicked the mule with his heels, and Shirley grabbed his belt as they lurched forward. In trousers, she could have dug into the animal's sides with her legs to stabilize herself. And she had to admit, he was right that learning to shoot a rifle or hop on horseback or even do occasional manual labor would be good for any woman's character—and perhaps hers in particular.

They headed out of town on rocky paths through the fields to the east. A cool breeze, bearing the first hint of autumn, came steadily from across the plains. She wrapped her riding coat around her and wondered if the damp air meant the possibility of rain, though no clouds obscured the moon as it rose over the distant mountains receding behind them to the west. The mule seemed to know the way over the terrain, the rhythm of its steps steady even in the dark. Shirley and Captain Hsu did not speak. The sky overhead was blacker than any she had ever seen before, and more filled with stars. Shirley shivered and couldn't help wrapping her arms more tightly around him as they pressed on.

After some time, they reached a butte surrounded by a tangle of rock outcroppings. The mule wove up the narrow trail until they came upon a hidden enclave of tents that, to Shirley's surprise, reminded her of the summer camp on Lake Erie she had attended as a girl. Several large, open-sided structures defined the perimeter, with smaller makeshift canvas ones dotted all around. Captain Hsu stopped the mule and called out. A young soldier trotted over and offered a quick bow, but when he lifted his lantern and noticed her seated behind the captain, the boy let out a giggle.

"Help Nurse Carson," Hsu instructed him. Then, in English, he said to Shirley, "These country boys have never seen a white person before, and certainly not a lady."

Shirley let the young soldier take her hand and did her best to slip down gracefully. Captain Hsu headed directly into the camp, and she had to hurry to keep up. They entered an area where some injured soldiers had been placed in rows, their feet facing a low-burning bonfire. A few were wrapped in thin blankets, but many lay directly on the rocky ground.

Shirley hurried to join Captain Hsu, who stood now with a group of officers. They hardly acknowledged her but seemed concerned with some important business. When Captain Hsu finally introduced her to the men, she bowed low and listened attentively for their names, some of which struck her as familiar. Several were among the Red leaders who had brought men, and even some women, all the way across the vast country in a mass military exodus. She had no doubt that her husband, and those who had joined their cause along the way in the Long March, admired these thin and ragged-looking men before her and considered them brilliant strategists and brave heroes.

Captain Hsu motioned her to follow, and they wove through an outdoor clinic area where several more injured lay on cots. While their condition appeared stable, and not requiring urgent care, no one was attending to them. A good many of the soldiers seemed in need of proper clothing. Some wore no shoes, and to Shirley, their cut and swollen feet were the saddest sight of all. Captain Hsu stopped just outside a tent and nodded for her to enter.

"What's this about?" she asked. "Where are you sending me?"

"He wishes to see you."

"Who?"

"Our leader."

"I see," she said and looked back at the rows of injured soldiers. "I'm honored to meet him but would much prefer to help as a nurse. Couldn't I do that instead?"

"No. You will see him now."

"But won't you come with me?" she asked. "I would feel more comfortable if you did."

Shirley searched for something in Captain Hsu's far-off expression. Was she right to think that he, too, considered her his charge and wanted to keep watch over her? To her surprise in that moment, his hand reached out and awkwardly brushed a stray curl off her forehead. He had never done anything so forward before, nor so gentle and kind.

"You will be all right," he said. "Everyone knows that you are the brave Nurse Carson."

A high, thin laugh escaped her lips. "Everyone except you. To you, I will always be a frivolous American woman."

His even gaze met hers, their eyes perfectly aligned, and she thought she saw a glimmer of warmth she had not seen before. "I do not praise you, if that is what you mean. But you have worked hard."

Shirley let the glow of his words wash over her. All her life, men had complimented her on her appearance or her cleverness, but she never valued their praise half as much as Captain Hsu's stingy assessment now.

"All right, Captain, I'll do as you say."

"Good," he said and held open the flap of the tent for her to enter.

In the dimness, Shirley did not notice the soldiers at attention just inside the door until one gestured for her to continue deeper into the shadowy room. She stepped around books stacked high on the threadbare Chinese carpet. On a rickety table lay maps and more piles of books. A young soldier poured tea from an earthenware pot. Shirley thought she was alone with the soldiers and wondered if she would have to wait long for Captain Hsu's leader. But as her eyes adjusted, she saw a reclining figure stretched out on a military cot tucked against the sloping back wall of the tent. A crackling red burst of light came as the reclining person lit a pipe.

"Please sit, Mrs. Carson. Thank you for coming to this remote camp."

She bowed but could not tell if he was even turned in her direction. His English was good, she noticed, though mostly she felt distracted by his peculiarly high voice. It had the reedy timbre of a young woman's. She looked about for a chair, but, not finding one, decided to kneel on the thin carpet instead. She spread her skirt over her legs and hoped that seemed respectful.

"What can you tell me about the noninterventionist movement in America?" he asked. "Do they hold much sway?" His pipe glowed again.

Shirley cleared her throat. "I know very little about politics, sir. My husband was more informed and involved than I am."

"We have reports that students are starting to rally on campuses, calling themselves America First."

"I'm afraid I never bothered with the news," she said. For a long moment, he did not reply, and she waited for him to ask something else, but when he didn't and went back to puffing on his pipe, she ventured to continue. "I believe, though, that if Americans had any idea what was going on here, they'd want to put a stop to the Japanese atrocities immediately."

He sat up, his high forehead catching the lamplight. She recognized his distinct profile from the papers. "You think so?" he asked.

"Absolutely. We have never cottoned to dictators. We can't abide countries marching in and oppressing their neighbors."

Still in shadow, the leader of the Reds reached for his cup and slurped from it. Then he let out a delicate belch.

His high voice cut through her thoughts again. "I understand that you are a nurse."

Shirley pulled back her shoulders and prepared for the real reason for her visit. "I have been honored to care for the people of my province and the good men who serve in the Red Army. They are fine boys, not educated, perhaps a bit simple," she said, and immediately regretted it, "but brave. Very brave. I'm sure you are exceedingly proud."

She could hear him bite down on his pipe stem and belch softly again.

"Now that I have seen the conditions closer to the front, I am prepared to help here as well, if it is needed," she said. "I hate to see patients go uncared for."

He stood. Shirley blinked in the dim light but felt quite certain that she was looking at his pudgy bare feet on the old rug. His pant legs were frayed, and he wore no uniform, just dark pants and shirt, like a shopkeeper in a poor provincial town.

"Help if you are asked to," he said, "but I do not think you are needed here." Then he bowed. "Thank you for coming, and good evening, Mrs. Carson."

She rose to her feet, too, and realized she was supposed to bow now, but she couldn't help feeling that nothing of significance had been said between them. "Is there anything else I can offer you or your men?"

"It is an embarrassing problem," he began as he stepped out of the shadows and set his pipe and cup on the table, "but I seem to have developed indigestion. No one must know that I would consider a Western remedy for my discomfort, but any suggestion you make is appreciated. We will keep it just between us."

This couldn't be the reason he had called her here, she thought.

"You have advice for me, Mrs. Carson?" he asked again.

"I'm sorry you're uncomfortable, sir. I don't suppose you can get your hands on antacid tablets?" she asked. "Plain baking soda would do. Sodium bicarbonate. Do you know it?"

He shook his head and poked out his bottom lip. "Not much is available here."

"Then the best solution is the old Chinese one. Ginger, finely chopped and taken in a cup of tea."

He clapped his hands. "Excellent. That remedy does me little good, but at least there is nothing better."

Shirley refrained from contradicting him. "But there must be something else I can help you with?"

He lifted a book from the table and began to leaf through it. "No, I don't think so. I assume you are going back to America soon?" he asked.

Shirley paused before answering. She had promised her son earlier in the evening that she would depart with him and the others when they left the mission for Shanghai. That plan remained her intention, but seeing the injured boys at this Red Army camp, not to mention having in mind those who might still arrive at her own clinic, made her waver yet again in her decision.

"That is my plan," she said. "But, to be honest, I've come to find the work deeply rewarding. I do still wonder if I can be of assistance here in North China, perhaps to continue my success at the clinic?" Her voice rose into a question, the pleading, unsure tone hard to mask. She wanted him to decide for her, this leader of the Reds so accustomed to issuing orders. But his nose remained buried in a book, and she wasn't sure he had even heard her.

"No," he suddenly said and slammed the book closed. "Absolutely not. You must go back to America right away."

Shirley took a step back. "I must, sir?"

"Stop calling me 'sir,'" he practically shouted. "Say 'comrade.'

201

That is what we are. Comrades. Do you understand the difference?"

For the first time, she felt frightened by the force of the man.

"You must go back to your people in America," he said and started to pace. "Visit your churches, and neighbors, and politicians. Tell them not to listen to the noninterventionists. Tell them we need America here and on our side. Now! Do you understand?"

Shirley nodded.

"You can do much more there than here," he said. "Now, go."

Shirley tried to compose herself. Whenever she had pictured herself stateside, she saw her stultifying childhood home in Cleveland, pointless lunches with her mother and her friends at the country club, or shopping with Kathryn and her mother at dull department stores. Going home meant a certain death of spirit, she was sure. But this Red leader was offering an altogether different vision of her future that seemed difficult to fathom.

"I'm not sure I understand," she said.

"You are an upper-class lady," he said. "You do not belong in the midst of all this. A revolution is not a dinner party, or writing an essay, or painting a picture, or doing embroidery! It is work." His voice remained jarring and loud and commanding. "Those superficial pastimes are all you know how to do, am I right?" he asked. "Not this."

She gathered up her courage and said, "Well, I am a trained nurse, you know. And proud of it now."

"All right, then, be a nurse. But in America, not here," he said. "First, though, go to your university president, your bank-owner friends, your fat-cat acquaintances. Raise money, and send it to us!" He rose onto the balls of his bare feet on the carpet. "Why are you here when you could be doing so much more for us there? Go!" he shouted. "Go back to America. You have a job to do!"

Her hand trembled as she brushed back hair from her brow. "Yes, of course, you're right, sir. Awfully right," she added, "I mean comrade."

He shook his head and said in a more measured tone, "Good evening, Mrs. Carson. Now, off you go." He waved her toward the door, snatched another book from the table, and threw his heavy frame down onto the cot.

She backed away but stumbled over a stack of books and then another. "I'm so sorry," she mumbled and knelt down to put them back in order.

"Leave them," he barked from the shadows. "I am finished with those, anyway. I have read them already."

Shirley stood and glanced around at the hundreds of volumes in piles all around her. "You have read all of these?" she couldn't help asking. "That's remarkable."

He let out a pleased chuckle. "Yes, it has been a productive summer. Earlier, we had skirmishes with the Japanese Imperial Army and won over the people by fighting an enemy they despise." His voice softened even more, as if they were old friends. "But of course, Mrs. Carson, the many wounded and dead Red Army soldiers seem a tragedy to you." He sucked air between his teeth and offered an apologetic sigh. "Yet it cannot be helped. We have let the Nationalists take over the battle with the Japanese, and they lose ten times more men than we do while we sit tight here in the North. But soon enough, we will reengage according to a new policy." He cleared his throat and raised the book into the air as if it could light the way forward. "I will declare that *Chinese do not fight Chinese!* We will act as a true United

Front, not just in name. Together we will rid our country of the dwarf barbarians. Peasants and landlords must fight side by side to throw off the imperialist yoke!"

He fanned himself with the book. "But in this miserable heat, my men learn to read and write and train to be better soldiers. An army without culture is a dull-witted army, and a dull-witted army cannot defeat the enemy. So we farm a little. We raise goats. And I read in order to become a more educated man. All in all, a most satisfying summer."

Shirley wished she could engage him further but bowed quickly and said good-night.

"Good night, Nurse Carson," he replied as she stepped out of the tent. "Safe travels back to your home county."

Twenty-one

Captain Hsu stood alone—solitary and quiet for a moment, a man usually surrounded by people. Shirley couldn't imagine what went through his mind as he gazed into the embers. From such different worlds, their paths had crossed and even joined for a time, but she hardly knew him and never would. She allowed herself to finally realize that she would be leaving soon.

"I hope you had a successful meeting," he said as she stepped closer.

"Did you know that he reads an extraordinary amount?"

"There is much to learn."

"He had advice for me. Rather stern advice."

"And you are actually willing to follow it?"

"I believe so," she said with a smile. "He has instructed me to go back to America right away and raise funds and awareness for your cause. He thinks I will be of more use there than here."

"That sounds correct," he said and turned her way. "But I will be sad to see you go, Nurse Carson. I will miss you."

He had never spoken so openly before, and it made her blush.

"We are friends," he said.

"Yes," she said, "and comrades."

They would say their good-byes soon, and she would return home to tell others about the worthy work of the Communists in China. But in her mind, and perhaps even her heart, she would be remembering this moment when Captain Hsu had confirmed their friendship and then gracefully let her go.

"I will take you back to the mission first thing in the morning," he said. "It is too late tonight to travel. You can sleep a few hours, and we'll depart at dawn."

"But I told Charles I'd be home tonight. I'd like to go now, please."

"I'm sorry, but I must attend a meeting. Our leader accomplishes a great deal in the dead of night. I will escort you to the women's tent. Comrade Li is in charge there, and she will give you a change of clothing. You can rest for a while."

She followed him through the camp, passing the injured soldiers and groups of men who sat chatting on their bedrolls and playing cards at makeshift tables. Many of them bowed their heads deferentially as Captain Hsu passed. She wanted to ask him about his role at the camp and the workings of the Eighth Route Army. If she was going to tell people about it back home, she needed to learn more. She would press Captain Hsu to fill her in as they rode back to the mission together in the morning.

But for now, she noticed that the men appeared content, despite their poor nutrition and lack of proper weapons, uniforms, and supplies. Shirley could tell she was being converted to the Communist cause, precisely what Reverend Wells and Kathryn had warned her against. And yet, she thought, if only they could see these soldiers, who did not swagger or misbehave. The rural Chinese boys seemed the opposite of the Japanese soldiers, who had been trained to lose their humanity in war. These young men, reading by candlelight and carrying on discussions in serious tones, appeared to be gaining theirs.

"Comrade Li is expecting you," said Captain Hsu. "She's a bit gruff, but I think you'll be fine. I will collect you at dawn."

He offered a quick bow and departed. Shirley stepped inside the long, open-sided building, where a sea of women soldiers lay asleep on straw mats. At the near end, several sat whispering in conversation by a flickering oil lamp. Shirley went to them and bowed to the oldest of the group, a matron with a waist as thick around as her chest.

"Good evening, Comrade Li," Shirley said in the local dialect and bowed again.

The younger women giggled, apparently amused by the sight of her. She looked down at her disheveled appearance. Her lace skirt was covered in yellow dust, and the linen of her riding coat appeared wrinkled and stained. Her untucked blouse was open low, exposing a gold necklace bearing the phoenix charm that Caleb had given to her. Shirley wasn't dressed formally, or particularly well, but these women in pale-blue uniforms and gray caps with thick belts to hold up their pants might never have seen a white woman before, or a woman dressed for anything but difficult work. The younger ones had narrow hips and hardly any breasts, and Shirley assumed they were underfed, even starving, farm girls who, like their brothers, had joined up when the army passed through their desolate provinces and felt lucky to be here.

"Captain Hsu brought me," she said with another bow.

"I know who you are." Comrade Li studied Shirley from the toes of her riding boots up past the hem of her skirt and the length of her long coat, then let out a disapproving grunt. "Uniform there." She pointed to a pile of folded clothing at the foot of a cot.

A strong body odor emanated from the older woman when

she lifted her arm, and Shirley told herself not to be prissy and particular. She thanked the matron and went to retrieve the clothing she had been assigned. When she looked about for a private place to change, Comrade Li gave a sharp look and Shirley understood she was meant to disrobe right there. The young women followed her with great curiosity and watched as she began to undress. When she removed her riding coat and placed it on the straw mat, the boldest of the girls reached over and ran a finger down the lapel.

Shirley said, "Try it on if you like."

The girl's eyes brightened as she snatched it up. She was about to slip her arm into the sleeve when Comrade Li sauntered over and reached out a hand. The girl gave it to her, and Comrade Li tried to fit it over her substantial frame, but the seams pulled across her broad back. The older woman took it off in disgust. Shirley gathered it and swung it over the matron's shoulders like a cape. The girls seemed to like that, and Comrade Li gave an approving nod.

Shirley pulled on a pair of light-blue cotton pants and a matching tunic. She cinched the belt at her waist. Finally she slipped into a pair of thin canvas shoes that were too small, so she wore them as sandals with the heels flattened. The other women watched as she set a green army cap with the red star upon her head. Although there was no mirror with which to check, Shirley could tell from their abundant smiles that it looked fine.

"If you stay long enough, we will cut off your fancy curls!" Comrade Li let loose a guttural laugh and tugged on a handful of Shirley's thick, wavy hair. "Western women wear hair every which way. Very decadent hair! But now we sleep," Comrade Li said. "You lie next to me, and I make sure you do not wander off."

Captain Hsu would have been proud of the restraint Shirley showed. "That is very kind of you, Comrade Li, but I would like to get some air before I sleep. I want to walk around. I ask your permission to go," Shirley said and bowed. Comrade Li looked repulsed by the strange habits of American women but dismissed her.

Outdoors again, Shirley was plunged into country darkness. The bonfire had gone out. Across the vast sky, the stars seemed to have only multiplied since earlier in the evening, a pale wash strung from horizon to horizon. Three swift shooting stars passed overhead in a period of minutes, each a small, startling miracle. They left behind tails that hung in the blackness long enough to become etched into Shirley's memory. She was in an army camp halfway around the world from where she had been born, in a danger zone, and yet she felt strangely at ease and even energized by the autumn air that rolled across from the distant mountains. So much seemed possible.

Captain Hsu stepped out of the shadows, a cigarette glowing in his hand. "Comrade Carson," he said, his white teeth showing as he smiled, "that uniform looks good on you. But did you not like your sleeping accommodations?"

"I was assigned a problematic bedmate."

"Soldiers do not usually have a choice in such matters. I believe you were treated in a special way again."

"Yes, I'm afraid so. There's no disguising it. I am a foreigner here, with all the privileges and complications that entails."

He took a drag on his cigarette and passed it to her, and she took it.

"We should get some sleep," he said, "even for an hour or two. Here, come with me."

She went with him into the second large, open-sided structure. In the flickering light, she saw the sleeping bodies of several hundred Chinese soldiers. Some lay curled on their sides on mats. Others lay on their backs on the hard dirt floor, their mouths open and snoring. Many pressed up against each other in a jumble, like puppies, Shirley thought. Captain Hsu did not pause but stepped over and around the sleeping men, and she followed.

When they reached an opening large enough for them both, Captain Hsu sat down and began to unlace his boots. Shirley glanced around and saw they were near the very center of the space. It made her uncomfortable to be surrounded by men on all sides, but no other spot appeared available. Captain Hsu took off his cap but left his boots on. Then he offered her his hand and gestured for her to wedge herself in beside him.

Shirley sat, too, and took off her cap and canvas shoes as the captain settled into a sleeping position on his side. Seeing no other options, she lay down on her side in front of him. He scooted forward and, as if it was nothing unusual, leaned his chest against her back and draped an arm over her shoulder. Shirley and Captain Hsu spooned. She lay stock-still, her limbs rigid, her mind buzzing with concern. As she was trying to think what to say to him to clarify their friendship and to make sure that he did not misunderstand her fondness for him, he began to snore.

Shirley smiled to herself as her tense and exhausted body leaned into the good captain. She listened to his breathing, then to the exhalations all around. Slowly she became quiet inside. Her own breathing blended with the waves of the many other breaths. As she started to drift off, she remembered Caleb's words: *We are one.* In a room crowded with Chinese soldiers, Shirley felt safer and more at peace than she could ever recall feeling before.

. . .

Voices woke her with a start, and she sat up, Captain Hsu no longer at her side. Only a few soldiers remained in the vast tent. Shirley couldn't imagine how she had slept through the departure of the others. Morning sunlight sliced over the nearby rocks, signaling that it was long past dawn. She yanked on her canvas shoes and cap and hurried outside. Soldiers ran in all directions, carrying supplies and rifles on their shoulders. She wove through them and did not stop to ask what was going on, hoping to find Captain Hsu at the center of the camp.

But at the entrance she was slowed by the sight of incoming wounded, some carried on stretchers, others stumbling against one another. Shirley knelt beside a new arrival, a young man shot in the shoulder. She would need hot water and pincers to remove the bullets and was furious again for having left her medical kit back at the clinic.

"Excuse me," she asked a passing soldier, "I need boiling water and surgical instruments. And bandages. I'm a nurse. I'm here to help."

The young man stared at her and finally gestured to a nearby tent before hurrying off. Through the open flaps, she could see several men leaning over a patient as they performed what appeared to be a surgical procedure.

"I'm here to help," she said to a soldier at the entrance.

He did not respond, and she remembered that these boys came from all over the country. There was no telling what version of the language they spoke.

"I'm a nurse," she tried again.

He motioned with his rifle for her to leave. When the boy

glanced away, she slipped past, but a different soldier stepped forward, his rifle pointing directly at her. He shouted in a dialect she didn't know, although his meaning was clear. More soldiers formed a circle around her. Shirley pushed away from them and marched off. She searched again for Captain Hsu. She felt useless without him. She wondered if she could possibly hurry to the mission that morning and return with nurses and supplies. The trip had not seemed long the night before. She spotted the old mule that had brought them and had known the route. Shirley headed toward it now.

But just then, a horse-drawn cart pulled up, and Shirley saw the strikingly blond hair of one of the passengers. She went to greet the foreigners and offer them assistance but stopped short. On the bed of straw in the back lay a pale man, his neck sliced almost all the way through and his chest punctured. If he wasn't dead yet, he would be very soon. His wife and daughters sat weeping over him. They, too, were splattered with blood, overly bright and gaudy in the morning light.

"Where are you from?" Shirley shouted to be heard above the many panicked Chinese voices. "How did this happen?"

The mother kept her arms around her daughters, who shook and wailed against her sides. She was a fine-boned blonde woman in a pretty calico dress ripped open all the way down, blood over her cheeks and legs. The daughters' dresses, too, had been torn, and their hair was matted with blood and their eyes glazed. The mother finally looked up and saw Shirley but didn't seem to recognize that she was a foreigner, too.

"We'll take care of you," Shirley said. "You're safe now." She reached over and closed the woman's dress. "Where did this happen?"

The woman's voice was hardly a whisper. "Our home."

An old Chinese man, their number-one boy or cook, had fall-
en against one of the wooden wheels. He had been badly beaten,
his shoulder dislocated, the arm hanging wrong.

Shirley crouched beside him and asked, "Where are you
from?" But his gaze did not rise from the ground. "The Anglican
compound to the west of town? Is that it?" she asked.

This must be the new British family that had arrived not long
before. She and Caleb had planned to invite them to tea, but then
he had gone on his expedition to the outlying churches and never come back. Shirley shouted for some Red Army soldiers to
carry the foreigners into camp. As stretchers arrived at the wag-
on, Shirley stood and went for Captain Hsu's mule but spotted
a horse tied up nearby. She unhitched it, grabbed the reins, and
mounted with ease. She dug her heels into the animal's sides and
galloped out of the camp, frantic to return home to her son.

As clouds crossed the sun, she followed the winding trail
down from the rocky ledge. After a half-hour descent, she was
able to see far across the plains, her destination of the town and
the mission a simple route through the flatlands. With some luck,
she could be there in another hour or so. She pressed onward and
tried not think about Charles and the others, although they were
all she could think of.

At a bend in the trail, a stream crossed, and Shirley felt the
frothing horse balk. She should have noticed it was already worn
out when she took it, probably having just arrived from some
great distance. She decided to let the animal have a quick drink.
She dismounted, and the horse hung its head over the bank. The
branches of a weeping willow skimmed the water, dragging thick
green tendrils of summer. The breeze was up, and the clouds had
grown darker, rolling in from the mountains to the west. She

needed to get home before the rain arrived. She needed to get home to be sure her boy was all right.

As Shirley started to gather up the reins, she heard fast-approaching horses and saw that Japanese soldiers rode them. Before she had a chance to mount, the cock of a rifle sounded close behind her. The two soldiers began to shout as they jumped down from their horses. A moment later, she felt the point of a bayonet between her shoulder blades. She lifted her arms, stepped away from her horse, and stumbled in the direction of the stream. They knocked her to the ground, and a rock cut her knee. Her canvas shoes slipped off, and the Red Army cap toppled to the dirt.

"I'm American," she shouted. "Not Chinese. See?" She tried to point to the whiteness of her skin, hoping it could save her.

With the butt of his rifle, the younger of the two soldiers rolled her onto her back. He reached down and yanked the gold chain Caleb had given her from around her neck and stuffed it into his pocket. The phoenix charm flew off and landed in the water with a quiet plop and was gone, never to rise again. The Japanese soldier pressed the wooden handle of his rifle between her legs and started to lift it to strike her. She had seen Chinese women with broken pelvises and now knew that this was how it was done.

"I'm American," she shouted again. "Not Chinese! Please. Don't."

The second soldier watched impassively as the younger one paused to unhitch his belt. She hoped that the older one wasn't in favor of the new barbarism of the Imperial Army. But as she tried to form the Japanese words to appeal to him, he surprised her by sweeping his bayonet past her face. A searing pain burned her cheek. Shirley covered the cut with her hand, and blood leaked over her fingers.

The younger man leaned down and ripped open her tunic.

She covered her exposed breasts as the two men laughed. She wanted to scream but had suddenly lost her voice. As the young one raised the rifle again to hit her, she opened her mouth and croaked out the words "General Shiga!" Hearing her own voice gave her courage, and she shouted again in English, "I am a friend of General Hayato Shiga. Do not harm me!"

The older one gripped the boy's arm.

"I am his nurse!" She scrambled away from them in the dirt. "I am Nurse Carson. Have you not heard of me? I am special nurse to General Hayato Shiga. Hal. We call him Hal. Shiga. You know the name. Shiga!"

She sensed that neither man understood anything she said except the general's name. She repeated it again and climbed up from the dusty ground. She wrapped the torn tunic around herself and rose to her full height. She towered over them, and even though she continued to shake all over and her heart was beating frantically, she glared into their anxious faces.

"General Shiga would not want you to touch a finger to me. General Shiga very angry if you harm American woman. General Shiga says no!"

This last point seemed to register. They conferred. She tried to think of how to escape, but it was impossible. With the exposed trail across the open plains, the Japanese soldiers would simply shoot her in the back as she rode away. The older one took over then. He pushed her with the butt of his rifle toward her horse. She climbed on, and he took the reins as the soldiers mounted theirs. The three started off. Shirley glanced back at the spot where she had been attacked, her shoes and the Red Army cap left in the dust.

Twenty-two

Charles woke to pounding on the door. He untwisted his pajamas and threw on the dragon-patterned silk top but didn't bother with the buttons. Before hurrying downstairs, he checked for his mother in her room. The bed appeared not to have been slept in, and he saw no signs of her return. Out the moon window on the stair landing, autumn sunlight struck the mission wall, less harsh than in summer, more golden. He assumed she was making her way back to the mission through that soft haze over the plains. But it wasn't lost on him that he now had not one but two parents missing out there. The thought no longer made him feel weak in the knees or panicked. Instead, a hard resolve tightened in his chest.

In the front hall, Kathryn and two of his mother's choir friends had been let in. Mrs. Reed and Mrs. Carr whispered to one another as the nurse's assistant in the Red Army trousers and cap eyed them, her arms crossed.

Kathryn called out to Charles as he joined them, "We have come to take you home, dear boy!"

He wiped sleep from his eyes with his elbow and pulled the loose shirt around his ribs. It had gotten too small, leaving his middle exposed. As Kathryn studied him from his bare toes to the top of his head, Charles regretted not dressing properly.

"My, he has grown, hasn't he?" Mrs. Carr said.

"We'd best lock up our daughters," Mrs. Reed whispered.

Kathryn planted a damp kiss on his cheek and took his hand. "Ladies, I shall take full responsibility for him from now on." Then she turned and patted his chest through the wrinkled shirt. "Are you packed?"

Charles nodded, his eyes on the hand that remained on his chest.

"We're counting on you to escort us. The men won't come along until later. The plan is for women and children to meet at the southwest gate at noon. Bring only what you can carry. Reverend Wells is trying to see if some of our possessions and furniture can be shipped home, but I'm sure your mother knows about that. Where is she, anyway? Somewhere around here, I assume?"

The ladies peered into the quiet clinic, where one or two assistants tended to a handful of patients. All but a few of the beds were empty now. No new influx had come for days, perhaps weeks, the military action having moved even farther away from town, Charles guessed. Just then, out of the corner of his eye, he noticed the muslin curtain rustle at one of the front windows. Dao-Ming turned at the dining room corner and headed for the basement steps.

Mrs. Reed peered into the clinic and said, "I had no idea Shirley had *this* going on."

"We were overrun with Chinese at first, too," Mrs. Carr said, "but I can't imagine still having them in my home."

"She lost her husband so recently, poor dear, and must have needed to fill the void."

Charles wanted to speak up on his mother's behalf but didn't. He hoped Kathryn might defend her, but instead she asked, "Any idea where she is, Charles? Or have you lost track of her like the rest of us?"

"I'm sure she's around somewhere. She's terribly busy and has a great deal to manage. We'll be at the gate at noon. No problem. Thanks for telling us."

He escorted Kathryn and the ladies out, shut the heavy door, and leaned against it. The smoky scent of the dark carved rosewood enveloped him, so familiar and commonplace here. He wanted to let out a shout. He was finally departing, leaving behind every strange, exotic smell and sight he had become accustomed to over the years. But where was his mother? She must be on her way home, he thought, and would surely arrive at any minute. At least he desperately hoped so, and he pushed from his mind any thought otherwise.

Charles strode to the top of the basement steps and called down for Dao-Ming, thinking she might know his mother's whereabouts, but no answer came. Perhaps she had helped his father with the pigeons, but he couldn't imagine how she had been of any use with the radio. Though now that he thought about it, he recalled her slipping into the cellar many times. He had always assumed it was to collect the root vegetables that Lian stored down there, but who knew the real reason? Charles headed into the clinic. He stood over the young Communist nurse in khakis and Red Army cap as she knelt beside a grandmother stretched out on a cot.

"Good morning, miss," he said to the nurse.

He didn't know her name but had overheard his mother and Captain Hsu discussing the diligent way she performed her work. She seemed all right, a little plain and far too serious. He wondered if he could get a smile out of her.

"So, what's the story, morning glory?" he tried.

She didn't look up.

"I bet you don't even know what a morning glory is. How about, hey, good-lookin', what's cookin'? Nothing, right? Hardly any food around here at all."

"Go away, we are busy," she finally said, still not looking up.

"I'll leave you alone, but I wonder if you've seen my mother?"

The young Communist nurse finally glanced up at him, and the edges of her lips rose slightly.

"Hey, I got a smile out of you," he said. "You like my outfit?"

Her expression became stern again. "No Nurse Carson here," she said and stood. "She has served her purpose and is no longer needed. We are better off without her."

"Gee, that's rude," Charles said. "She set up this clinic, you know? It's our house."

"This is not your house. Never your house."

"How ungrateful. After all she's done for you."

The young woman turned back to her patient. "You are a young, insignificant boy. Leave us alone."

"Now, wait a minute," he said and touched her shoulder.

The woman jumped up and put her hand on the butt of the pistol tucked into her Red Army belt. She began to shout, "Get out! No more foreign devils here! America business steal North China coal, become rich, while we Chinese starve. You and Mother do nothing to stand up to the yellow sons of whores from Japan! You are bad people, not good! Get out before I shoot you!"

The woman waved her pistol in the air as Charles stumbled out the front door and onto the porch. He held on to the column, his head dizzy from her crazy words. A searing hunger bit into him. As he caught his breath, he noticed that only a few Chinese passed by in the empty courtyard below. For days, he had seen them packing up and departing. The ground they left behind was hard and cracked from their many footfalls. As the last of the campfires died out, litter remained strewn throughout the compound—scraps of newspaper, old sheets of tin, wooden planks, and piles of rubbish everywhere.

Across the way at the Reeds' house, Charles saw the Reverend lugging his wife's and daughters' straw suitcases down the porch steps. The vegetable garden to the side of their home had been trampled and used as a bathroom for weeks, but one lone sunflower still hung its dried head over the churned-up soil.

Each spring, Caleb Carson had been the first to farm that small plot. Charles would follow his father outside and helped push the seeds deep into the thick yellow clay, patting down the soil and shaping it around each thin stalk. He could practically feel the dampness of it between his fingers. Charles rubbed his hands together now. His father had been swallowed up by that same entrapping earth. Charles wrapped his shirt tighter around his ribs and knew that the unsettled air meant rain.

When he was young and the autumn storms finally came, he and Han used to splash in puddles that formed quickly in the parched dirt. They painted each other's faces with mud in great slashes like war paint, becoming Indians on the American Western plains and doing war dances in the rain. Charles wondered why they had never pretended to be characters from Chinese lore. He had insisted on cowboys and Indians, and Han, being a good guy, had gone along with it, playing Tonto to Charles's masked man. They never switched parts because why would they, when Charles was the leader and Han the follower?

Charles felt his cheeks flame. As they grew older, Charles had imitated suave leading men, Cary Grant or Clark Gable, while Han was always cast as his trusty manservant. He spat over the side of the porch now and slapped his palms on the railing. "Damn," he said to no one and let himself wonder if maybe the Communist nurse was right: he and the other Americans had been squatters all along. Outsiders who never knew the truth but barreled ahead anyway, insisting on their way. His mother had tried to help with the clinic, and the Chinese had followed her instructions, but she had never been in charge. Captain Hsu, and now this young Communist nurse, and perhaps other Chinese whom Charles didn't even know about, actually ran the show. Charles and his mother had thought they were the leading actors, when really he could see now that they were but extras in China's fast-moving play.

He set off down the steps and across the courtyard, slipped down the alley, and came out in the servants' quarters. The same eerie emptiness met him there. He didn't bother to turn toward Han's house. He knew that his friend would be on the front lines by now: happy to choose his own role and not have it assigned to him by his American friend.

Han had been the braver of the two, Charles realized now. Han had worked hard since he was a boy, been loyal to his father, and always performed his duties with care and respect. By comparison, Charles had never been leading-man material at all. He caught his breath and leaned a hand against the rough-hewn wall of Lian's quarters, as he had that day when he had stood over Li Juan and tried to appear handsome and debonair. The poor girl had just come from the dangerous countryside, and he had tried to impress her with his new sneakers.

He turned and peered into the darkened room. Lian stood with her hands on her hips in front of her mother, who lay on a straw mat with her arms crossed over her chest. The old woman had finally died, Charles thought. As he joined Lian, he wanted to offer his condolences and for once be of help to her and not the other way around. But he pulled up short when he saw that the old woman's eyes remained open, her face set in a grimace.

"Mother," Lian said, "you are behaving like a stubborn old mule."

"That is what I am. Nothing more."

"Hello, Lian," Charles said softly. "Everything all right?"

"Do not bother us now, Charles-Boy. We must leave right away, but Mother refuses to go another step. She prefers to lie here and be raped and murdered. She wants my two precious daughters to be kidnapped by dwarf bandit soldiers and taken away on their trains to a life of servitude and misery. This is what happens when you are stubborn, Mother, and refuse to do what is best for all!"

Charles didn't know what to say, but a bright voice responded from the kitchen area.

"I say we leave her," Li Juan said.

Lian snapped her fingers hard. "If you think that, you are no child of mine. We bring her."

Li Juan stepped closer. "I'm not carrying her."

"We will find a way. This cot will serve as a stretcher."

Charles cleared his throat and ventured to ask, "Can she walk at all?"

Li Juan ignored him and headed for the door, dragging a bundle made of a sheet with his mother's initials monogrammed on it. Charles followed close on her heels as she stepped into the alley.

"I came to say good-bye," he said.

Li Juan finally looked at him and giggled. "What are you wearing?"

He looked down at his ill-fitting colorful pajamas. "Nothing, it doesn't matter. I just want to say thank you."

"For what?"

"I—" he glanced into Lian's small, dark room and then up the rutted path with ditches on both sides that stank of human waste. He wanted to say for everything. For absolutely everything. "I'm not sure," he offered. "But thanks."

"My stubborn grandmother is going to get us all killed."

"Please take our horse if it's still there." He reached for Li Juan's hand. "And our cart. Yes, take it, too."

Lian appeared on the threshold, and Charles stepped away from Li Juan, who didn't seem to mind one way or the other when he let go of her limp fingers.

"The horse and cart are long gone, Charles-Boy. Weeks ago."

"How about the mule?" he asked. "I want you to have our mule."

"We were going to use it, but somebody stole it last night. But thank you," Lian said and smiled very slightly. "You must go. Mission women and children leave at noon."

"I know. I'm ready."

"You are not such bad boy after all," she said.

With that compliment, Charles found himself throwing his arms around his old amah. He had to bend far over to do it, but his large hands held on to her sturdy back. He wanted her to know something very important. She had kept watch over him and spent years setting him on the right path. But now she pushed him away, and he didn't mind. That was just her curt manner. When he stepped back, he saw that she had tears in her eyes, too.

"Thank you, Lian," he said and bowed.

She did not bow in return, which struck Charles as somehow right. Instead, she appraised him.

"Charles-Boy, you look like monkey in that outfit. Go home and change right away. You disgrace the family name. I did not raise you to look a fool. Go!"

"I'm sorry. I'll change right away. I apologize, esteemed Lian," he said and started to leave but then stopped again and asked, "But do you know if my mother got back to the mission last night?"

"She is not back yet?"

Charles shook his head.

"That's very bad news. We received word about trouble at camp out on the plains."

Li Juan took her mother's hand.

"But even if she is not back in time, you must leave."

"I will. But how do you know what's going on out there?"

Lian waved his question away. "What matters is Captain Hsu and others will protect your mother. I will radio them to say that she has not returned here."

"You know how to do that?" he asked. "Who else used that radio?"

She wiped her hands on her apron as she always had when it was time for him to stop pestering her. "Charles-Boy, there is much you do not know and much you will never know. Off you go, now."

He bowed for a final time and dashed up the alley again. He would change out of his childish clothing, gather his things, and meet the others at the southwest gate at noon.

Twenty-three

Yellow dust blew in sideways from the Gobi. Shirley held an arm up to protect her eyes and kept her mouth shut to avoid swallowing loess, the sticky topsoil that was inescapable at this time of year. Scraps of paper, dried leaves, and other detritus whirled across the desolate streets. For days the Chinese had been packing their belongings and fanning out into the countryside, but she couldn't imagine how they had fled so completely. The Japanese Imperial Army had returned to town, its soldiers standing in shadowed doorways and on street corners.

The two soldiers motioned for her to dismount. The older one used the butt of his rifle to push her up the steps of the former municipal building. Yellow light poured down from the open door, and Japanese soldiers streamed in and out. None of them seemed to notice the thinly clad foreign woman holding on to her torn shirt, blood and bruises dotting her limbs. Shirley feared that they considered her just another body, a nameless victim to be finished off when the order was given. She wondered if the British missionary mother had thought the same thing or if she and her family had been set upon too suddenly.

Once inside, they prodded Shirley down a hallway and into a storage room, the door abruptly locking behind her. She crumpled with her back against a damp wall. As in the antique shops she had browsed in Peking, Chinese furniture was stacked to the ceiling—teak tables with angular legs, high-backed scalloped chairs, and even old Tupan Feng's elegant daybed. She had heard that like hedonistic emperors of ancient times, he used to lie upon it when meeting his subjects here in the government building. His sins of excess and greed seemed childlike to her compared with the Japanese now.

Fear and exhaustion swirled over Shirley, and before she knew it, she was asleep. After some time, Japanese soldiers returned and pushed her back into the hall, where more soldiers hurried past. Someone had her arm and yanked her to stand before Major Hattori. His eyes roamed down her body. Shirley held her tunic closed and tried to control the shaking. Hattori signaled for the soldiers to prod her up the steps and into the general's office. As the two officers chuckled at her, Shirley did not lift her eyes from her bruised and dusty feet. Her knee had bled down her leg in shocking red rivulets, and her arms trembled as she squeezed her ribs. The major turned and left the room, closing the door behind him. Shirley felt certain that no one would question the general—Princeton-educated or not—if he chose to finish the job the soldiers had begun by the stream.

"You have wasted our time," he began in his perfect English.

Shirley finally dared to look up. General Shiga sat in the banker's chair with his boots on the desk, his uniform as crisp as before and his lip curled back. Only his eyes seemed different. They appeared gray and unflinching and dull. She tried to remember him as a boy back in college but could not. This man before her had become as impenetrable as that foreign Asian boy in America had once seemed vulnerable.

"We are done with you." He took a sip from a fine white teacup and set it on his orderly desk. "I should let my men do as they wish."

A shiver started in her shoulders and made its way swiftly down her back. Her knees began to buckle, but she righted herself. She wanted to stand tall as she always had in moments of difficulty. She felt a tear roll down her cheek, and when she wiped it away, blood stained her fingers. Words had fled her mind. Only one thought raged.

"I need to find my son," she whispered.

The general tapped the cup with his heavy gold class ring—a cruel and taunting sound. "They have left the mission," he said. "We let them go. We have other concerns."

"But I must go with him," she said, trying to regain her voice. "Please, General, help me."

He lifted his legs off the desktop and set his boots on the floor with quiet finality.

"I will be your nurse now. I can tend to your officers."

"It is too late for that. Your son will travel to Shanghai and board a ship out of China and away from his mother forever. He will make a new life in America and will be fine without you, probably better off. Americans are far too sentimental about such things."

As she gripped the edge of his desk to catch her fall, her shirt came open, and she hunched over quickly to cover herself. The British mother had no longer cared, so Shirley had reached across to close the woman's blouse and wiped the blood from her pale skin. The bodies, Shirley recalled, so many wounded bodies that she had helped, not once feeling squeamish or frightened. But she understood now that she had seen too much suffering. She had held the hands of Chinese boys as they took their final breaths, their own mothers far away. She could not bear to have it end like that for her and her son—to be separated and torn from one another like the women and soldiers she had tried to save.

"Please," she said again, "I must go to him."

General Shiga stood but remained behind the desk, and Shirley was grateful that he didn't come closer. She feared she might faint if he did. Although he wasn't threatening her, his presence filled her with the terrible dread and panic that she had held at bay for weeks.

"You will tell me the location of the Red Army camp and help us find Captain Hsu," he said. "Then you may see your son."

Shirley's head throbbed, and she blinked several times. "Captain Hsu?" she asked. "I hardly know the man."

The general slammed a hand on the desk, and Shirley flinched. "I give you one chance," he said. "You lie to me again, and I no longer care what happens to you. Now, tell me, where is the Eighth Route Army camp?"

Her voice came out high and thin. "Your soldiers found me on the trail that leads to it."

"We already know the location of that Red Army camp out on the plains to the east. We attacked it this afternoon."

Out the window, the dust-clogged sky grew dimmer. Shirley realized that hours must have passed while she had slept in the storage room. Night was falling rapidly now. "You attacked there today?" she asked.

"We did away with it. Even the Reds with their unmanly guerrilla tactics are far inferior to us." General Shiga strode to the window, and Shirley studied his unrelenting reflection in the glass. "But their leaders escaped. They are a wily bunch and know the countryside better than we do. We simply finished off the wounded. There is no point in taking prisoners. We have orders to destroy all."

The general's words cascaded over her as one thought drowned out all others. She needed to see her child and escape this madness together. She held the wicker chair to steady herself and brought forth the courage to ask, "What do you want me to do?"

He turned to her. "Tell us the location of their headquarters in the mountains. We could bomb the whole range, but that would be a waste of our resources. You will get me the coordinates of the Communist camp."

"But I have no idea where it is, General. I'm not a Red Army soldier. This foolish uniform I wear is just a costume. You must know that." She cleared her constricted throat and made herself continue. "You know me, General Shiga—Hal," she added, with trepidation, but he didn't seem to take offense. "My stepfather is a successful capitalist. He owns a chain of shoe stores in Ohio. I couldn't possibly believe in all this Communist nonsense. You know my alma mater. You graduated with distinction from one of our brother schools." She dared to let go of the chair and started toward him, as if finally making her way across the dance floor of her youth. "You know I am a Vassar girl. We attended that spring social together, you and I. Now, please, just let me find my son and go home. I have no business being here. It's been an awful mistake. I should never have stayed so long."

Sweat trickled down her sides as Shirley joined him at the window. "Come, now, help us return home to America, where we belong."

"Vassar girl," he said with a snarl.

The wind whipped great clouds of yellow dust across the

gloaming sky, giving the air a deep ochre tint. The Japanese flag on the pole snapped frantically, the shutters of the old municipal building banged, and the windows rattled. Then, in an instant, the rain began. Shirley thought she heard the general let out a pleased sigh, as if hearing the opening chords of a concert he was fond of remembering. She wished that the initial gentleness of the rainfall would bring him back to his former self. She would have liked to reminisce about the band that night. The gay lanterns on the campus lawn. The girls in their springtime dresses. She would have liked to be her former self—a carefree young woman who thought the world was safe and hers for the taking.

"Get me the location of the Red Army camp in the mountains, and I will see that you join your son before he leaves Shanghai," the general said as he continued to gaze at the storm that was starting to rage outside.

Torrents always marked the change of season here. Shirley remembered Charles playing in the sudden mud puddles with his dear friend, Han. Her husband would dash home so they could press their rocking chairs close together and watch the great, sweeping power of the storm as it rushed across the plains. For so many years, rain had made all things new. Shirley wished for that now, for them all. To wash away the sins of violence and misery.

But the rain would do nothing of the sort, especially not for her. Shirley understood in that moment that if she did what the general asked and betrayed her friend and his cause, nothing could wash her clean. No matter how empty or terrified she might feel, or desperate to be reunited with her son, nothing could justify such a decision. And yet she felt she had no choice.

"I will try," she said.

"Don't play games with me, Mrs. Carson. If you do not come

through with this information, you will not see your son, and I will leave your fate to my men."

The general called for his soldiers. They pushed her out of the office and through the maze of other soldiers, then left her on the steps of the municipal building to make her way home in the driving rain.

Twenty-four

Caleb watched the rain as Han and Cook conferred at the back of the cave. They had set it up so nicely, with a fire and two cots, his own and one for Cook. All summer, Caleb had been grateful for the dampness inside the cave as it had helped keep him cool through night sweats. He was coming back to life. He felt certain of that. But then he heard their voices, and despite the pounding rain and their quick tongues, the crucial information reached him. Han whispered to his father that an update had come over the radio: Mrs. Carson was missing, perhaps taken by the Japanese or simply lost in the countryside. The night before, she had visited a Red Army camp out on the plains with Captain Hsu. Early that morning, an unexpected Japanese attack had struck nearby, and in the confusion, Mrs. Carson had disappeared. She had not been seen since, and subsequently, Han explained, the camp had been destroyed, only the Eighth Route Army leaders and some of the troops escaping in time.

Caleb wanted to shout above the sound of the rain and beg them to tell him it wasn't true that Shirley's whereabouts were now unknown. But instead, he bit his bottom lip and squeezed his hands together in an exercise they had devised to help him regain strength in his arms. Cook had overseen his recovery so well, and Caleb understood that the older man was protecting him from any painful news that might impede his recovery. He listened intently for any further updates and heard Cook say that he would confirm Mrs. Carson's absence with Captain Hsu.

They were all out there, Caleb thought: his wife, his son, and his friend and comrade Captain Hsu. They all existed beyond the veil of water that separated him from the rest of the world. As the rain fell, swirling him in its embrace, he shut his eyes and tried to appear as placid as he could, though his mind roiled with worry and his body felt more infirm than ever.

"You have rested well," Cook said. "But now you must sit up. The humors must move. Stir blood. Very important."

For weeks now, Cook had tried to teach Caleb the Chinese understanding of the body. It was so foreign to him, and he was such a slow learner since the accident, unable to grasp the many rules and distinctions of his care. But he had come to believe that Cook's approach was right: his blood had grown too still. Now, after overhearing the news of his missing wife, Caleb sensed that even his heart was slowing. Perhaps it would stop altogether. His tears started again, and Cook frowned.

"You feel much pain?" he asked.

"No, I'm just happy that my family is going home to America."

At this, Cook nodded briskly and appeared satisfied. "It is best."

He then stepped away and left Caleb to wonder how he could possibly go on living while she was out there alone in the countryside. He remembered the old phrases he had used to cheer his wife when she felt unhappy, which had been quite often here in China. *Stiff upper lip*, he had said. *Carry on*. How had he ever believed it possible to carry on, unscathed? He had thought he could come to China to make a difference, first with teaching at the mission and then with the Communist cause as well. He had wanted to help redirect the stream of history here, when in actuality, it had washed over him like the rain over the lip of the cave. How had he ever thought that he and his family could escape the shifting and slippery ground around them in a country not their own?

He fell asleep to the pounding of rain and awoke later to see the unmistakable silhouette of Captain Hsu by the mouth of the cave. Caleb sensed other men nearby, too. A great tiredness overcame him. He was not well. The rain had slowed to an even pace. Caleb knew it would go on like that for days. It made his bones ache even more than before. The pain seeped through him the way the water leaked from cracks in the cave walls. His wife was missing and he hurt all over. He raised a finger and tried to make his voice heard above the insistent rain.

"Captain," he called.

It took several more tries before his comrade heard him and left the other men to come to his side. He knelt down and pressed Caleb's hand.

"You are feeling better?" Captain Hsu asked.

Caleb wanted to smile but felt too feeble to do so. "I'm no better than I was," he said.

"That is not what Cook tells me." The Captain's strong voice echoed off the watery walls.

What a vital man he was, Caleb thought. That scar over his eye and other marks on his face did not take away from his overall handsome and positive appearance. Captain Hsu would have stood out in any country but seemed especially unique in this setting, where hardship crushed the spirits of lesser souls.

"I have heard about my wife," Caleb whispered. "Is she still missing?"

The captain bowed his head, his silver hair catching the lamp-light. "I am sorry, my friend. We tried to spare you this news."

"Don't tell Cook that I know. He will worry about me."

The captain looked out at the night. "We did not see the raid coming until it was almost too late. Our leaders barely escaped. And now, Imperial Army troops line the main roads and fill the town. Everyone who can has left. We are unable to return there without great risk. I have to assume that the Japanese took Mrs. Carson, though honestly I don't know. But I will try to investigate."

"Please don't put yourself in danger, Captain," Caleb said.

Captain Hsu patted the Reverend's chest. "Danger is every-where. It cannot be helped." He stood and started to step away, but Caleb called him back.

"I'm sorry, Captain, but I have another favor to ask."

"In addition to trying to find your wife?" The captain finally smiled. "Isn't that enough?"

"Yes, and I'm eternally grateful to you."

"I don't believe in eternity, so don't bother. What else do you want, old friend? Another blanket? The air is colder now with the rain."

Caleb motioned for the captain to bend closer, and he did.

"I want you to shoot me," he whispered. "Will you do that for me?"

The captain straightened up fast. "You don't know what you're saying."

With great effort, Caleb tried to reach for the captain's hand, but Hsu did not take his.

"You should know I would never do such a thing," he said. "We are not barbarians. I will ignore this insult because you are not yourself. Now, sleep. That is an order."

Then the good man—a better man than Caleb thought himself to be—left the cave. Sleep came quickly and with it relief from the shame he felt for having asked his friend to commit a mortal sin, even if the captain did not believe in such a thing.

Twenty-five

Rain blotted out the night sky and made every surface slick. Shirley wove through the deserted streets and felt the dust turn to mud beneath her feet. A Japanese soldier followed a short distance behind, and she wondered if he was rogue and would attack her, although the longer he did not, the more she allowed herself to believe that he had been sent to protect her instead. When she glanced around again, he was gone. But then he reappeared in the destroyed market and later by the compound wall. She didn't know if she could do what she had been asked to do, but for now, she simply walked, one cut and bruised footstep after the next.

The gates to the compound had been left open, and a pack of emaciated dogs stood over the body of the blind grandfather who had guarded the entrance. Shirley looked away quickly but had already seen too much. Though soaked through, she did not hurry or seek shelter. She wandered up the brick pathways in a daze as rain cascaded down her hair and fell in a wall around her face. At her home, she stumbled through the moon gate and up the wide wooden steps of the porch. The rocking chairs were gone from their usual places, and Shirley had no idea how long ago they had been taken. There was so much she had not noticed. The screen door had been stolen, and the handsome carved front door stood open, the small statue of the door god no longer keeping watch. She stepped over the threshold and nearly let out a cry at the familiar sight of her piano. It stood exactly as before, though the bench was missing. She longed to play it now, to hurl herself into a sad and stirring piece, but didn't dare make noise or draw attention to the house. She had seen no one since entering the compound, though she had sensed movement in the dark.

She wandered into the clinic, where only a few cots remained. The supply station had been tipped over, the medical instruments taken. Used bandages and other debris lay tossed on the wooden floor. Hanging on the coat tree, along with several aprons, she found a rumpled sweater that had belonged to Charles when he was a younger boy. She pulled it over her head and breathed in the scent of him—neither sweet nor unpleasant but simply his. With the wind up and the season changing, she was chilled all the way through but began to feel warmer, sensing her son with her.

She hung a white apron around her neck and tied the sash at her waist. She had come to feel such purpose when putting on her nursing garb and entering the clinic. She stepped into the former parlor now. The cots and chairs had been taken, too. Only the wicker sofa remained, tipped on its side, the cushions gone. Dry newspapers and other rubbish littered the corners. Ashes from a recent fire glowed in the hearth, and she wondered if any Chinese people were hiding out in her home, a thought that would have once terrified her but now seemed almost a comfort.

She pressed her bare toes into the faded coral cherry blossoms on the sea of blue carpet. The gold screen painted with the image of the rising phoenix no longer stood in the corner. She had complained to Caleb that all the decorations in their formal rooms should be as fine as that elegant piece, one of her prized possessions. By having high-quality Chinese antiques and Oriental bric-a-brac, she had hoped to convince herself, as well as the Chinese, that she knew them and their world. She understood now that she had hardly known them at all.

"Oh, Caleb," she whispered to the barren room, "you tried to tell me, but I wouldn't listen."

Outside, the rain continued, insistent and hard. It would go on like that for days, mesmerizing and casting a spell over everything. Shirley wondered how she would manage without her husband here to light a fire as he always had. How would she manage anywhere without him, and without her son, too? Without them, her life was as empty and eviscerated as this house. She needed to leave China, and not alone. She didn't belong here any longer. She didn't know where she belonged. But she understood that she must find Captain Hsu and do what needed to be done in order to join Charles, no matter the cost.

Light-headed and exhausted, she stepped outside and folded herself down onto the porch floorboards, leaning against the yellow-brick exterior. Out of the corner of her eye, she sensed the Japanese soldier at the side of the porch, hidden behind a post and a shrub the name of which she had never learned, its delicate yellow blooms just ending. Some part of her assumed the Japanese soldier would kill her whether she did General Shiga's bidding or not. But as she started to drift off to sleep, she let herself consider that the presence of the soldier might actually mean Shiga intended to keep his word. With that conflicted and yet dimly promising thought, Shirley shut her eyes, tipped back her head, and within moments was asleep.

Some time later, she felt tugging at her arm and tried to knock whomever it was away. Her mind filled with an image of the dogs standing over the old man at the entrance to the mission, their teeth bared and growling. Shirley awoke with a shriek and scrambled to her feet. No dogs surrounded her, but before her stood Captain Hsu. She threw her arms around him and said, "You're alive!"

He pushed her away gently and took her hand. "We have to get inside. It's not safe out here."

"Wait, I need air," she said as she took him by the sleeve.

Shirley brought him to stand at the railing so that their voices could be heard above the rain streaming down the tiles. This would be the moment, she thought. If she did as the general asked, would the Japanese soldier take Captain Hsu to his execution in the town square or shoot him right there on her front porch? Would he kill them both simply to have it over with?

"I want to help the injured troops at the camp in the mountains," she said. "Charles is gone with the others, and I can't make it to Shanghai in time to join him. Please, Captain, let me be a real Red Army nurse."

"You must come inside. You have a fever."

"Please, for my husband's sake," she made herself continue. "I want to carry on his good works."

Captain Hsu studied her hard, and Shirley wondered if he could tell that she was deceiving him. But then a surprising and kind light came into his eyes as he said, "Yes, I think you're right. The Reverend would want that."

"But where is the camp located?" she asked. "By what route will we travel?"

So the good captain told her. He said the road and the pass they would take to get there. He mentioned the name of the range and the distance. He spoke casually, helpfully, not knowing how his words would be used against him and his comrades. Shirley's mind reeled with the magnitude of her betrayal. When he finished, she grabbed his hand and hurried him over the threshold and into the house. She expected the sound of gunshots but heard only the front door slamming and the scrape of the heavy bolt as it fell into place.

Captain Hsu placed his cool palm on her forehead. "You're burning up. We'll have to leave while it's still dark, but you can rest for an hour first. Here, eat this."

He pulled an oatcake from his pocket. She bit down on the hard surface, chewed, and swallowed with a dry throat. She started to follow him upstairs, but when they reached the landing, Shirley's gaze drifted down, and she saw the curtain rustle by the front window. Then the basement door creaked closed. On the dusty floorboards in the front hall, she thought she recognized small footprints where there had been none before. The captain raised his pistol.

"It's nothing," she said, "only the storm. Someone left a window open in the clinic."

But she prayed that it was not the wind but instead the miraculous young woman, Dao-Ming. She prayed that the girl would somehow know to warn her comrades. That was Shirley's only hope to reverse what she had done.

In her bedroom, she was startled by her reflection in the vanity mirror. Bent and ghostly, Shirley looked as old as Lian but thin and drawn, the way her mother appeared after one of her benders. Shirley turned away and ached for bed. The blankets, quilts, and even the sheets had been taken. Captain Hsu led her to the mattress and helped her down. She curled on her side, and he covered her with his Red Army jacket. Shirley longed for the peacefulness she had felt at the Communist camp. Her life, and the lives of the Chinese around her, had seemed so full of promise then.

From the bed, she looked across to the window, where outside everything was monochrome darkness. All light had been snuffed out in the night, and she started to close her eyes. At that moment, from the southwest wall, a sudden flurry of pale wings caught the air as the flock of pigeons that Charles and Han had trained flew off into the pelting rain. Shirley sat up and followed them with her eyes as they flapped frantically against the harsh night.

Captain Hsu saw them, too, and looked across at her, an urgent question on his face.

"Run!" Shirley whispered.

Captain Hsu held his pistol high and, without a word, hurried from the room. Shirley heard his soft tread as he descended the steps and then fled across the front hall. She listened for the grating of the bolt on the door, but it never came. Nor did she hear his footfalls on the creaking porch floorboards. But then, in the quiet, she heard a shot, then another, and finally a third.

Shirley raced to the window, Captain Hsu's Red Army jacket falling to the dusty floor. She saw nothing outside except rain battering the glass as night sealed the courtyard. She pressed her fingers to the pane and waited for something to tell her what had transpired below but saw no movement and heard no further sound. Her fingers left a ghostly print on the fogged glass, but that was all.

Some time later, from far off, she heard the low rumble of an engine. Approaching bombers, she was sure, come to finish off the mission. General Shia had not ordered her shot because, as he had boasted, he preferred to destroy all. The tangled history of this foreign outpost would finally and fully be obliterated. But instead of aircraft overhead, a black car drove in through the southwest gate. The beams of yellow light pierced the fog and rain. The car slowed to a stop in front of her home and idled ominously, waiting, she realized after a long moment, for her.

Shirley raced to her closet and pulled down a small valise from the shelf. Her husband's gold monogrammed initials caught the car light as it reflected off the mirror. She put her only two remaining dresses inside the small suitcase and closed the latch. Next, she crouched before the empty fireplace and removed a brick from the back, then reached into the opening and pulled out a tin box. From inside it, she stuffed Chinese and American currency and her family's papers into the pockets of her apron. She found her raincoat and hat on the hook by the door and pulled on socks and high Wellingtons. Shirley cinched the belt of the mackintosh around her waist, lifted the valise, and headed downstairs. She looked about for Dao-Ming but saw no sign of the girl.

Twenty-six

The train slowed, delayed once more by Chinese storm-ing the tracks. They clung to the windows and climbed onto the couplings between the cars. More Chinese mobbed the corridor outside the compartment and pressed their faces to the inside glass. Charles barricaded the door with suitcases, and Kathryn pulled the frayed curtains closed. Then he hunkered down on the bench and pulled his father's driving cap lower over his eyes. He knew he was lucky to have a seat, lucky to have made it this far through the dangerous countryside. Lucky, really, to be alive.

Despite the commotion, Kathryn fell asleep with her head resting against his shoulder. Charles pressed his forehead to the window and watched the blurred fields pass by. He wondered where Han was at that moment.

White steam unfurled as it drifted past the window and dissolved into wet air. He shut his eyes and let the rhythm of the train lull him until he remembered his father's words again: *Keep your wits about you, son. Steady nerves. Don't fire till you see the whites of their eyes.* Charles had no pistol, and his father had never meant for him to carry one. But Caleb Carson wanted him to be on the lookout for danger in a country fraught with it. Han, too, had tried to teach Charles to stay attuned to signs and signals, to listen more, and, as he had politely insisted, jabber less. Both his father and his friend seemed better suited than he to handle the adversity around them.

Charles shifted in his seat, and Kathryn finally stirred. Her charming little hat tipped off her head and landed in his lap. Her sleeping face under the dark bangs was cocked up toward him at an odd angle, and he couldn't help noticing that even though she wasn't close to his age, she also didn't seem so old, like his mother. She had insisted he call her Kathryn. And as he whispered it now, it occurred to him then that she was his one and only friend. That seemed such a forlorn thought that it made Charles long once again to see Han. Kathryn continued to snore softly, so he nudged her harder this time. She swung around abruptly, tilted her head back further, and, with eyes still closed, pushed herself up to kiss him. Charles's eyes opened wide, while hers remained decidedly shut.

"Hey, now," he said as he gently pushed her off, "what have you been drinking?"

She snatched her hat back and placed it on her head.

"How about sharing?" Charles asked. "I'm dying of thirst. Give me a slug or two, and we'll really pucker up."

She pinched his rumpled sleeve and offered an embarrassed laugh but opened her silk purse and handed him a tarnished silver flask. She had already finished off a third of it. Charles was determined to catch up. The booze burned the back of his throat, heated his chest, and plunged deep into his empty stomach, sending heat straight to his brain. A minute before, he had felt friendless in this world. Now he had a girl on his arm and hooch in his hand. He'd been around people who drank but had never tasted liquor before. He'd also never kissed a girl before and felt it was long overdue. He was finally a young American, headed home.

"That's fine Kentucky bourbon, not some lousy Chinese fire-water," Kathryn explained as she straightened her skirt. "My father gave it to me, and I kept it in the back of my closet the whole time I was here. There were temptations galore to break it open, but aren't you glad I waited until now?" She took the flask from Charles, screwed it shut and dropped it into her purse. "But not a word about any of this, kiddo. It was just a little dream you had." Kathryn shut her eyes and rested her head against his shoulder again. "Go back to sleep."

Charles looked out the window at the rice paddies and wished he could melt into the wet earth pockmarked with rain. He wanted to get out of the stuffy compartment but knew he should relish this moment of peace and privacy. Instead, he felt trapped and ashamed. It would have been grand if Kathryn James had been his girl. But she wasn't his girl. She was just some older woman at the end of her rope. When everything was going to hell around you, you went that way, too.

His father didn't believe in hell. He said it was an invention of zealots intended to frighten people into believing. Reverend Caleb Carson didn't care for mumbo-jumbo to fool the ignorant masses. *We behave well on this earth,* he had said, *because that is our nature. Humans are inherently good and cooperative, and when we are not, stories of devils with pitchforks won't make us rise to our higher selves.* Charles had heard his sermons about human goodness all his life and had always assumed they were true. But he wished he could show his father what he had seen over the past weeks. Hell is real, Dad, Charles would have said. And it's here in China.

On the muddy road beside the train track, the throngs marched forward, stumbling and fighting their way to safety.

Charles hadn't seen any Japanese soldiers for a while but knew they were out there. At first, the rain had come as a welcome surprise, but already it was making matters worse. He had seen farm trucks and the black sedans driven by officials stuck deep in watery ruts. But somehow the people pressed onward, unyielding against the wind and slashing rain. The goddamn unlucky Chinese, Charles thought. Nothing ever seemed to go their way.

How his parents had ever thought it was a good idea to live in this country, Charles couldn't imagine. He supposed he had his father to blame for that. But he couldn't blame him for the way the earth had given way under him and he had died in a landslide. Caleb Carson had been pursuing his cause, riding out into the countryside to check on the churches up in the mountains. His father had died doing his Christian duty.

Charles hoped that someday he would be as dedicated to a good cause as his father had been to his. A doctor's calling was like that—done for the sake of others but with the possibility, Charles hoped, of a fine-looking automobile parked in the driveway. No harm in that, he thought. He had every intention of growing up to be like his father, but not quite so dedicated as to get himself killed.

It was his mother Charles would never understand. The more he thought about how she had taken off for the Red Army camp, the less likely it seemed he would ever forgive her. His father had sacrificed his life out of the goodness of his heart. His mother, on the other hand, was just plain foolish, selfish, and wrong. His jaw tightened as he used a finger to follow a raindrop down the windowpane. Dusk descended, and he pressed his palm against the window and removed it quickly, leaving a ghostly print suspended for a long moment.

He recalled how they had sat together on the window seat in the parlor and watched rain fall in the mission courtyard. She pressed her hand to the pane, then removed it, and in their game, he would quickly place his own much smaller palm over the shadow of hers. As the mark of his mother's hand faded, he had tried to catch it before it fully disappeared. Charles assumed that he would never hold that hand again, nor would he want to. He squinted at the rain rolling down the window beside him and swallowed with a dry throat again. He was on his own now with nothing but the fast-fading memory of his parents, both gone for good in China.

Charles felt certain that his mother must have known she was going to stay at the Red Army camp when she had gone there. Captain Hsu had probably convinced her. Shirley Carson wouldn't come to Shanghai before his ship departed or even meet him later in America. She might never return from China at all. He would search for her in future newspaper photos standing alongside the Communist leaders—one lone, tall American woman, her eyes bright with zeal. It burned Charles up inside to think of how she had been willing to sacrifice everything for the Reds.

The train jolted, and from the corridor came voices raised in a heated altercation. The Chinese were always shouting about something, Charles thought. The compartment door inched open, and an ancient grandfather pushed his way inside, somehow managing to shift the suitcases piled before the door. Bent nearly double over his cane, he shuffled toward the empty seat. Kathryn hopped to her feet and was starting to shoo him out when Charles spoke up.

"Tupan Feng? Is that really you?"

The old man dropped onto the bench opposite and did not

reply, his wheezing breath his only answer.

Charles whispered to Kathryn, "He's like the ghosts in Lian's bedtime tales—he never dies."

"Not ghost," Tupan Feng said, his voice, like everything else about him, surprisingly strong.

"Sure looks like one to me," Kathryn said as she pulled the flask again from her purse, tipped it to her lips, and took another drink.

Tupan Feng's bony claw swept the air. He pointed at her but said nothing more.

"Now I'm spooked," she whispered. "Maybe he's just a figment of our imaginations, the booze going to our heads."

"Not figment," Tupan Feng said.

"Sorry, honorable Tupan," Charles said. "We don't mean to be disrespectful, do we?" He nudged Kathryn.

She didn't take the hint but muttered, "What do you bet he dies right here on the train, and we have to deal with it."

Tupan Feng shouted, "I die when ready to die—in America!"

"America?" Kathryn asked with a laugh. "Is that so?"

Tupan Feng nodded and announced, "Charles-Boy takes me."

Kathryn slapped Charles on the knee. "Good luck with that, sonny."

In every tale Lian had ever told, Charles recalled that those who ignored the signs of the spirits met their downfall swiftly and painfully. Han had explained to Charles many times the importance of honoring one's elders, respecting the way fate unfolds, and accepting that what must be must be. So although Charles's head felt woozy, and he was getting a kick out of Kathryn's bad manners, he rose to his feet and bowed before the wizened warlord.

"I apologize, esteemed old one, for our rudeness. We are honored to have you join us here in our compartment. I will escort you wherever you want to go."

"Oh, for heaven's sake," Kathryn said.

Tupan Feng looked Charles up and down. "American boy will not die a fool." Kathryn started to snicker until the old warlord added, "Not so for American woman. She is putrid turtle egg of the lowest order."

She raised the flask to toast him, but this time, Charles took it from her and screwed on the cap. He then helped Tupan Feng stretch out on the bench and tucked his father's driving cap under his head to serve as a pillow.

"You sleep now, old one," he said.

But Tupan Feng's eyes remained opened and unnaturally bright. "Charles-Boy, do not search skies any longer for Fenghuang. The Chinese phoenix will never land again in this country. Never, I say!"

"Okay, take it easy," Charles said. "I won't look for it again."

"No more good fortune here! Just pain and suffering from now on. The emperor of all birds has flown!"

Charles nodded as he laid his topcoat over the thin and trembling shoulders, and the old man's eyes finally shut. Then Charles sat again beside Kathryn. She shut her eyes, and before long, she, too, had started to snore softly.

Charles reached deep into his khakis pocket and pulled out his father's chop. He studied the red ink-stained phoenix carved into marble, its wings partly spread and its head thrown back in defiance. Charles recalled that his father had used it on envelopes and papers written with Chinese characters in his spidery penmanship. He had seen the image stamped on files and telegrams hidden in the secret drawer at the back of the Reverend's antique scholar's desk, which Charles had come upon by accident when playing at his father's feet as a boy. And Charles recalled the same small red stencil of the phoenix flying across the wall beside the two-way transistor hidden in the basement.

He pressed the chop into his open palm now, but it left only a hint of pink, the red phoenix fading. An undeniable thought billowed upward in Charles's mind along with the steam that fogged the train window, making the countryside out there more shadowed and indecipherable than it already seemed: his father, and not just his mother, had most certainly been a spy. Charles wondered how he had ever thought he knew his parents at all.

Twenty-seven

Rain continued to stream over the lip of the cave all afternoon and evening. Caleb slept fitfully on his cot near the back wall, his bones chilled by the change of season. Deep in the middle of the night, he awoke and heard men whispering at the entrance. He did not call out and interrupt their meeting. He had already been too great a burden. He would be forever grateful to the Eighth Route Army for seeing to his recovery and knew he was still being cared for on the orders of Captain Hsu. Caleb had helped the captain by gathering information about the Japanese, but Hsu's loyalty since his accident had far outweighed Caleb's significance as a spy.

With some difficulty, he reached across to light the lamp and tried to see the soldiers' faces in the dimness. But the men disbanded just then, and Caleb spotted Hsu's profile as he departed, no doubt occupied with urgent business. Cook appeared abruptly beside Caleb's cot and looked down on him with sorrow in his clouded eyes.

"We must leave now," he said. "Very sorry, Reverend." Cook pulled the wool blanket higher around Caleb's neck, bowed, and started to back away.

"Wait," Caleb called after him. "Please, what's happening?" He tried to sit up.

"Much danger. Troops now depart. We come back when we can. God bless Reverend. Very good Christian man." Cook bowed a final time and hurried out of the cave.

Rain pounded the rocky ground on the cliffside as dawn broke over the opposite mountain. Silver rivulets caught the first sunlight, growing wider and stronger with each passing moment. The cascade over the cave's entrance resembled a true waterfall, as frothing and relentless as the one Caleb had stood under as a boy in summer in the White Mountains. He was inside it now and tried to imagine his brothers beside him. Their shivering bodies had been vivid with delight, unlike his body now, which shook with cold and fear. Caleb told himself to hold close the memory of his brothers. They had always looked after one another, and he prayed for that now.

The lamp, he noticed, had only a small amount of kerosene left. The fuel would burn down, but luckily dawn was almost here at last. Caleb watched the small flame and enjoyed the shadows it cast on the back wall. He thought of Plato's "Allegory of the Cave" and chuckled to himself. Of course it would come to this: a cornerstone of Western thought reenacted here in a distant Chinese cave. He had traveled all the way to the other side of the world, hoping to broaden his understanding of life through Eastern ways, but still remained saddled with a Western perspective. Though enlightened by liberal interpretations of the Bible and an eager proponent of Chinese communalism, Caleb knew he was no different from the ancient Greeks of Plato's allegory. He remained chained to his cave with nothing to do but watch light flicker on the wall and long for his freedom. All knowledge was subjective. All life, a narrow illusion.

From overhead, he heard the swift, heavy footfalls of the Eighth Route Army as they marched out of camp. After a while, he heard nothing except the pounding of the rain again. The Reds were gone, and he was alone.

Caleb shifted on the cot to find the right position. He wove his hands together, raised his arms toward the lamplight, creased his thumbs, and flapped his palms. The shadows on the wall took shape as he hoped. A bird began to take flight in the manner his son had always loved. He watched the shadows of the wings soar and longed for Charles's high and happy voice to beg him to continue.

He had used the name Red Phoenix yet was nothing but stagnant, barely healed bones now. He had no wings. He had no fine plumage and no myth to carry him upward. He was nothing but feeble hands folded in prayer once more. The bird on the wall took off in a cloud of pale wings, carrying with it the hope that he and his comrades had created here. Then his arms drifted down to his sides. Caleb rested and waited.

Some time later, he awoke to the hum of aircraft flying low. Reverberations of their engines echoed off the cave walls. The first bomb went off a short distance away, perhaps down in one of the ravines nearby. The planes whined as they circled. The second bomb landed closer. The third was a direct hit at the center of the camp, just up the cliff from Caleb's cave. The mountain rumbled, and he sensed what was happening before it began. Rocks began to fall, slowly at first and then with greater force as they landed in front of the entrance.

Through the dimming lamplight, he watched the landslide begin. The heavy rain brought down the rocks, but it was the bombs that had done it. The Japanese had finally discovered the location of the secret Eighth Route Army base in the mountains. Caleb was grateful that the troops had escaped before the bombing began. Someone, he realized, must have intercepted word of the imminent attack and saved them. A spy had done his or her duty, and the soldiers, including Captain Hsu, had been spared. The excellent Eighth Route Army was safe, or at least would not perish in this air raid.

Caleb watched as rivulets of mud turned to thick streams that oozed into the cave, pouring over the boulders that continued to settle. The giant rocks stacked one on top of the next with surprising ease, and the mud formed a bond between them. Quite quickly the rising wall blocked out gray daylight. The boulders shifted as they were washed over by silt, and Caleb saw the entrance become sealed.

The lamp sputtered, the oil almost used up. Jesus had known the cock would crow and rose to meet his destiny. Caleb could not stand but knew his fate was fast approaching. But still he held out hope that his spirit could lift up from it like the majestic phoenix from the ashes, like his Lord. Caleb recalled Captain Hsu bestowing his code name upon him. "You will have many lives here in China," the good captain had said. "Whatever you do to help the people will help you to change as well." So it had come to pass. Caleb was a changed man, and for the better.

He let out a long, stuttering sigh, but the tears had dried from his eyes. No longer limp with weakness and fear, he felt his heart growing stronger in his broken chest. He was not sorely afraid. He would be embraced in heaven, or high on some desolate, craggy mountain perch. Soon to be released from the suffering of this world, he would be rewarded with God's goodness. Washed away, yet not abandoned, Caleb would die in this cave in North China.

The light was snuffed out then, and all went dark. He could not see what happened next but heard the lamp topple from where it had rested on the ground. The mud flow knocked it over and carried it away with some force. He felt the earth rise up under the cot, wet and chilly on the underside of his legs. He pulled in his hands from the sides and crossed his arms over his chest, but the mud webbed between his fingers, and he felt it rise higher against his ribs. It sloshed over his chest with alarming speed. Quite quickly, the coldness cradled his chin.

He tried to sit up, but the surface of the cot was too slippery. There would be no escaping the mud. He allowed himself to finally think of her, his wife, Shirley, whom it pained him to leave behind. He pictured her as she stood tall and proud with her arms crossed, her hip cocked, and that saucy, inscrutable expression on her face that he had both adored and tried endlessly to correct. She would stride deeper into her life and carry on, her heart, he knew now, expanded by her time in China. She would do good works going forward, which gave Caleb great comfort.

And Charles, dear Charles. He would never know the man his son would become, so he thought back to the sensation of holding him in his arms when he was young. Caleb bent down to say good-night, and Charles gripped him tightly around the neck and planted a kiss upon his cheek.

The mud clogged his nostrils now and slid into his ears. The thick earth covered his eyes and oozed into his mouth. Caleb swallowed out of reflex, choked, then simply let his jaw hang open. He tipped back his head. The wet, moving earth became his pillow, releasing his spirit to take flight.

Twenty-eight

When she reached the top of the gangplank of the *Grip-sholm*, the Swedish liner that had been assigned to take foreign women and children out of war-torn China, Shirley did not pause but pressed deeper into the crowd and finally made it to a railing overlooking the water. Dizzy from lack of sleep and hunger, she shut her eyes and steadied herself. When she opened them again, she saw shards of a new day dancing on the fractured surface of the Huangpu River as it led out into the East China Sea. She leaned back and peered into the blinding dawn. Its warmth on her cheeks felt like a reproach, an insistence that the natural world had carried on, unconcerned with all that she and others had survived.

In the North, she had grown quickly accustomed to living in rain and knew it as her element. Foggy, impenetrable night and damp shrouds during the day had suited her. The gloomy landscape mirrored her troubled conscience. Here in vivid Shanghai, the colors were too sharp, the voices too loud, the crowds impossible to comprehend. Shirley had been shocked to see that so many still lived, but that was only because those who had died were but a fraction of the sheer mass of humanity in China. The people had somehow carried on, she thought, in spite of the violence, and the mistakes, and the losses.

On deck, passengers crowded the port side several deep, and

she sensed the ship listing that way. Although they were mostly foreigners, she assumed they were leaving behind family and friends and lives they had built here in China. They peered down on the frantic crowd below and counted their blessings. She wondered if many of them were leaving China with a mix of sorrow and elation but also, like her, with shame in their hearts.

As the first departure horn blared from the bridge and filled the air with electric excitement, she snatched up her valise and slipped into the crowd, in search of Charles. She wove through passengers from amidships to the stern but still didn't see him and told herself not to panic. Not to fear the worst. She had hardly slept on the train from Peking, her body rigid with worry as she had tried to will herself to make it to the ship safely. But now that she was here, she began to fear that she and her son might not be reunited in China after all.

So many faces, the bodies pressed close together, all blended into a feverish mass. What if Charles was stuck on shore and unable to make it on time? If she left China without him, she could never forgive herself. As she continued to scour the strangers, she decided that if she did not find her boy soon, she would have no choice but to head down the gangplank before they pulled it up. She would charge back into chaotic Shanghai to find him.

Her eyes drifted over the many faces until the profile of a young redheaded man came into focus. He had taken up a prime position at the very center of the stern and stood in a jaunty pose. Charles did not notice her, so Shirley had a long moment to soak up the sight of him, her handsome boy who rested a new leather shoe on the railing and tilted his head in a cocky way. With his hair cut and slicked back, he looked so much like his father that Shirley felt a pang of both sorrow and pride. Charles seemed as charming and irrepressible as ever, she thought. At least, she hoped that was true. For now, she was just happy to see him happy.

Then she noticed her dear friend at Charles's side. Kathryn's cheeks, which had always had a rosy plumpness, hung like gray shingles. She had lost weight, they all had, and her gentle, girlish curves had been replaced by sharp contours. Although she wore a new Oriental-cut silk skirt and matching jacket in an elegant orange chrysanthemum print, her hair was tousled, and the bangs had grown jagged. She still wore a familiar hat to the side, though its velvet brim was crushed.

Shirley was watching them both when Charles suddenly tossed his head forward and spat over the side of the ship. She thought that wasn't a polite thing to do at the start of a voyage and intended to tell him so but also felt relieved that he still had such boyish habits. Kathryn took Charles's arm and scolded him playfully. Not the mother figure her son needed, Shirley thought, but not a bad friend to have, either. She began to elbow her way through the crowd to join them.

"Pardon me," she said, "I need to see my son. Excuse me, I must get through to be with my son."

A mother with a child in tow stepped out of her way, as if understanding the urgency of her request. When Shirley finally stopped before Charles, she lost all words. She stood paralyzed as she let the look on his face wash over her. For a brief moment, he conveyed the love that she had sacrificed so much to feel again. Shirley realized how terribly she had longed to see that light in his eyes.

But then, in an instant, his expression narrowed, and he squinted down, his forehead forming a tangle of lines. He glared at his mother, quite furious.

She moved closer anyway and threw her arms around him. She pulled him into her and held on for too long, she knew, but couldn't help it. Charles felt so sturdy. His body not depleted like hers. He stood tall and with a broad back and wide shoulders that did not bend to hug her in return. He remained stiff, unforgiving, a plank of resistance. He pulled her hands from around his neck and stepped back. She stared up into his face with moist eyes, but he glanced off toward the shore.

Kathryn placed herself between them and wrapped her skinny arms around Shirley, a bony cheek pressing against hers. As her friend held on in an awkward embrace and almost toppled them both, there was no mistaking the alcohol on her breath. Shirley knew she should be concerned about Kathryn, but she couldn't take her eyes off Charles.

"Thank God you made it," Kathryn said, squeezing Shirley's hands. "Aren't we all the worse for wear? I haven't seen a mirror, but I know I must look dreadful. You poor thing, is that all you have?" She pointed at Shirley's flimsy valise.

"The clothes on my back," Shirley said. "I gave my last two dresses to Chinese women on the train. They had nothing. My suitcase is empty." Shirley glanced down at her raincoat and rubber boots and realized she still wore the apron under it and Charles's sweater, which she had refused to take off for days, even as the weather grew warmer in the south.

"Not to worry," Kathryn said. "The other ladies and I will share our new outfits. We had a chance to shop in Shanghai before boarding. Everything was contraband, our money going to the White Russian mafia, I'm sure. It felt criminal to contribute to the downfall of this sorry country." Then she dipped nearer and whispered in Shirley's ear, "You'll have to give the ladies another chance. Teetotalers, I'm afraid, but not so bad otherwise. I hope you'll join me for a little toast up on the main deck? You always were more game than anyone else. I'm sure that's what made you such an excellent spy." She pressed a finger to her lips.

Shirley saw Charles flinch at the mention of spying. She remembered the tantrums he had staged as a child and the silent brewing that had taken place before they occurred. She had always known him so well—sometimes better than he knew himself—and yet not any longer. She couldn't be sure what he was thinking now.

"I just wish you'd told me sooner," Kathryn continued. "I do so love a story."

Shirley didn't bother to correct her friend's mistaken notion. It was Charles she needed to get to. Shirley reached across to pat his chest with an open palm, but he pulled back, leaving her hand stalled in the air.

"You must explain absolutely everything once we get away from this dreadful place," Kathryn carried on. "Charles and I have been trying to piece it together, but now that you're here, you can fill us in on the true goings-on."

Shirley wished Kathryn would stop talking and finally spoke up. "What a handsome new suit, Charles," she said. "You look sharp."

He straightened the lapels of his seersucker but did not reply.

"I was so worried about you," Shirley continued. "You have no idea how frightened I was that we might never see each other again."

"Don't be overly dramatic, Mother. We would have found one another eventually, although I was set to make the trip without you. When you didn't return to the mission, I assumed you'd decided to stay with the Reds."

The coolness of his tone rocked Shirley back onto her heels. "No," she said. "I always wanted us to be together."

He offered a sharp laugh. "Is that why you went off on the back of Captain Hsu's mule?" he asked. "I watched you out my window that night. You looked perfectly content to be leaving."

Shirley's face went hot, and her dizziness returned.

"Kathryn and I both tried to convince you to leave your clinic," he continued. "But being Florence Nightingale seemed more important to you."

"That's not true, Charles. You're what's important to me."

"Or maybe you didn't want to give up the perks of being a spy? I saw them drop you off down at the port in a fancy black car. Everyone knows those are only used by top officials."

"I got here the only way I could," she said, her gaze lowered and shoulders hunched.

The crew of Swedish sailors positioned around the ship shouted suddenly in various languages for the passengers to prepare for departure. The gangplank rose with a deafening clatter. The second horn blared, more a warning than a hopeful call. Below in the port, traffic remained stalled as trucks, carts, rickshaws, and tens of thousands of Chinese on foot blocked the way. Sirens and shouting rose from the crush below, frenzied and wild.

Farther up a boulevard that led away from the ship, Shirley thought she saw the black sedan that had dropped her off as it wedged back through the throng. She would never have made it on time if General Shiga hadn't arranged her ride. When the train from Peking had finally squealed to a halt in the Shanghai station and the panicked passengers elbowed their way down the iron steps, Shirley had stumbled through great clouds of steam and out onto the platform. She stood stunned and knocked about by the Chinese until a Japanese soldier took her elbow and pulled her through the crowd and into a waiting sedan. As she settled on the slick leather seat, the driver stepped on the gas and cut a swath through the mobs. Chinese of all ages pressed against the car windows.

At first, she made herself look into their terrified faces. But there were too many of them for her to help, too many to even comprehend. She had squeezed her husband's passport to her chest and found herself praying. She hardly knew how any longer and wasn't sure to whom she prayed—God or Jesus, her husband or Captain Hsu. She prayed for forgiveness, even though she felt she did not deserve it. Still, she whispered her prayer and hoped that her words could be heard above the muffled cries beyond the closed windows that kept her safe inside the Japanese car.

Earlier, on the train, she had been taken to a private section at the back and given a Western-style meal. When the silver dome was removed from her dinner plate, she almost fainted at the sight of steak pooling in its own blood. A formal card accompanied the dish: *Compliments of General Shiga*. The note written in elegant English penmanship promised that he would look her up the next time he was in the States. Below his name he had written, *Princeton, '15*, a final seal of their secret, insidious pact.

"Charles-Boy," she said now, "I brought you some steak. I thought you might be starved." She pulled a white cloth napkin from deep in the pocket of her raincoat and began to unfold it.

"Don't call me that. Don't ever call me that. That was Lian's name for me, not yours."

"But are you hungry?" Shirley tried again. "I have something for you." She held out the steak on the napkin in her open palm.

"Where'd you get that?" he asked. "No one has food like that anymore. Not even the fine hotels along the Bund."

Kathryn leaned in and said, "I'll eat it if he doesn't want to."

"Don't take it," he said fiercely to her. "It's poisoned."

Shirley wrapped the steak and stuffed it back into her pocket. "Don't be so righteous, son," she said, and tried to stand taller but couldn't muster the strength. "I just thought you might be hungry."

He glared down at her. "It's corrupt, Mother. That steak is corrupt. Like the black car you arrived in. You left me to join the Reds, but now you show up in an official's car with a Japanese driver. I saw him when he opened the door for you." Charles shook his head in disgust. "I don't know what you've been up to. I don't even know whose side you're on, anyway. I think you're on no one's side but your own, that's what I think."

"Jesus, Charles," Kathryn said and swatted his arm, "That's enough. If you were my son, I'd wash your mouth out with soap."

"It's all right, Kathryn," Shirley said.

Charles was correct, she thought. She had made a decision for no one's benefit but her own and her family's, and at the expense of others. What she had done was a sin, and she didn't need her husband here to remind her of that fact. Though not a highly religious person, she now understood in a biblical sense that she had crossed over into some vast, desolate valley and must spend the rest of her days wending her way back. Any mild impulse she had felt to do good for others seemed trivial in light of her treachery toward Captain Hsu. She would have to carry on his, and her husband's, good works in repentance.

"I didn't see her get out of any car," Kathryn said as she swung toward Charles and rubbed a finger on his lapel. "You must have eagle eyes, Charlie. How did you spot your mother with the thousands of people down there? I think you were looking for her awfully hard." Then she turned to Shirley and leaned on her arm. "You see?" she said. "There's a good sign. Your son was searching for you, right at the same moment you were searching for him. Come on, now, you two, time to make up."

Charles's jaw remained set, and his arms stayed crossed tightly over his ribs.

"Is that true?" Shirley asked as she gazed up at him. "You were looking for me, son?"

Charles put his fine new shoe up on the ship's railing and shrugged.

"Who knows, Charles," Kathryn said in a slurred but cheerful tone as nudged closer to him, "someday you may even be proud of your mother. She's our own Mata Hari."

Shirley wanted to peel her friend off her son and might have done so, but Charles elbowed Kathryn away himself, and rather harshly. Shirley wondered what had gone on between them, though, whatever it was, he had no business treating a lady like that. Then something occurred to her about her boy that seemed even more disturbing and wrong.

"Charles, let me get this straight," Shirley began. "You saw me from up here on the ship, and yet you didn't come to greet me? What if I hadn't found you in this crowd? Would you have simply waited until we bumped into one another like a couple of strangers?"

"Of course we'd find each other, Mother. We're going to be on this damn boat together for over a month."

With his raised chin and imperious tone, Shirley realized that he sounded just like her at her worst. Charles was behaving arrogantly, dismissing her in the way that she had dismissed others in the past. "Do you know that I would have left the ship if I hadn't found you? Then what would have become of us?"

"Well, I wasn't going to give up my spot here at the stern," Charles explained. "We nabbed it two hours ago, and I've had to push people away ever since. We'll get the best view as we leave old Shanghai, won't we, Kathryn?"

Kathryn nodded, but Shirley sensed that her friend was as perturbed as she was.

"You couldn't be bothered to meet me after all I went through to get here?" Shirley asked again. "I sacrifice any last vestige of goodness and now receive this in return?"

Before Charles could reply, a sudden giddiness began to overtake her, and she started to laugh. He seemed startled by her outburst, and although Shirley tried to control herself, a strange and pleasing lightness rippled through her body for the first time in weeks, perhaps months. She had lost her husband, betrayed her Chinese friend, and come frighteningly close to losing her son as well. It was all too much.

But she had not lost her son. And she would not ever risk that again. From now on, she had no intention of letting him go astray.

"Oh, thank heavens," she sputtered, "I see now. I understand. You still need me. I believe you really do. You may be a young man," she said as she straightened her spine, pulled back her shoulders, and spoke as sternly as she could, "but your behavior, Charles Carson, is completely unacceptable. Do you hear me, my boy?"

He lowered his chin in direct proportion to how high she raised hers.

"I don't ever," she said and poked his chest with a finger, "ever want to hear that you have disregarded other people as if you couldn't be bothered with them. You learned that from me, and it is high time you unlearned it."

The cocky, know-it-all expression slipped from his face. Before her stood the good boy that he truly was.

"It isn't right for us to put ourselves first at the expense of others," she said. "Do you understand me?"

He nodded.

"After all our years in China, I would think that you might know more about filial piety than you have shown me today. Would Lian have approved of your behavior?"

Charles shook his head.

"Would Han?"

"No, Mother."

"All right, then," she said and stepped closer and lowered her voice. "The truth is, I'm a poor example for you. But without your father here, we must help one another to stay on track. *We are our brothers' keepers*, as he used to say. *We are one*. We must remind each other of that. But I think we can do it if we put our minds to it, don't you?"

He offered another nod.

"Good." Then she held open her arms and said, "Now, give your mother a proper hug."

He fell toward her more gladly than she could have hoped.

"I love you, my dear, and always will," she said.

"I know, Mother," he said and dipped into her embrace.

After a long moment, he stepped back and said, "Here, come stand with us. It really is an excellent spot to wave farewell to China."

The three Americans stood side by side at the railing. Shirley placed her hand around the metal, and to her happy amazement, Charles set his much larger one on top. Very few things in life, she thought, would ever feel as satisfying as that sweaty, strong palm on the bony back of her hand.

An image came to her in that moment, as it would often from then on: Captain Hsu smoking as he leaned against the wooden railing on her front porch, a wry, knowing smile barely raising the corners of his mouth. He would forever be pointing out to her her weaknesses and the weaknesses of her people. He would serve as her insistent reminder that she rise to be her better self, as she had, however briefly, on these shores.

The enormous ship began to rumble. Deep in the hull, its engine spun the massive propellers as ocean water frothed at the stern. The final horn blasted over their heads, startling Shirley so badly that she gripped Charles's hand. He laughed and squeezed hers in return.

"We're going home, Mother. We're finally going home."

He looked as excited as a small boy, the one she had known so well and still knew even now, though differently. A roiling wake formed behind them as they left the chaos on the shore. The boat created a fierce and unyielding undertow—so strong that if a person slipped and fell into it, he would be sucked downward and drowned in its thick embrace. History had done the same here in this country they were leaving behind. Her husband had slid into it and died instantly in a landslide, while Captain Hsu, Shirley feared, had met it in an enemy bullet on a wet and lonely night in the mission courtyard, with herself to blame.

And yet, despite her sorrow, Shirley had come to love this vast and maddening cipher of a country. The Middle Kingdom, as

China had called itself from ancient times, Center of All Under the Vast Heavens, was known as encompassing all things in all seasons: the brick walkways and dusty grounds of the mission compound, the grassy plains where peaceful streams ran past willows, the purple-shrouded mountains in the distance, and even the teeming, desperate streets of Shanghai. As she and her son left it behind, morning sunlight sliced the air over the masses, coating the foreign bank and merchant buildings on the shore in a fiery wash.

Acknowledgments

My grandmother Gertrude Chaney Pye was a missionary in China from 1909 to 1942. When her husband, Reverend Watts O. Pye, died in 1926, Gertrude did not return to America but instead chose to remain in Shanxi Province to raise her son, my father, Lucian W. Pye. When the Japanese invaded Manchuria in 1931, then occupied North China in the lead-up to the Second Sino-Japanese War that started in 1937, she stayed. When my father went off to college in the United States in 1939, Gertrude still stayed. Only Pearl Harbor finally forced her to leave. She made passage in 1942 on one of the last boats out, the *Gripsholm*, a neutral Swedish ship. As a child, I heard many stories about her, but one in particular stood out: during the Japanese occupation, she shooed Japanese soldiers off her front porch with a broom.

When I mentioned this anecdote about my grandmother to my editor, Greg Michalson, who I was fortunate to work with on my first novel, *River of Dust*, he suggested I write a new novel inspired by her experience. I'm deeply grateful to him for his literary wisdom and keen editorial eye and for his excellent team at Unbridled Books. I'm also thankful to my delightful publicist, Caitlin Hamilton Summie, and to my generous agent, Gail Hochman.

China and Japan scholars Patrick Cranley, Prof. Richard J. Samuels, Virginia Stibbs Anami, Rick Dyck, Jeanne Barnett, and Pat Barnett Brubaker helped me grasp the history of North China in the 1930s. My story was informed in particular by the biographies and journals of three American women who lived in China during that era: Agnes Smedley, Helen Foster Snow, and Nym Wales. The China experiences of my father and his closest friends, Charles T. Cross and Harold R. Isaacs—uncle and grandfather figures to me as a girl—were also crucial, as were seminal texts by Edgar Snow and Jonathan D. Spence, numerous other personal accounts of that time, and several studies of warlords, including one by my father.

This novel was written in his memory and is also for Eva and Daniel, who show me the way as they blaze forward in life.